# Ghost in the Wind

# E. J. COPPERMAN

BERKLEY PRIME CRIME, NEW YORK

**BERKLEY PRIME CRIME**

**An imprint of Penguin Random House LLC**
**375 Hudson Street, New York, New York 10014**

GHOST IN THE WIND

A Berkley Prime Crime Book / published by arrangement with the author.

ISBN: 978-0-425-26927-5

PUBLISHING HISTORY
Berkley Prime Crime mass-market edition / December 2015

PRINTED IN THE UNITED STATES OF AMERICA

10 9 8 7 6 5 4 3 2 1

Cover illustration by Dominick Finelle.
Cover design by Judith Lagerman.
Interior text design by Kristin del Rosario.
Photography: flock of birds © Alexuss K / Shutterstock;
painted background © istockphoto / Thinkstock.

Penguin
Random
House

*For John, Paul, George and Ringo.*
*Maybe especially Ringo.*

# ACKNOWLEDGMENTS

This is the seventh Haunted Guesthouse novel. Just typing that sort of amazes me. The reception to these books has been utterly astonishing to their author, and I can never repay the trust some people—mostly you readers—have shown in me.

The first among those readers is Shannon Jamieson Vazquez, the stalwart and indispensable editor of the Haunted Guesthouse series, without whom you would be reading someone else's book right now. Shannon saw the potential in the series at its idea phase and has shaped everything you've read in it up to this very moment. She'll probably have a few changes to suggest after I submit these acknowledgments, and she'll be right about those, too. Can't thank you enough, Shannon.

Also improving those rough first drafts is Yvette Grant, production editor, for making this look like a book. When I'm done with it, the thing looks like a collection of random words cut out of magazines like a ransom note. And thanks to my copyeditor, Deborah Goemans, who did her very best to make sure things made sense and were spelled correctly, and who curbed my compulsive use of commas. I can't help it. I'm just a comma freak. Thank them for what they do, or you'd be reading a book two hundred pages longer just for the commas.

Dominic Finelle came up with yet another amazing cover that manages against all odds to surpass the ones that came before it. One of the best days in the process is seeing what he's come up with this time based on my wholly inadequate suggestions. I'm not responsible for the covers on these books, folks. He is. If a book cover could get a standing ovation, these would be the ones I'd be out of my chair applauding.

Of course, the usual thanks to the people who made this series begin and continue. Christina Hogrebe of the Jane Rotrosen Agency read the manuscript for the first book in my Double Feature series, and asked Shannon to look at it. Here we are ten books later.

Josh Getzler, Danielle Burby, Tanusri Prasanna and all the gang at HSG Agency make it possible for me to do this for a living and are actual human beings at the same time. It's nice to do business with people you like. When they're also really good at what they do, that puts it over the top. And no one is a better companion than Josh for a trip to the Yogi Berra Museum and Learning Center.

To all the reviewers (even the not-as-happy ones) who take the time to read and discuss the books, thanks for your dedication and your honesty. Writers will tell you they never read reviews. They're lying.

Most of all, thanks to the loyal readers of the Haunted Guesthouse series. You make this happen, time and time again. Prepare to be thanked for the eighth time, right around this time next year in a page remarkably similar to this one. You are never unappreciated.

# One

Let me just state for the record, right at the top, that I was against the plan to show *Ghost* for the first movie night at my guesthouse, but I was outvoted.

By the ghosts.

I had chosen the coming Sunday night to inaugurate my newly renovated movie room, which was at one time going to be the fitness center but had originally been the game room (it's a long story). The room was finally done the way I wanted it to be, with light chestnut stain on the paneling, beige room-darkening drapes for better projection, a very large HDTV connected to the Blu-Ray player and a killer surround-sound system. Everything was exactly the way I wanted it.

But Maxie Malone, who'd been a rising interior designer before her life was ended for her at the tender age of twenty-eight, had insisted that I was wrong. "The wood floors are too hard and shiny," she said. "You really want an area rug in here to absorb some of the sound or the movie will echo."

Maxie likes to play oil to my water, but although I hate to admit it, she usually makes the right suggestions about décor in the guesthouse. I'd bought the place roughly three years earlier without knowing she and Paul Harrison, a then-newly-minted private investigator who'd been poisoned while working a case for Maxie, were already inhabiting the place. It took a hard shot to the head—administered by Maxie herself—for me to develop an ability to see and hear the ghosts, and there have since been plenty of times I have regretted not ducking out of the way faster.

Anyway, after much debate, I'd finally (as usual) acquiesced to Maxie's judgment and bought a six-by-nine-foot rug in maroon and brown for the room. It looked perfect, which only made me resent Maxie more.

But that was not the argument about the movie.

I had chosen a classic film, *Lawrence of Arabia*, for our first showing. Its gorgeous vistas and sweeping scope would best show off the terrific flat-screen TV I'd bought, and its themes of enigmatic heroism would feed the soul of everyone who viewed it.

"Booooooooring," Maxie said, and to my horror, I saw my daughter Melissa, eleven years old but wise beyond my years, nodding her head in agreement.

"It's like four hours long," Liss sided with Maxie. "By the time it's over I'll be twelve."

"It is a long film," Paul agreed. You'd think someone existing through eternity would be less concerned about elapsed time. "But it is a classic." That was better.

While my ability to see ghosts was a relatively new occurrence after the "accident" that led to my discovery of Paul and Maxie (among others), the blow—not the one to my head, but to my sensibility—was compounded by the revelation that my mother and my daughter had both been able to see and communicate with ghosts all their lives and had concealed it from me for fear that the knowledge would make me feel inferior, when in fact it would merely have made me think the two of them were delusional.

With only three days before the premiere would take place, this insurrection was throwing a severe monkey wrench into my plans. Including the three ghosts present at the moment (Maxie, Paul and my dad), there were seven of us: Melissa, me, Mom and my boyfriend, Josh Kaplan, (who can't see or communicate with ghosts himself, but luckily didn't run for the hills when I told him about them).

I looked to my dad, hovering about two feet above the floor and admiring the paint job on the ceiling, for moral support. "What do you think?" I asked him. Dad always backs me up.

"I wasn't listening," he said. "What's the question?" He looked to my mother, who raised an eyebrow and cocked her head to one side: *What's the difference?*

"It's about a movie," Mom told Dad, smiling at him. They have a great marriage that lasted thirty-three years while my father was alive and six years since. That's quite an accomplishment when you think about it.

Dad shrugged his shoulders and floated up closer to the ceiling so he could admire the corners and see I'd done the job right. Dad, who taught me all I know about home maintenance (which is approximately one-seventeenth of what he knows), takes great pride in my every accomplishment.

"What do you suggest?" I asked Maxie. If it was something wholly inappropriate for Melissa, I could shoot down her suggestion easily and Peter O'Toole would be mounting his camel in no time flat.

But Maxie's smart. "*Ghost*," she said. "It's perfect because the place is haunted, and people like that."

Perhaps I should explain.

I came back to Harbor Haven, the Jersey Shore town where I'd grown up, after my divorce from Melissa's father, a man

I refer to as The Swine because using more accurate language around my eleven-year-old daughter would be inappropriate. I'd also gotten some money from a lawsuit I'd settled with a previous employer and sunk it all into this great big Victorian at 123 Seafront Avenue. My intent had been to create a unique vacation experience for people year-round, something which doesn't happen that much down the shore, but which is possible when the building is properly insulated. Sure, it makes sense to come down here in swimming weather, but the shore is also beautiful and peaceful in winter and offers a relaxing trip when the crowds dissipate in fall and spring, too. In the early fall, like now, there is foliage to look at, but the waves still hypnotize with their sound and their beauty, and the air is crisp but salty. We get the occasional hot day, but the ocean water has cooled to the point that swimming in the Atlantic is really more for the very brave or the incredibly crazy.

But it turned out that what really drew in guests was being haunted. They love that.

I was approached just before the place opened by Edmund Rance, a representative of a company called Senior Plus Tours, which offers adventurous people over a certain age vacations with "value added" experiences.

Like hanging around with a couple of ghosts.

Senior Plus guaranteed me a number of guests in exchange for at least twice a day contact with the spirits, and they don't mean alcohol.

In order to secure Paul and Maxie's cooperation in what we call the "spook shows," I had to make a bargain I would have preferred to avoid. It turned out that Paul wanted to keep doing investigations, not letting a little thing like being deceased stand in his way. But as he is incapable of leaving my property (Maxie has since developed the ability to travel around and now shows up wherever and whenever it's inconvenient for me), he needed someone living to do the legwork for him. In short, I agreed to sit for a private investigator's license to help with Paul's cases if he'd convince Maxie to perform in the spook shows. Let's just say investigating crimes is not my favorite thing, but since they've held up their end of the bargain, I'm stuck doing the right thing. The moral high ground can give you nosebleeds.

"*Ghost*?" I asked now. "It's such a cliché, don't you think?"

"What?" Maxie came back. "You have a sign outside the front door that says 'Haunted Guesthouse.' You want to promote the place based on subtlety?"

I hate it when she has a point.

"Let's take a vote," I said, assessing the room. I figured on votes from Mom, Dad, Josh and maybe Liss in addition to my own, so I had confidence in my suggestion.

Except Maxie was grinning, and that's rarely a good thing. A mischievous poltergeist, she is emotionally a little young and unlikely to get any older, considering her not-so-alive status. She exists mostly to make me cringe, but will defend me to the . . . well, let's just say Maxie will stick up for me if someone else takes on her role of antagonist. It's an odd sort of friendship. I guess.

"Great!" she said. *Uh-oh.* "Who wants to see—"

"*Lawrence of Arabia*," I shouted out. Get my choice in first and cut this charade short, I figured.

The problem was that only three hands went up: mine, my mother's (she'll back me up on anything I ever want to do because she lives under the deluded notion that I'm perfect) and Paul's.

I couldn't speak. The feeling of betrayal was . . . okay, it wasn't that serious, but I was still a *little* hurt.

"How about *Ghost*?" Maxie said, her smile now wide enough it seemed to be the only feature on her admittedly transparent face. Melissa repeated the question aloud for Josh, who can't see or hear ghosts.

His hand went up. So did Melissa's, Dad's and hers.

"That's a win," Maxie crowed. "Four to three."

Dad shrugged. "I've never seen *Ghost*," he said.

I looked over at Josh, whose expression was that of a six-year-old boy caught standing on a kitchen chair to reach the Oreos on the top shelf. "Josh?" I said.

"I like Whoopi Goldberg," he said sheepishly.

I was about to suggest he date her in that case, when something in the far corner of the room caught my eye. There was the indication of movement, something going from the outside wall abutting the driveway (to our right) toward the hallway to the front room (left, for those of you drawing maps at home). Very fast motion, so that I really couldn't make it out, but I thought it might be a person.

"Did you see that?" I asked Paul.

He nodded. "I think someone just passed through the house," he said, and headed in the direction of the movement.

"See what?" Josh asked, now anxious to get back into my good graces.

"There's another ghost here," Melissa told him. "They don't usually just barge in like that."

Dad followed Paul toward the intruder, who must have been in the front room by now. He moves more slowly than Paul, I suppose because he was older when he died. "Let me see what's going on," he said.

Mom looked concerned, despite the fact that as far as we know, there is no possible way that harm can befall my father anymore, but she didn't say anything.

"It's probably nothing," I told Josh and by extension Melissa, who wouldn't have admitted to being concerned. "Ghosts do pass through every once in a while. We've found others in the house before."

"Yeah, but this one looked like it was trying not to be noticed," Liss said. She didn't sound worried, but had that "woo-ooh" tone kids get when they're trying to make more of a situation than is there just for the drama it can generate.

Maxie looked annoyed. "Why is somebody always ruining it when I get the attention for a second?" she whined.

"Calm down, you won," I told her. "We'll show *Ghost*, but over my protest."

Maxie brightened up. "Of course you will. I won the vote!" It takes so little to make her happy—just me not getting whatever *I* want.

"Maybe I should go see, too," Josh said, squinting in the direction Liss indicated Dad and Paul had gone. He likes to feel useful, but he sometimes overlooks certain facts.

"You wouldn't see anything," Melissa pointed out.

Josh grinned a little sheepishly, which is one of his better grins. "Touché, Melissa," he said. He stayed put.

From the entrance to the movie room came a somewhat tired voice. "Is there something going on in here?" Maureen Beckman, one of my younger Senior Plus guests this week, moved her walker into the room as I went over to meet her. Maureen didn't move around all that well ("My hip. As soon as I finish this vacation I'm going into the hospital to get a new one."), so I was trying to minimize the amount she had to walk in the house. She was game, though, and had already spent a full day on the beach, something younger, sprier guests don't always find enjoyable in September.

"Nothing special, Maureen," I said as I reached her, only a few feet into the movie room. "Something I can do for you?" This is how you learn to talk in Innkeeper School. I assume.

"Well, Alison, you know I don't like to complain." Of course, Maureen loved nothing better than to complain; but she did it in an ingratiating way, and since I'm from New Jersey, a little complaining doesn't bother me. "But it gets a little chilly in my room at night."

I had put Maureen in the largest room I had, which was located on the ground floor and wouldn't require her to climb stairs, and had not charged her the extra fee I usually ask for that room. It does get a hair cooler at night, though, especially at this time of year. "I can put another blanket or two in there for you," I told her. "Do you need a space heater?"

Maureen waved a hand. "Oh no," she said. "I'm sure extra blankets will do it. Thank you, Alison." As she turned to leave, I saw Paul and Dad hover back into the room. There was another ghost behind them, not being dragged but certainly lagging behind. I could barely see him.

Maureen turned back. "There's just one more thing." With Maureen there was always just one more thing. "Do you know of a reliable taxi service in the area?"

Of course, I knew of several, and was about to give her the name of one that would accommodate her needs (and perhaps get me a small percentage in accordance with an agreement I have with a few local businesses that I know are reputable).

But suddenly I found myself unable to speak.

"Um . . . um . . . um . . ."

Melissa, immediately keen to such things, looked up at me with a perplexed expression on her face. "Mom?"

I wanted to tell her it was okay, because it *was* okay, but the words weren't coming. "Ahhhh . . ." I said instead. At least it was a variation.

Josh came to my side. "What's going on?" he whispered in my ear. "Is it a ghost thing?"

"I'll just check the phone book," Maureen said, shaking her head a bit and heading out of the room, walker clacking as she moved. There went my commission.

My mother looked at me, then followed my line of sight and chuckled a little. "Oh, *that's* it," she said.

"What?" Josh wanted to know. "What's it?"

Maxie, her face even more sardonic than usual (mouth curled to one side, one eye narrowed), lowered down to look me directly in the eye. "What got in your drawers?" she asked. Maxie is the very picture of restraint and demeanor.

I was staring at the new ghost and my mouth was moving. That much I knew. But nothing coherent was happening.

Have you ever met an idol of yours, face-to-face? I mean someone you absolutely adored from the time you first saw them, someone whose every work you collected religiously, someone who seemed to absolutely understand your nature and communicate directly with you although you'd never actually met?

I was currently staring upward at mine: Vance McTiernan, lead singer and songwriter of the Jingles, maybe the least appropriately named band to come out of England in the 1960s. I first became aware of them more than twenty years after the band split up, but once I'd been introduced to the Jingles, and Vance especially, I was devoted for life. There was a time I would have gladly sued for my independence from my own parents if Vance McTiernan had expressed an interest in adopting me.

"Mom?" Now Melissa was starting to sound worried. "What's wrong?"

I have evidence of my strength of mind, because I forced myself to relearn the entire English language in one second. But what I was thinking came out as one word, as a thirteen-year-old girl (something Melissa will be in two years, and if you don't think I'm dreading that, you are incredibly wrong) would say it: "OhMyGodThat'sVanceMcTiernan!"

Vance himself looked surprised. "You know me?" he asked, just as Josh was saying, "Where?" and Maxie was saying, "Who?" Josh's expression indicated he remembered the name but couldn't place it, and Maxie's indicated she was Maxie.

"Yes," I answered to the only one I was listening to. "I'm a big fan. It's an honor, Mr. McTiernan."

He was a great physical specimen (before the heart disease had weakened him) for someone who had died at least one president ago: he looked lean and somewhat better defined than he had been late in his life. This must have been a slightly younger version than the final Vance, but certainly not the one I'd seen in magazines and concert footage from before I was born. He'd abused drugs and alcohol in an attempt to prove he was a real rock star (according to the biography I'd read) because his deep, intelligent lyrics had moved some critics to argue that he actually wasn't crude enough for the Jingles music to be considered rock 'n' roll. The fact that they'd jokingly called themselves the Jingles hadn't helped his case.

Now he smiled the most charming smile since Cary Grant gave up smiling, and floated down toward me. "But you're much too young," the charming accent said, making the words that much more endearing. "You couldn't have even been born when I was working."

My mind was still operating on something lower than its usual level, so although I grinned foolishly back at him, I couldn't get it together enough to respond. Mom picked up the slack. "She got the records from me, Mr. McTiernan," she said.

He diverted every ounce of his attention to her, reached for her hand with both of his and said, "You call me Vance. All of you." His arm swept the room, including us all, living and . . . otherwise.

"Swell," Maxie mumbled. Maxie truly hates it when attention is on anyone but her.

Josh touched my arm gently and asked, "Where should I be looking?" Josh is a very understanding man who is fascinated with all the ghostly goings-on at my house but knows it's best to ask about them after the fact, when I can explain everything at once rather than fielding questions as events unfold.

I pointed, and Vance (what the hell, we were on a first-name basis now) looked down at him.

"Nice to meet you, sport," he said to Josh.

"He can't actually see or hear you," I explained to Vance when Josh didn't react.

Vance blinked and looked around the room. "Oh. I thought it was the house that was special." He focused those laser eyes in my direction, and something odd happened inside my stomach. "Turns out it was you, love."

It was my definite and deliberate plan to bask in that moment for about two weeks, but I was wrested out of my reverie by, of all people, my daughter.

"No, Mr. McTiernan. My grandma and I can see you, too," Melissa said.

I did not feel resentment toward Melissa for refocusing Vance's attention away from me. I didn't. Not even a little.

That's my story and I'm sticking to it.

Vance swooped over and looked Liss in the eye. "Of course you can, my dear," he cooed at her. "You are all very special ladies indeed."

Paul, with a concerned look on his face I didn't understand, coughed theatrically (which is the only way he can cough. I don't think it's possible for him to catch a cold anymore, which he would no doubt say was one of the few advantages to being dead).

"Mr. McTiernan—" He checked the singer's look in his direction and began again. "*Vance* says he came here following a message I sent out some time back." I knew that Paul sometimes sent out mental advertisements about what he truly sees as our detective agency, since he can communicate sort of telepathically with other spirits, a system we call the Ghosternet. (Okay, *I* call it the Ghosternet. Paul just isn't as hilarious as I am.)

"I understand you offer investigative services," Vance said. "I am in need of such a professional, alas."

This was the first time I'd ever been glad to be a PI. "What can we do for you, Vance?" I asked. For once, here was a client I'd happily take on.

"Mr. . . . Vance said he wants us to investigate a murder," Paul said and, very uncharacteristically, shook his head *no* just slightly.

"Of course we will," I said, looking at Vance. "Let's have a seat."

# Two

Those of us who weren't floating led the way to the area where I'd collected some sofas, armchairs and other furniture gotten from garage sales and thrift shops to serve as unusually comfortable theater seats. Mom, Melissa, Josh and I sat down while Paul, Maxie and Dad (who seemed distracted by the ceiling fan, at one point taking an adjustable wrench out of his back pocket and tightening something) floated within earshot. Vance brought up the rear, seemingly taking in the atmosphere.

Josh did a quick double take at seeing a wrench repairing the fan on its own, then nodded and turned back toward the front of the room, despite his not being able to see or hear what was going on. Josh seemed less than amazed at Vance's presence. He was leaning a little heavily on me and staring up, pretending to look in the direction of the ghost, but his gaze lacked focus. Then I realized he'd been up since five this morning and probably wasn't as much of a Jingles fan as I was, because nobody is.

Vance McTiernan took center stage, directly over the flat screen.

"I'm a brokenhearted man, that's for sure," he began. A true showman, he knew how to get a crowd's attention. "It's a murder, pure and simple, and I'm powerless to do anything about it."

I did some quick math in my head. "Surely not you," I said to Vance. "You've been . . . that is, it's been eight years since . . ."

Maxie rolled her eyes at my insensitivity. Most ghosts balk at words like *dead*. They're such babies.

"It's true, I've been gone quite a while, and it was my own excesses did me in," Vance admitted. "No, I'm here begging for some closure, some clarity in the death of my only child, my little girl, Vanessa."

I knew the name. Vance had been involved in some intrigue in the seventies when a woman brought a paternity suit against him and it was determined the child, a daughter named Vanessa, was indeed Vance's.

Maxie vanished into the ceiling. I figured she was heading up to Melissa's room in the attic, the one Maxie sort of shares with my daughter, to get her laptop. Maxie is in charge of online research for our investigations and she's a whiz at it.

"As Vance was explaining, apparently his daughter passed away about four months ago," Paul said, seeming anxious to get to the gist of the matter. His abruptness was somehow unsettling because it was so unlike him. "He believes she was a victim of foul play."

"There's no 'he believes' about it," Vance said, a tiny suggestion of anger in his voice. "It was definitely murder, and I want the bastard found and punished."

I looked at Paul, who was hovering above Vance, as if being higher would make him right. "I think the question is open to debate. Before you ask, Alison, no, I have not been able to contact Vanessa. Either she is deliberately not responding or she is one of those souls who didn't land on this spot in the continuum."

Paul tells me that there's no rule book for the afterlife, and often notes that while some people die and become ghosts, others seem to move directly to whatever the next thing might be. Paul and Maxie have seen other ghosts evolve past this point, but there seems to be no rhyme or reason to the process.

Paul is convinced there are other stages of existence past the one he and Maxie have found themselves occupying. We have seen other ghosts vanish into what appears to be some sort of metamorphosis, although we don't know what type of dimension that might be. And Paul is envious of those who, as he puts it, "don't have to spend eternity in one place." Toward that end (moving on to whatever the next thing is), he had been experimenting with the energy that seems to make up his and Maxie's bodies. He thinks it's the key, but so far all he can do is run appliances that aren't plugged in, which came in handy for a little while when the power went out during a thunderstorm during the summer. The ice cream in my freezer never melted, but Paul needed to rest in the basement for six hours afterward.

"Maybe she just doesn't recognize your voice and doesn't think she should answer," Mom said to Paul.

He cocked an eyebrow. "It's possible, but what harm could come from responding? She can't get any more dead now." He caught himself and looked at Vance. "My apologies."

"No worries, mate," Vance said in a fake Australian accent. He was a performer, all right.

"How did your daughter pass away?" Mom asked Vance, trying to defuse the situation.

"They said she had an allergic reaction," he spat out, as if the words tasted bad. "They said she had eaten Chinese food with soy sauce, but she was terribly allergic to soy and she knew it. She was careful." His voice trailed off and his lower lip flattened out. Ghosts can't cry, at least not real tears, but the impulse is still there, Paul tells me. Vance burst out, "So it can't be true. Somebody poisoned her, as sure as I'm standing here!"

He wasn't actually standing there, but the point was made. Before anyone could react, Maxie dropped down through the ceiling wearing a bulky trench coat. When the ghosts hide objects in their clothing, said objects have the ability to pass through walls and ceilings. Cuts down on the guests asking about books walking up the stairs and such. Of course, most of my guests come specifically to see the ghosts but this way Maxie's route was more direct.

As soon as she got through the ceiling and into the room, the trench coat disappeared and Maxie returned to her usual uniform of tight jeans and a black T-shirt with white lettering. This one read, "Unexpected." She was holding her laptop computer and clacking away at the keys.

"Poisoned?" I said. "Are you sure? How do you know?" Clearly Vance had some inside information. Maybe he'd been there watching helplessly as it happened.

"I know," he said. Well, that was helpful.

"Where did this take place, Vance?" Paul asked. Paul is all about gathering information and putting the puzzle together. Sometimes he also notices that people have feelings. He's a very nice guy with a good heart—okay, he *used* to have a good heart—but he gets so caught up in the hunt that he occasionally overlooks the emotions that surround it.

"Here, in Harbor Haven," Vance said, with a tone of *how-could-you-not-know-that* in his voice. "Nessa had just moved here before . . . it happened. That's why I came here. It's why I responded when I got your message, mate. Because you were here."

That must have nicked Paul a little bit. He likes to think

we have a reputation as the go-to sleuths of the ghost world. He did not show the wound, though. He plowed on through.

"So we can check with the Harbor Haven police and they'll have records," he said, not necessarily to Vance. "But if the medical examiner found that there was no foul play . . ."

"Oh, there was foul play," Vance intoned, his accent taking on a slightly threatening tinge. "And I know who played it foul, too."

Maxie looked up from the computer screen. "You know who killed your daughter?" she asked.

"If I knew, I wouldn't need you." Vance floated back and forth, like pacing but without moving his feet at all. "Whoever did it would be dealing with me at this very moment, no doubt."

Maxie, having clacked away a while longer, shouted, "Aha!" before Paul could respond to Vance's pronouncement. "I've got it here." She pointed at the screen. "Vanessa McTiernan, daughter of the front man for the Jingles—"

"Front man?" Vance interrupted. "I *was* the Jingles. The other three played what I told 'em to play."

"But Phil Leeds was a genius on the bass and Louie Calhern never missed a beat, even when your rhythms got complicated. Morrie Chrichton's name is even listed on a bunch of the songs as a cowriter." I hadn't intended to challenge Vance, but the music geek in me emerged when I wasn't looking.

Vance's lips took on a sneer and his eyes cooled down considerably. "Morrie Chrichton." He said the name with what could only be described as contempt. "Phil and Louie were basically session guys, but Morrie! That untalented old tin-pot couldn't have written his own name if I hadn't shown him how. He got credit on the songs because we made a stupid deal when we were twelve years old and I was too much a gentleman to dissolve it when we started making money. Don't talk to me about Morrie Chrichton."

I decided not to talk to Vance about Morrie Chrichton, possibly ever again.

"Anyway," Maxie went on, "it says here that police responded to an anonymous 911 call about loud music in the apartment. Vanessa McTiernan was found dead in her home four-and-a-half months ago, in April. Initial reports indicate natural causes, probably a severe allergic reaction."

Vance McTiernan's daughter died in Harbor Haven less than five months ago and *I didn't know about it*? I was a disgrace to obsessive fans everywhere.

"It's *not true*," Vance interrupted.

"We know," my mother assured him. She's a champ at getting people back under control. She learned to do it when I was about Melissa's age. "But Maxie isn't responsible for what was written in the newspaper."

I knew who *was* responsible for that, and she was going to be my first phone call.

Vance eyed Maxie up and down. "I can tell you what she could be responsible for," he said. It's part of the rock star persona to be a ladies' man. He probably couldn't help it. But it would have been nice if he'd had better taste.

Maxie ignored him and went back to reading. "Vanessa, forty years old, had been a singer and keyboardist for the local band Once Again until two years ago. She was currently employed as a coding specialist for a medical records firm in Asbury Park. Survivors include her mother, Claudia Rabinowitz, and a half brother, Jeremy Bensinger. The brother's in Marlboro but there's no address for Claudia." She looked up at Vance.

"Claudia," he said almost wistfully. "I met her on tour. We played the Garden State Arts Center and she was backstage. We hit it off." (Just to be accurate, the venue is now called the PNC Bank Arts Center. The name change hasn't made any difference to the music.)

One of the later Jingles albums included a song called

"Claudia" that I'd especially loved in my early teens. It sang of new love, possibilities and devotion that would never die.

"How long were you married?" Mom asked.

"Married?" Vance said. "We were only together that one night. I didn't see her again until she filed the paternity suit."

"What's a paternity suit?" Melissa asked.

"Something fathers wear for special occasions," my own father said, coming down from the ceiling to shelter his granddaughter, who clearly knew he was lying. "Come with me into the kitchen, peanut. I want to talk to you about what you're making for dinner tonight." Melissa has been taking cooking lessons from Mom, who has finally realized I'm a lost cause in the kitchen and moved directly on to the next generation.

Liss, who is a very intelligent girl, gave her grandfather a suspicious look. "You're just trying to get me out of the room, aren't you?" she asked Dad.

"That's right," my father said.

Melissa thought that over. "Okay," she said. She loves her grandfather and finds it hard to say no to him, especially since he is deceased. Besides, we both knew that no matter what inappropriate subject matter might arise after she left the room, Maxie would clue her in later.

I looked up at Vance as soon as Liss and Dad went into the hallway, presumably to go to the kitchen. "Vanessa," I said. "She used your name? Not her mother's?"

"Only professionally. Her mother's name wasn't going to open any doors in the world of music, love," Vance said. "Her mother was a girl from New Jersey and I was the Jingles."

That was the second time he'd chosen to say it that way. There's a certain braggadocio among performers and artists, but in this case Vance wasn't just being an egotist. It was common knowledge among those of us who loved the Jingles that he was not only the heart and soul but the brains of the outfit. He wrote (until two minutes ago I would have said cowrote) all the songs, arranged and sang them, and although Martin Wellspring got credit for producing the band's recordings, all the interviews in later years—even with Wellspring himself—admitted that while Vance might not have been physically turning the knobs, he was charting out exactly when and how far they should be turned.

"Okay, so, please, explain what you think happened and what you want us to do."

"Indeed," Paul chipped in. "I don't see how we can help you much in this case." Paul and I had apparently undergone one of those mind-switching things that happens in some of the cheaper live-action Disney movies—I'm usually the one trying to get out of an investigation, and he's the one being patient and polite with our (usually ghostly) potential clients, in the hopes of getting the case.

As if there were so many other spirit detectives on the Ghosternet Craigslist that we had to compete.

"I think you can," Vance answered. "See, here's the thing: I was in England when I died, and that's where I showed up like this." He gestured toward himself in a sweeping motion.

I remembered when Vance had died. I'd read about it in the newspaper and sat stock-still for I don't know how long. The Swine had come down from our bedroom and looked at me carefully. Then, being a swine, he had asked if I'd gotten any Honey Nut Cheerios for breakfast.

"So what are you doing in New Jersey?" Paul asked.

"We were always bigger in the UK than here, so Vanessa's death was news. When I heard it on the telly, I had to come here to find out what really happened," Vance said. "It's funny what you can do when you don't have to actually follow physical laws at all."

"Still, you couldn't have flown here in minutes from the other side of the Atlantic Ocean," Mom said.

"Of course not," Vance admitted. "It took months for me to walk here."

"Walk?" Maxie said. "From England?"

"Absolutely. It's not like I could drown, is it? And I have to tell you, there are some amazing sights down there, when there's still light enough to see. Sometimes I'd float to the top and hover a bit, fly over the water and watch the whales jump. But mostly it was walking."

"Couldn't you have taken a plane or a cruise ship or something?" Mom asked. "It would have been faster."

"Needed time to think," Vance said. "Needed a *lot* of time. To think."

"But you didn't find out everything you needed or you wouldn't be talking to us," Paul reminded Vance, bringing him back to the subject at hand. Paul is a master at staying on topic.

Vance pointed a finger at him. "Absolutely right, mate, absolutely right," he said. His accent got a little thicker when he talked to Paul. His manner was more jovial, too, as if he momentarily forgot the reason he'd been talking to us in the first place. "I don't know who did it and I don't have a guess about how, but the problem is, I have no information. I was back in England and Nessa was here. So I need professionals like yourselves to find out who killed my little baby daughter."

Maxie looked up from her screen. "Your daughter was forty," she said. Maxie will never be forty, so she thinks that's old.

"They're always your babies, love."

Paul raised his finger, no doubt to lecture Vance on the finer points of investigation and motive, that one needs reliable, verifiable evidence and so forth—but I jumped in before the professor could begin to profess. "We'll do everything we can," I said to Vance. Paul looked at me with an expression of utter amazement on his face but no way was I going to let him turn down a case with *Vance McTiernan* just because he clearly was jealous of our client.

The man who might have had slightly more justified reason to be jealous—my boyfriend, Josh—would certainly take my side of the argument. That is, he would if he were awake. Right now, he was nestled against my shoulder like a puppy, eyes closed and breathing regular. He even had the good taste and breeding not to be snoring. But I couldn't count on him for support just now.

"What Alison means," Paul countered, "is that we will try our best to determine if your daughter's death was actually a homicide. We're not going to enter into a situation where we find some patsy on whom you can take out your frustrations. Is that clear?"

"Crystal," Vance agreed.

"Very well, then," Paul said, settling the matter. "We will report back to you as soon as there is news about the case."

"Right," Vance said.

I got the impression Paul expected Vance to leave at that point but the rock 'n' roll ghost stayed put and watched my friend, the detective, float in place.

Paul studied him. "Is there anything more you can tell us that might help?" he asked.

Vance made a show of thinking about it—I was noticing that he made a show of just about everything, not that I minded—and shook his head. "I don't think so."

"Very well," Paul repeated.

"Okay." This was getting tedious.

"Okay, fellas," I said. "Let's get the ball rolling. Vance, we have a client form we'd like filled out. It gives us information about you and the case and fills in all the information we'd want to ask you later when you're not here."

"When I'm not here?" Vance asked. "Where am I going, love?"

"Don't you have a place to stay?" Mom asked.

"Why would I? I just strolled in from the Atlantic. I'm sure you'll find this hard to believe, but now that Vanessa's gone, I don't actually know anyone else in New Jersey. Except you."

Paul's eyes widened. Mom's narrowed. Maxie, as ever when the situation didn't involve her, was distracted by her own thoughts and was circling the ceiling slowly. Her rate of speed increases when she's agitated but now she was downright tranquil.

"I can stay here, can't I?" he asked.

"Of course!" I answered before Paul could object. My inner fangirl was screaming, *Vance McTiernan's going to stay in my house! Vance McTiernan's going to stay in my house! Vance McTiernan's going to stay in my house! Would I get to hear him sing? What if he wrote a song about me if I found the truth about his daughter's death? Was that too much?*

Next to me on the sofa, Josh stirred a little and his eyelids fluttered. I lowered my voice a little to let him sleep—the man owns a paint store and has to be up at the crack of dawn to open in time for all the painters stocking up for a day's work—and added, "I have a room that's not being rented if you want to set up shop in there."

Maxie's mouth twisted on one side. "He's a ghost," she said from the ceiling. "Do you think he brought bags with him?"

"Would be nice to have a base of operations," Vance said, looking me straight in the eyes, just as he once had from the vintage poster I'd had tacked up on my wall as a tween. "Please take me there."

"Follow me." I figured if I hustled him out of the room, Paul's noticeable irritation at Vance's residency might not be vocalized.

I was wrong. "You intend to stay here for the duration of the investigation?" Paul demanded of Vance. "To watch us every step of the way?"

Vance, who had been following me out of the room, turned and looked back at Paul, who had dropped about calf-deep in the floor but was still advancing toward us. "Well, yeah," Vance said. "Why not? Is there something you don't want me to see about the way you're going to find my daughter's killer?"

Paul stopped. You can make fun of his Canadian politeness.

You can question his priorities. You can even tell him he wasn't the best investigator ever when he was alive, as Maxie often does.

But you don't dare question his integrity on any level.

"Of course not," he got out through essentially sealed lips.

"All right, then. I'll be here to help if you need me, but I promise I'll stay out of the way when you don't, okay? You won't even know I'm here."

We turned back toward the hallway and I walked, Vance floated toward the stairway so I could show him his room.

But as we made it to the movie room archway (there is no door there), I heard Paul mutter, "I'll know."

# Three

I was immediately annoyed that I couldn't give Vance (*I got to call him Vance!*) my best room because I'd rented it to a living, breathing, paying person. I continued to ignore Paul's uncharacteristic arguing against taking the case, but aside from that, the rest of the night proceeded more or less as usual. Josh woke up and went home to sleep. Melissa and Dad arrived back from the kitchen with plans for dinner that included ordering a pizza.

I also helped two of my guests, Roberta and Stan Levine, find a suitable restaurant for dinner. I don't serve food, so my guests are on their own in that department, but it doesn't mean I can't throw a little business in the direction of the Harbor Haven Diner or Rascal's for dinner or the Stud Muffin for breakfast. I like to support local businesses, especially the ones that support me by sending a small percentage of the profit they make on each customer I send their way.

Roberta and Stan headed out, as did the rest of the guests,

including Maureen after I called a taxi for her. The walk into town would have been too difficult, but she wasn't going to stay in the house all week, she said. This was a shore vacation!

Maxie cut out right before dinner, saying she had a date with Everett, a ghost for whom death had actually improved things. Everett had been a homeless man on the streets of Harbor Haven in the last years of his life, but had reverted in spirit form to the clean-cut, disciplined military man of his past. Maxie announced that the two of them were going "down to the mini golf course to move the balls around when people aren't looking."

The five of us left in the house (Vance had stopped by to say that he was going to "gallivant about town by way of exploring") gathered in the kitchen when the pizza arrived for Mom, Liss and me.

"I've never seen you like this, Alison," Paul said from his perch over the stove (he knew there was no danger it would be used and besides, what damage could it do to him?) as I was getting paper plates out of the cabinet. "You've never actually wanted to take a case before and now suddenly you want *this* of all cases?"

"What's wrong with this case?" Melissa was finding cups in a cabinet closer to her reach, under the countertop by the fridge. But "her reach" is growing and Dr. Stewart, the pediatrician, insists she'll be taller than me in a couple of years.

"For one thing, I don't believe one word that man says." Paul was looking at me as he said that, and all I was doing was getting a pitcher of water out of the fridge. "He *walked* here from England? He has it on 'good authority' that Vanessa didn't die of natural causes? It's so clear he's lying. I don't understand it, Alison. Why are you trying to talk me into doing the bidding of a man I wouldn't trust as far as I could throw him, *if* I could throw him. What makes you so sure about him?"

I stopped and considered it.

*"The tide of love and truth/*
*the idea of love in the sea/*
*was the only bright part/*
*of my misspent youth/*
*that meant the world to me."*

I looked up at Paul and folded my arms.

"That's it?" he asked.

"It's from the Jingles song 'Misspent Youth,'" Mom informed him.

"It's a terrible lyric," Paul insisted. "It strains to rhyme and confuses the number of items it describes. What has that to do with the murder—if it was a murder at all—of Vance McTiernan's daughter?"

"A man who can write with that much sensitivity is open to pain," I said. "Imagine how he must feel with his only child dead by someone's hand and powerless to do anything about it?"

"He's not interested in evidence. He doesn't need proof. He wants us to help him get revenge," Paul said. "He wants us to identify a killer and then you can bet Vance will take matters into his own hands."

I turned on the oven because I like to keep a slice or two warm. It was a very mild September, but the heat from the oven wouldn't be oppressive and warm pizza, while fabulous, is not as fabulous as hot pizza.

I had put two slices in the oven on a piece of aluminum foil (keeping with the fully disposable theme of the dinner) and was taking another out of the box to put on my plate. Liss was already set up with a slice and we sat on bar stools at the center island, a pitcher of filtered water between us.

"Vance is in deep pain," I said. "Maybe it's his unfinished

business on earth. Maybe he needs to solve this crime so he can move on to the next stage, did you think about that?"

Paul's lips straightened out into a horizontal line. "Vance has shown no sign whatsoever of any mental anguish," he said. "So far, all he's done is tell us a fragmented story, put off filling out our intake form and charm you into letting him stay in the house. You're being played, Alison, and I even think you know it."

I didn't answer Paul because, frankly, what he was saying hit a little close to home. Also, I was busy eating. (The pizza tasted great, but then, when does it not?) I had never been enthusiastic (or even willing) to take on an investigation before. But Vance McTiernan wasn't just some guy who'd sang on records. He was the guy I'd listened to in my adolescence when nobody understood me—but *he* had understood. He was the singer whose voice would echo my angst, whose lyrics spoke the feelings I couldn't express. Even as an adult, when Melissa's dad, The Swine, had left me for a younger, blonder woman, I had spent two full weeks listening to nothing but the Jingles.

I was halfway through my slice when I asked Paul, "What reason would he have to con us?" Defensive? Moi? "What's his motivation? You're the one who advertised our services on the Ghosternet or Vance would never have known to come here and talk to us. And if his daughter wasn't murdered, what possible reason would Vance McTiernan have to look into it?"

Melissa said, "He could just be wrong. He might think the evidence supports the conclusion of murder when in fact all he has is circumstantial evidence and innuendo."

It's possible Melissa has spent a little too much time around our investigations.

Paul was pacing, which is always weird to watch since his feet don't touch the ground. I've seen it many times before but it's still a little disconcerting, as was how I could see the calendar on the wall behind him despite the fact that his body was in front of it.

"My recommendation is we tell Vance we've looked into his case but it's too tough and we can't help him," Paul was saying now. "He really can't argue with that. We'll just seem slightly incompetent rather than dishonest. He'll move on."

"Who are you and what have you done with Paul Harrison?" I asked. "'We'll just seem slightly incompetent'? Isn't that, like, your worst nightmare, ruining your reputation on the Ghosternet? What is it about this case that scares you so badly, Paul?"

He stopped pacing and put his hands in the pockets of his jeans. "I have a bad feeling about it," he said.

"Really, Obi-Wan? You have a bad feeling? You know how many bad feelings I've had about cases you were all gung ho about us taking on?"

Dad, who had been back in the movie room contemplating last-minute touches, floated in through the wall just as Mom stood up and went to the fridge to refill her orange juice. Orange juice with pizza. No, I can't explain her, either.

"Sometimes a detective has to go on a gut instinct," Paul said. "Sometimes that's all we have. And my gut instinct about Vance McTiernan is that he's hiding something, and it's something we don't want to see."

"He's *Vance McTiernan*," I said for approximately the ninety-seventh time. "His every emotion is in his work. Hiding something? The man's incapable of hiding anything. Besides, he's a ghost. He's transparent by definition."

Paul ignored my last comment entirely. "His music is not the issue. It's a mistake to take on a case when you can't trust your client. And Vance is clearly lying to us about something, which could be a simple matter of ego or could hide his desire, not for justice but for revenge. That can be a very big problem. I don't want to see you in danger, Alison."

"Oh man! That's a laugh coming from you. How many

times have I been in danger on cases you found interesting, and my safety never seemed to be a problem then!" I stopped eating and handed my crust to Melissa; that's how upset I was. Paul was trying to ruin the Jingles for me and in the process was even putting a damper on pizza. "What about *my* instincts, Paul? I think Vance is an artist and a poet and he's asking for help with his broken heart over the death of his daughter. *My* instincts say we should do everything we can to help him. Why isn't that as important as your gut instinct?"

Melissa is eleven. She's starting to see signs of the woman she'll be someday and it occasionally freaks her out. So I know she's looking at me and measuring exactly how much of her mom's personality she's going to want to emulate. She was watching me intently at this moment, and I think she looked proud. It made me bolder.

"This is about an investigation," Paul said. "That's why my instincts are more pertinent to the discussion."

"Why? Because you don't think *I'm* a detective, right? Well, the state of New Jersey disagrees. You want to see my license?"

Paul is a gracious and gentle man at heart. Despite evidence that in life he'd had enough muscle to have torn me in half like a piece of pumpernickel, he is polite and he is sensitive. In many ways, he could have passed for a singer-songwriter like Vance McTiernan.

That's what made it so much more devastating when he bluntly stated, "You only have your license because I told you the answers."

I stopped dead in mid-motion (getting another slice of pizza because my confidence had returned). "So you're saying you don't trust me on an investigation?" I asked.

"Don't make me say it, Alison."

Melissa's eyes widened but she said nothing.

Mom held up a hand, but Dad spoke first. "Let's not cross

any lines here," he said. "You two are good friends. You don't want to change that. Okay, so you disagree on a case; it's not like that's never happened before. You'll probably disagree again. Don't start saying things you can't ever take back."

Mom reached over and patted Dad on the arm. Sort of. She can touch the ghosts, while I get more of a feeling from them—Paul is like a warm breeze, Maxie like a refreshing one, at least when she's in a good mood.

I heard what he was saying. I processed it and I agreed with it intellectually. Dad was right. Paul and I should not let emotions rule our actions and we should not do anything that might jeopardize our friendship.

But then Paul said, "This is not about friendship, Jack. It's about business. And I know this business better than your daughter does."

So he really did see me as a poor investigator. I'd always been self-deprecating about my detective skills, and with a good deal of reason. But the truth was, I *have* actually solved a couple of cases practically all by myself. Sometimes the self-deprecation is just for show. I may have gotten my private investigator license under duress, and it's true that I wasn't as proud of it as the day I got my innkeeper's license, but that was because I had never considered being an investigator before I met Paul. I had always wanted to own a guesthouse.

I take pride in doing everything I do well. I care about doing a job right, whether it's restaining the paneling in the movie room, making sure my guests feel comfortable during their vacations or doing the inevitable legwork on one of Paul's investigations. His attitude now was hurting me.

"If you don't want to help me on this case, Paul, you don't have to," I said. "I'm sorry you don't believe in me, but I wouldn't want to make you do something that you feel is wrong. Just as I'm sure you'll understand why I'm taking this investigation on by myself."

I saw Paul's astonished expression briefly as I stood and turned away. Mom's jaw dropped, Dad looked puzzled and Melissa looked back and forth between Paul and me as if trying to see which one would break first. But there was no time for that. I walked out of the kitchen before anyone could try to talk me out of it.

I took my slice of pizza with me, though. I'm not crazy.

# Four

*Friday*

"Do you smell something?" I asked Melissa the next morning. Then I sniffed.

I was getting dressed while Liss, almost ready for school (something she was just now getting used to again after summer break), was sprawled face up on my bed, watching the ceiling fan and doing her best not to mention what had happened the evening before.

Mom and Dad had left for Mom's place roughly five minutes after my dramatic exit from the kitchen. Luckily, cleanup from dinner was remarkably easy and quick, consisting mostly of throwing things away. Melissa had wrapped up the leftover pizza in aluminum foil and put it in the fridge, where it was undoubtedly feeling very lonely. I think all we had was milk (for cereal and coffee), some baby carrots and two bottles of beer. In a former life, I was undoubtedly a frat boy.

Melissa had come out of the kitchen as soon as it was under

control, but Paul had remained out of sight, so I couldn't have apologized to him even if I had wanted to.

But to be honest, I didn't want to. It wasn't just that I was hurt by Paul's lack of confidence in me—I more or less understood that. It was more that Paul didn't believe in Vance, the man who had helped me get through such difficult years with his sensitivity, his understanding and his adorable smile (on the album covers and in magazines). His music had been out for decades before I discovered it, but it had spoken to me in a way that few other artists had ever managed, even to this day.

It occurred to me to explain to my daughter, early in her sixth-grade year, why I had been so quick to fly off the handle the night before, but she had never really embraced the Jingles and might not understand. Melissa is open to all kinds of music and loves some of my favorite bands—she has three Beatles T-shirts—but had never really warmed to Vance and his less-direct poetry. It was okay; she could still be my daughter. I was magnanimous about such things as long as she didn't play any serious rap when I was around. I've never warmed to it and usually take refuge in my oldies. I'm a throwback.

I love a lot of oldies bands, but to me the Jingles were just as up-to-date as anything on your radio this morning. (Not everyone feels this way—approximately one in every six thousand people appears to have heard of the band, which confuses me. How could they not recognize the genius?) Nobody's adolescence is easy, and mine was not worse than most, but there were nights when I turned off the lights, closed my window and let the glow from the cassette player (Mom wouldn't let me keep the albums in my room, so I recorded all of them) be the only thing I could see and Vance McTiernan's voice the only thing I could hear. To this day I get a warm feeling in my chest when "Claudia" or "Misspent Youth" or the Jingles masterpiece "Never Again" plays on my radio or my iPod. Some things just don't die.

Which brings me back to Paul.

Of course I had been impulsive about kicking him off the case and stomping out of the kitchen in a huff. He'd attacked my idol and my pride at the same time and I hadn't had a moment to sift through my feelings. But he also wasn't allowing for the idea that I might be right or that Vance might actually need me—us—so much that turning him down would be an act of cruelty. Sure, he was dead, but that didn't mean he was without feelings.

"Smell what?" Melissa asked. She closed her eyes and sniffed. "I don't smell anything."

"I don't know. Maybe my nose is playing tricks on me." This is the kind of thing you say when you don't want to discuss something else.

On cue, Maxie descended through the ceiling, even though she knows I prefer she knock before entering my bedroom. "What's with Paul?" she asked as she floated down. Maxie's sensitivity extends only to all things Maxie, so it was a surprise to hear that she had actually noticed her fellow spirit acting strangely. "He hasn't said a word all morning."

"Mom's mad at him because he won't take Vance's case," Melissa informed her "roommate." Whatever issues I have with Maxie, I know she adores my daughter and I think Liss looks at her as the rebellious older sister she never had.

"I'm not mad at Paul," I said, and it was mostly true. I wasn't mad at him *anymore*. Now I was mostly feeling a little hurt and a little worried about how I'd impulsively taken a case on my own, but I wasn't mad.

"Oh," Maxie said. That was odd. Maxie, not questioning something that could potentially be a source of irritation for me? The small hairs on the back of my neck didn't stand up, but they were definitely crouching at least.

"Do you have an opinion?" I asked. It was the first time I had asked Maxie that question, mostly because it was the first time she hadn't offered one without being asked.

"I dunno. I was more into the punk scene, so I don't know anything about this guy. I've never heard his music."

I felt my brow crinkle. "That's your criteria? If his music is to your liking, we should find out who killed this poor man's daughter, but if it's not, we should just ignore his pain?"

"Chillax, Mom," my daughter said. She's a lovely girl, but she is still rather seriously eleven. "You were the one who said we should take the case because Vance is such a sensitive songwriter."

As usual, she was right, but what was different this time was how annoyed it made me. "Don't you have to get to school?" I asked.

Maxie and Liss exchanged a look I wish I hadn't noticed before my daughter got off the bed and headed downstairs to make herself a rudimentary breakfast, which would undoubtedly have exceeded my cooking skills. I can't properly toast an English muffin.

Maxie did not follow Melissa downstairs, which I found curious. She waited, then pulled a pencil from behind her ear and picked up a pad of paper I had on my dresser. "So what's the assignment?" she asked.

"Assignment?"

"Yeah. When Paul makes you take a case, I always get some research stuff to do. I figured even without him, you were going to give me some stuff to find out."

This was serious. Maxie was the sensible person in this conversation.

"Okay. Yeah. Um . . . find out whatever you can about Vance's daughter, Vanessa."

There was a long pause. Maxie said, "That's it?"

Right—I should have more for her to do! "No. No, I also want you to find out where and when she died, who she was with, anything about this band she was in and who survives her." That sounded pretty good. Thorough. Professional.

What Paul would say.

"I told you most of that last night, remember? She died four-and–a-half months ago, she played in a band called Once Again, worked at a medical records firm, she had a mother and a half brother." Maxie floated directly over my head to the point that I lay down on the bed to avoid neck strain looking at her.

"Well, find out more about the band. If she was following in her father's footsteps, that might have caused some rifts, maybe with her mom. There were lawsuits over her when she was a child. See if you can find out where Claudia Rabinowitz is now." I closed my eyes. I'd gotten up at five to clean before the guests got up, something I do most days. But having my eyes closed seemed such a good idea now because of that early hour.

Some might say I should go to bed earlier. Some wouldn't know that I can't sleep until all the guests are in their rooms. It's a rule I established for myself when I opened the guest-house.

"Okay, but Paul would have told me to find out more stuff." Maxie rose up into the ceiling and vanished before I could tell her how much I cared what Paul would have told her. Because the fact is, I really was starting to care what Paul would have told her.

I sniffed again and sneezed. I hadn't bothered to ask Maxie if she'd smelled anything because ghosts can't smell or taste. They can see and hear, and I know they can interact with things, but whether or not they feel is something I'm still a little fuzzy on.

*I* smelled something, or at least was reacting to it. I felt allergic, the inside of my nose and the back of my throat itching. I wondered if a stray cat had wandered onto the property; I'm allergic to cat dander and dog fur. That was one of the main reasons I don't have pets in the house (the other being that it would be awful for business if we had to turn away anyone who was afraid or allergic). But I hadn't seen any unfamiliar animals around the place lately. Was I allergic to something else?

There wasn't time to think about that because Vance McTiernan floated in through my bedroom mirror and boomed out, "Good morning, love! Any news on the investigation yet?"

It still stunned me to be talking to *Vance McTiernan*. I was a little in awe of him—you don't get used to seeing one of your idols in the . . . ectoplasm . . . right before your eyes very quickly. It was like looking at an album cover and having it talk to you.

But I was a little thrown by his unannounced appearance in my bedroom, so I played it casual. "Not yet, Vance. Besides, I do have to sleep. For a few hours a night, anyway."

"Of course. It's just very hard for a parent to wait. I'm sure you understand, don't you?" He moved into a sitting position that was probably more for my benefit than his. It looks natural, but the ghosts aren't actually sitting; they're just floating in a different configuration.

I didn't want to think about what a parent might feel under such circumstances, so I decided to change the conversation.

"Vance," I said, "from now on, don't come in here unless you ask first, okay? It's one thing in the rest of the house, but this is my bedroom."

He grinned impishly. "There was a time when I was a welcome presence in some ladies' boudoirs, you know."

"I know. That's how you got Vanessa. But this is now and I'm me, and I'm asking to please be careful about coming in here, okay?" I stood up. "I have to get ready to drive my daughter to school, and then I promise I'll be right on your case."

"Of course, love. Pardon me for not knocking, but it's hard to do when you don't have real knuckles, isn't it?" He was still smiling as he floated down through the floor. I was somewhat relieved he hadn't risen, because Melissa's attic bedroom is right above mine. I was in awe of Vance McTiernan, but that didn't mean he didn't worry me a little, too.

I went downstairs and checked on Melissa, who was having a cup of coffee (she's a little too advanced sometimes, but puts lots of milk in it) with a few minutes to spare before we had to leave.

After checking on the guests, two of whom were already heading to the Stud Muffin for breakfast (the Levines, a lovely couple in their sixties from Maplewood), I did a quick scan of the downstairs, making sure the movie room looked ready for the grand opening in two days, the library had all its books shelved neatly (or close to neatly) and the den, my largest room (probably once a dining room), looked homey, welcoming and clean.

Who am I kidding? I was really looking for Paul so I could apologize, and he wasn't around.

He'd undoubtedly be present a little after ten, when we did the first spook show of the day. Paul never misses one, although Maxie does occasionally "forget" to show up and is then outraged when I scold her for it. Lately, she'd been more reliable. I wondered if it was due to Everett, with his military training, having a positive influence on Maxie.

But that didn't solve the Paul question for right now.

"Gotta go, Mom." Melissa appeared at my left elbow (okay, my left shoulder—she'd grown a decent amount in the past year) checking her cell phone. "I see there's an accident on Ocean Avenue; we'll have to take the long way today." My daughter is so responsible it's a little bit frightening. I know she didn't get it from me, and as *responsible* is not a word one would ever dredge up when thinking about The Swine (something I try not to do whenever possible). I'm guessing she got it from my mother, and it skipped a generation. Like cooking and being able to see ghosts without suffering a concussion first.

I took another quick look around the room and smiled at her. "Okay, let's go," I said.

Melissa looked at me sideways. "Paul's not here. I saw him out in the back before, floating around the beach."

"I wasn't looking for Paul."

"Sure you weren't."

Liss chatted on about school while I drove her there. She had a science test on Tuesday, which was so unfair because now she'd have to spend her whole weekend studying and why couldn't teachers just take that into account when they were planning out their marking periods, and also her best friend, Wendy, had a crush on some boy whose name I was supposed to recognize and was therefore acting "weird."

I was thinking about Vance McTiernan's daughter, Vanessa, and decided that I'd check with my best source of information on such things after I dropped Liss off at school.

"You're not listening, are you?" she asked, bringing me out of my stupor.

"Sure I am. Wendy. Weird. Test. Unfair. I got it all."

"I was talking about quitting the Tech Club." Melissa looked at me with something approaching pity. It's so hard raising a mother these days.

"Okay. So my mind was elsewhere for a minute. I admit that." I don't believe in lying to my daughter unless she asks me questions about her father, because telling her the truth would be too upsetting. She knows it, but she doesn't need to hear it from me. "I'm sorry. Why do you want to quit the club?"

"It meets twice a week." Liss was already looking out the window to see which of her friends would be available immediately after escaping from the bowels of my car. In sixth grade, friends are your world and your mother is the chauffeur. It's important to have priorities.

"Are you really that busy?" Something sounded fishy.

"I don't like getting home that late when we have a—" She caught herself.

That was it. "Because we have a case?" I asked.

"Yeah." She still wasn't looking at me.

"Don't quit the club for that, Liss. You're not a detective, you're a sixth-grader. Be that."

We'd reached the entrance. Melissa got out of the car and fled as fast as she could without giving me a response. Luckily, I had stopped the car at the school entrance or that could have gotten messy.

Well, at least I had stopped sneezing for the moment and I didn't smell anything unusual anymore. Maybe whatever was giving me an allergic reaction was back at the house. I'd have to get the antihistamine out of the medicine cabinet when I got home.

But first I was heading back toward the center of town, and I had enough time before the upcoming morning spook show to squeeze an invaluable source of information for everything I could get.

"Vanessa McTiernan?" Phyllis Coates looked over half glasses at me and scrunched up her mouth into a small circle. "I don't remember the name."

"I hadn't heard about it, either, which is weird," I told her.

"Honey, let's be real. It's much weirder that I didn't know about it than you."

Phyllis was right. Well, no she wasn't. I was the major Jingles fan, and she had never heard of Vance McTiernan (which came close to damaging our relationship but I had to be magnanimous about such things or I'd have no friends at all). But under almost any other circumstances, Phyllis would know more than me about virtually anything. As the editor, publisher, reporter and custodial staff (the one area in which she was badly unskilled) of the *Harbor Haven Chronicle*, she knew everything and everybody that had anything to do with my hometown.

The minute I'd mentioned Vanessa's name, Phyllis had yanked a binder off a shelf just to her right and found all the information she had on the death from the past spring. Some people have computers; Phyllis has knowing where everything is in her suffocatingly cluttered office. But she wasn't looking at her notes now. One glance and she could access the part of her brain that already had it memorized. Ask her what she had for lunch today and she'd have no idea. Ask her where the strand of hair that produced the DNA evidence in a six-year-old murder was found, and she wouldn't hesitate for one second. Phyllis, as much as I love her, is scary.

"So what else do you know?" I asked her. If she wanted to show off, I could only benefit from it.

"I know enough not to tell you anything unless I'm going to get a story out of it." Okay, *that* could have gone better.

"I promise the minute I find out who killed Vanessa, you can have the story," I said. "You know I'll completely snub CNN."

"Ha! Nobody watches them anyway." Phyllis smirked at me. "You really think she didn't just die from the allergic reaction? There wasn't anything crazy in the autopsy report." Phyllis has a source in the county medical examiner's office with whom she shares "information." Well, in the broadest sense of the word. Phyllis gets information and her friend gets . . . let's leave it at that. "Besides, it happened months ago. How come you're all hot and bothered about it now, all of a sudden?"

She sipped from the Dunkin' Donuts iced coffee I'd brought her. Phyllis's office, which is among the greatest firetraps in the land, is covered in paper, but it does have a lovely hot plate on which a pot of coffee has been brewing since Jimmy Carter was in office. It would be safer to face Vanessa's killer armed with a toothbrush than to drink a cup of Phyllis's office coffee.

"A family member came to me with questions about Vanessa's death," I said. That was true. "I agreed to look into it. So you're my first stop because you know everything. Are you saying there's no chance whatsoever that Vanessa McTiernan was forcibly fed soy sauce?" I took a sip of my own Dunkin' Donuts iced coffee. I was just as worried about my own health as about Phyllis's, after all. Maybe even a touch more.

Phyllis waved a hand. As a retired reporter for the New York *Daily News*, she's seen everything at least twice and knew enough not to make definitive statements about something being completely impossible. She's the same way about the ghosts in my house—what she couldn't confirm was just a rumor, and Phyllis was interested in facts. "You know perfectly well there's always a *chance*," she said. "But the odds are against it. Vanessa had an allergy, the thing she was allergic to was present in her system, there was no sign of forced entry to her place, no sign of a struggle and no record of anybody being mad at her."

"A perfect setup," I argued. "The cops didn't really give it much of a look because it was just someone who showed up dead with an easy-to-explain medical condition. Why even look over the scene of the death? File it away, call the case cleared and move on to the next thing. Right?"

Phyllis shook her head no. "The primary detective on the scene after the uniforms called it in was Anita McElone."

For once, I did not groan at the mention of Lieutenant McElone (with the long *e* at the end, rhymes with *macaroni*). McElone and I had a somewhat complicated relationship, in that I always came to her for help and she always thought I was a nut who was going to get in the way. But lately McElone and I had found a touch more mutual respect—as in, she now respected me a little, and I continued to respect her a lot—after I'd saved her life. Technically.

"She's good," I said. "McElone should know if there was anything sketchy about the way Vanessa died. But why did they call a detective if everybody thought it wasn't suspicious?"

"That's a good question," Phyllis answered. "You should ask McElone that when you talk to her."

My gut still had a little twinge of butterflies when I considered that. McElone might finally regard me as within driving distance of competent, but she still acted like I was a total screwup, and that fed into my natural insecurity. I didn't like asking the lieutenant for help when I didn't have to. Now it seemed I'd have to.

"That's the best you can do?" I asked. Sometimes prodding Phyllis a little gets you information, and sometimes it's just a way to put off seeing McElone. "You tell me it's routine and I should go ask the cops for anything else? What happened to being the source of all information down the shore?" I tried to say that with a twinkle in my eye so Phyllis would know it was gentle teasing. Have you ever *tried* to get your eye to twinkle? It's very hard to do.

Phyllis scowled, as if denigrating my twinkling ability. "You think that's all I've got?" she asked.

"No. Clearly I think you've got more and you're just not telling me." Playing up to her ego couldn't hurt, either, especially since the whole "prodding" tactic had fallen flat on its face.

"You're right," she answered.

"So what is it? What have you got that you're not sharing?"

"If you hadn't been so snarky, maybe I'd tell you."

Well, that was hitting below the belt. I apologized profusely and explained that I'd only been kidding. Phyllis graciously accepted my apology, patted me on the head (really!) and then kicked me out of her office without telling me anything else.

Sometimes being Phyllis's friend is hard.

I was halfway out the door and regretting that I'd even bought her an iced coffee when she said, casually and offhandedly (unless those both mean the same thing), "There's something in the ME's report."

Right at the door, I stopped and looked at her. "What did you say?"

Phyllis's back was turned. "You heard me."

"Well, what is it?" I took a couple of steps back into the *Chronicle* office. Mostly because I realized I'd forgotten *my* iced coffee.

"Too much soy sauce. Either she was trying to induce a reaction, or somebody made her drink it."

# Five

Even after I'd picked my iced coffee up off Phyllis's desk, she wouldn't tell me anything more. Which, I realized, probably meant she didn't know any more—Phyllis likes to be seen as a tough cookie (and she is one), but she loves me and will help me when she can. Especially if she suspects she'll get a story out of it.

I pestered her for a full three minutes but she just kept telling me to go see Lieutenant McElone. It was getting close enough to the morning spook show, however, so I decided it was smarter to go back home first and see the lieutenant later.

That's my story and I'm sticking to it.

Harbor Haven is a small town, so it normally takes no more than five minutes to drive from the *Chronicle* office to my house. But I had barely made it a half mile back to Seafront Avenue, where my stately mansion is located, when I noticed a ghost on the side of the road.

Now, I don't see anywhere near the same number of ghosts

that Mom and Melisa do; they tell me it's because my "talent" is new and not as developed as theirs. Which is a nice way of saying they're good at something I'm lousy at, but this is one instance in which I don't mind being the second runner-up. However, as time goes on, I have been seeing more ghosts than I did when this wondrous adventure (I speak fluent Sarcasm) began.

This particular ghost looked especially forlorn, and that always gets to me. She looked to be in her sixties, and was alone (which isn't wildly unusual but isn't always the case either. Sometimes ghosts travel in pairs or packs). But this one just looked lonely.

She was walking (okay, floating—you feel better?) along the side of the road, staying out of traffic, which is more than most living people do. Behind her she dragged a wagon by the handle, a child's toy which appeared to have been crafted out of wood. It made no sound as she moved for a number of reasons, not the least of which was that both the ghost and the wagon were about six inches above the ground.

I stopped along the side of the road, noting that there were no other cars or people in the area, and lowered my passenger window. (No small feat, by the way, because my Volvo wagon is the last car on earth to exist without automatic windows. I had to lean over and crank it down manually. Yes, I'm a pioneer.)

"Can I help you?" I asked the ghost.

She did not respond, probably used to people talking to each other nearby but not knowing she was there, and slowly continued on her way. Ghosts know for a fact that they don't need to be in a rush for anything.

"Excuse me, ma'am—I can see you and your wagon and I'm wondering if there's anything I can do to help you," I said again.

The ghost turned, startled, and looked at me carefully. Then she pointed to herself. "Me?" she asked.

"Yes. You looked like you might be upset about something, and I wanted to see if there is anything I could do." I mean, what were the odds? I was being a Good Samaritan and probably wouldn't actually have to follow up on my offer at all.

And okay, she just looked a little sad. I can't explain it, but she got to me.

"Yes, there is," the ghost said. Karma is a bitch. "Can you find Lester?"

It seemed tactless to inquire as to whether Lester might be living or not-so-much, so I started with something easier.

"Who is Lester?" I asked.

"Lester is my friend," she said. Well, that settled it; I'd begin looking immediately. The woman's eyes were a little too wide, a little too focused, like she might not have been in her best state of mind when she'd died and had not reverted to anything better when she'd made the transition to ghost-hood. I was starting to regret that I'd stopped the car and moved my foot closer to the gas pedal just in case.

"What does he look like?" I asked.

"He has light hair and is not very big," the woman said. "He has brown eyes and a very generous mouth." I wasn't sure I wanted to know what that last part meant.

"Where did you see him last?" I doubted I could find Lester, but it would help if I had some idea of where to look.

"In Topeka, Kansas," the ghost said. "Can you find him?"

"I'll do my very best, ma'am," I said. "But I can't make any promises."

The ghost looked at me as if I were very far away. "All right, then."

"How will I find you if I have any news? What is your name?"

"Yes," the woman said, then turned and pulled her wagon farther down the road.

I felt like an idiot.

Back at the house, I made sure that everything was set

for the morning spook show. Today it would be in the library, which is one of the smaller rooms but one with lots of bookshelf space. As for the spooks themselves, Maxie was on hand, which was unusual. She usually shows up at the last minute, running a comb through her hair for no reason and complaining (naturally) about having to be on a schedule. Maxie sees herself as an artist (she was an interior designer in life) and believes she should be experiencing a bohemian existence. The fact that she exists only in theory doesn't seem to make a difference.

More unusual today was the fact that Paul was *not* present. Under normal circumstances, he is the more reliable of the two by far, with a strong sense of responsibility and the knowledge that he'd engineered the deal linking my interests (the spook shows) with his (investigations).

I guessed these were not normal circumstances.

I was straightening a few books that guests had taken out to read and either returned incorrectly or not returned at all. Keeping the shelves organized had been one of Melissa's tasks over the summer, and I hadn't yet adjusted to her being back in school.

Maxie looked distracted, which isn't unusual. Maxie is better when distracted; it keeps her from dreaming up things you'd (okay, *I'd*) prefer she not think up.

"You know a ghost named Lester?" I asked her.

"Huh?"

"Lester. You know a guy named Lester? Light hair, short? 'Generous mouth'?"

She squinted at me. "Are you taking some medicine or something?"

No, but I wondered if I should have been as I sneezed again.

"Gesundheit," Maxie said.

"Forget it. Is Paul boycotting the show this morning?" I asked Maxie as I tried to remember whether I had *Ulysses* classified as classic or foreign language.

"He didn't say anything to me," she answered helpfully. "Maybe he figures if he's not on the case, he doesn't have to hold up his end of the deal." She lay down on her side, one of her favorite poses; like Cleopatra floating down the Nile sans barge.

"If Paul's not going to make it, can you get Everett?" I asked. Maxie's boyfriend, Everett, with his military bearing, sometimes "sat in" on the shows and did some drill maneuvers that wowed the guests. I thought of trying to get Dad to fill in, but I knew he'd be spending some time at Josh's paint store today. He loves the painters, even if he doesn't know most of the current crew, and Josh's grandfather, Sy, in his nineties, still comes by most days. He can't see Dad, but Dad doesn't care. I'd hate to impose if it wasn't absolutely necessary.

"Nah. He's at the Fuel Pit. It's too far away for him to get back here in time." Everett stays fairly close to the Fuel Pit, a local independent gas station, much of the time. It's where he died, and ghosts sometimes take a while to break free of their final resting spots. It's been three years for Paul and Maxie, and they still get all their mail here at 123 Seafront.

(They don't get any mail. They're ghosts.)

I let out a sigh. Maxie could probably handle a rudimentary spook show on her own, and with two-a-day shows, the guests could stand one slightly skimpier entry.

"I could help," came a voice from behind me. A voice that had the power to make my stomach quiver. "If you tell me what you need, I'll bet I could handle it," Vance Mc-Tiernan said when I turned to face him. "I imagine I'm still a fairly decent showman, I don't mind sayin'."

My mind raced. A private Vance McTiernan performance for me and my guests! The closest to a musical section any of our previous spook shows had come was Paul hitting a bongo drum a few times and strumming the strings on a guitar without changing their pitch—it was more an "ooh, scary" thing than a real musical display.

But before I could respond, Paul rose through the floor and gave Vance a stare just a touch short of dagger-like. "That won't be necessary," he said. "I have an obligation and I intend to fulfill it."

I'll confess it: I was disappointed. "Um, we could do both," I suggested.

"I don't think that will be an advantage," Paul insisted. "Maxie and I have done this hundreds of times before."

"Yeah," Maxie said ominously. No doubt the tedium of actually having to do something that made people happy was wearing on her.

Vance looked at Paul for a long moment. "Another time, then," he said, and rose up into the ceiling and through it. I tried calling after him to ask if he knew Lester but he was gone already.

I tried to remember that my purpose when I'd gotten out of bed this morning had been to apologize to Paul for my emotional and rash behavior the night before. But I had just had the opportunity to present *Vance McTiernan* in concert in my own house and Paul quashed it because he had marked his territory in my library, or something.

"What were you thinking!?" I demanded of Paul, who had the unmitigated nerve to look surprised. "Are you that insecure?"

He didn't have time to answer because just then, two of my guests—Roberta Levine and Maureen Beckman—arrived at the library door. Maureen, leaning on her walker, looked into the room and asked, "Isn't this where we get to see the ghosts today?"

Maxie swooped down from her orbit to a position about two inches from Maureen's face. "You don't get to see me at all," she mocked.

"That's right," I told Maureen, trying hard not to give Maxie a poisonous look (what good would poison do on a dead person?). "Please, come on in. We'll be starting in just a minute."

Maureen, Roberta and Tessa Boynton came in and sat in three of the easy chairs I have for reading in the library. The fourth remained unoccupied, but I was sure that Stan Levine would not be far behind his wife. Tessa's companion, Jesse Renfield, seemed to keep to himself—I'd only seen him once so far. He was young for the Senior Plus set, technically not a senior at all (a junior?) in his late forties. Twenty years ago, he had probably been a surfer off Sandy Hook. But he still had his hair and his teeth (at least in the sense that he held the receipts), and he seemed to know the art of keeping an older woman interested.

Hey, anything can be an art. Jesse was an artist. Just keep in mind that not every artist is a *good* artist.

My sixth guest, Berthe Englund, was out for the morning because she said it was easier to get a good Skee-Ball lane at the boardwalk if you showed up early, especially when school was in session. What made one Skee-Ball lane better than another was a question I hadn't felt the urge to ask.

"If you're truly upset, Alison, I can tell Vance to come back and I'll sit this performance out," Paul suggested. He seemed more puzzled than upset.

I shook my head. The guests know I frequently talk to people who technically aren't there, but the spook shows are about their (the guests') experience, and I was concerned with putting on a good performance. I didn't want to be seen arguing with the "talent."

This group of guests had seen only one spook show the afternoon before, so there was no need to mix it up too much. We could rely on our usual staple, the "floating" objects, and move on from there. As they'd pointed out, Paul and Maxie had done these bits quite a number of times now, and could probably do them in their sleep. If they slept.

"Let's just wait for everyone to be here," I said to the assembled group.

"Stan isn't coming this morning," Roberta informed me. "He's taking a nap, but he'll be here this afternoon."

Maxie huffed an irritated sigh. She actually believes the guests come to the house merely to irritate her, as if it said on the brochures, "Don't pass up your chance to annoy a dead person!" Maxie, as I've said, might be a tiny touch self-centered.

"So then should we wait for Jesse?" I asked Tessa.

"Oh, I don't think so," Tessa answered. "He's probably just wandering around the beach. He doesn't seem that interested in ghosts."

"The feeling is mutual," Maxie volunteered. Again, I pretended she hadn't spoken.

Instead, I sneezed. I had stopped sneezing when I'd left the house, but now that I was back, I felt itchy and allergic again. I wondered if one of the guests was wearing a perfume that might have irritated my sinuses, or something. Mom has told me how she had to stop wearing White Shoulders when I was little because it made my eyes tear and my nose run.

Don't picture it. You're better off.

"Well then, let's get started!" I said, doing my best to sound enthused. When we'd first begun these performances for my guests, it had felt like a scam, presenting Paul and Maxie as scary creatures for the sake of my fledgling business. But I realized over time that the guests didn't want to be frightened. They just wanted some interaction with the unknown, with beings who had crossed to another plane of existence that nobody—not even Paul or Maxie—understands.

Hey, it's a way to make me feel better, and it's not hurting anybody.

I stood in the center of the room and took a deep breath. It wasn't because I was nervous, believe me. It's part of the act. "I'm clearing my mind," I said. "I have to be able to concentrate so I can locate the spirits of the guesthouse."

When I looked up, I noticed Maxie mouthing the speech along with me. Maybe we needed to freshen up the shows a little bit.

"As I clear my mind, I invite you to open your own," I intoned, stifling another sneeze as my brain sent urgent "itch" messages. "Think of nothing at all." (That is, by the way, impossible to do.) "Allow any possibility in your imagination to become real. Consider life and death and what changes come with each step along the continuum of existence." No, I don't know what it means, either, but it sounds profound, doesn't it?

"I sense two presences here in this room," I told the guests. The three women didn't appear to be especially nervous, which was good. Even with all the assurances I offer, some people are scared about being in a house with ghosts, despite having gone out of their way to pay for the privilege. The jumpy ones can get everyone else a little on edge, and then the show stops being fun for anybody.

"Yes, they're here, all right," I continued. "And their names are Paul and Maxie." I pretended to be exhausted by my "connection" with the ghosts, and moved back toward the door of the library. I knew what was coming and wanted to give the ghosts as much room as they needed.

"How come he always gets top billing?" Maxie asked. She knew I wouldn't answer, and it wasn't the first time the question had come up, but she has her agenda.

I felt the urge to sneeze again but I wanted to be sure the show was completely in progress before I could step into the hallway, so I put my index finger up under my nose and pushed. I learned in third grade that could suppress a sneeze and no matter what you think, it works for me.

Paul began by choosing a book—*Team of Rivals* by Doris Kearns Goodwin—and taking it off the shelf and moving it around the room. Not that impressive when you can see the ghost, but to the guests in the library, it appeared that the large volume was flying by itself through space. Their eyes widened and their mouths opened just a little. Roberta actually stood and felt for wires holding the book up, and Paul responded by dropping the book to her eye level and opening it to the title page.

"See if she wants to read it," he said. That's Paul's idea of a joke.

Not to be outdone, Maxie picked up an armful of paperbacks and began tossing them gently onto the laps of the guests. Tessa started just a little, then said, "How did you know I love Danielle Steel?"

"You seemed the type," Maxie told her, but of course only I could hear her voice.

Paul, smiling slyly, took three books in his hands and started to move them around as if he were juggling. To the audience, of course, it looked as if he *was* juggling (Paul isn't anywhere near that coordinated, nor would he ever take the time it would require to learn something so frivolous, despite his literally having all the time he'd ever need), so the women broke into a round of applause when he stopped the "juggling" and stood still with the three books.

"Big deal," Maxie said. She retaliated by buzzing around the room taking bookmarks from the side tables. (I figured a library should have bookmarks, largely because I object to people who leave books, especially paperbacks, open on flat surfaces and break their spines. And dog-earing the pages is a desecration, if you ask me. So there was quite an assortment.)

Maxie took the bookmarks and moved to an old child's toy easel I use to put up announcements for the guests. It made a perfect bulletin board now; too bright to be ignored, but didn't seem imposing or impersonal. It lent a nice touch to the cozy quality of the room.

Maxie now arranged the bookmarks on it to spell out: IS

THAT ALL YOU GOT. She tried to make a question mark at the end but found the task too difficult and left it at that.

Once the guests saw what she had written, they laughed. They didn't know where to look for the competitor—Paul— who would have to meet and exceed the challenge, but I could. And he looked just a little concerned. But then I saw him nod, presumably after having gotten an idea, and fly up to the ceiling fan, where he attempted to get it spinning on its own. Lest the guests think I had simply activated it myself, I took the opportunity, now that the show was in full swing, to head out into the hallway and indulge myself in a truly impressive sneeze.

It actually turned into four consecutive sneezes, followed by massive itching in my throat, which required my making some truly horrendous noises to soothe. So I moved myself farther down the hallway to the movie room and made sounds like a lovesick sea lion for a minute or so. That, unfortunately, clogged my ears. Right after the spook show, I promised myself, I would search the house for some antihistamine, because I was surely having a reaction to *something*.

The congestion in my ears, however, was even more regrettable once I made my way back to the library. Because there in the doorway, holding an acoustic guitar and playing "Claudia" from the Jingles album *Electric Spur* (ironic because it was all acoustic music) was Vance McTiernan. And it was mesmerizing the group, wide-eyed and rapt in their attention.

It was the fulfillment of a dream for me. I literally couldn't move my feet. But I knew what I had to do: I held my nose and blew through it to clear my ears. I didn't want to miss this.

*You faded out like far church bells*
*Your lipstick smeared and caked*
*You never stopped to say farewells*
*But left my heart to break*

The consummate performer, Vance was still revising his technique, putting twists into his intonations and holding notes he hadn't held on the recording. His lovely baritone filled my ears but the guests only heard his intricate but simple guitar accompaniment. Though that was still enough to hold them all in thrall. And I, getting the whole performance, was speechless and awed.

Vance was a real pro.

He made sure to look my way as I reentered the room but did not smile through his lyrics of regret; he was either acting the song or feeling it. And at the end, he performed a special guitar run that I knew wasn't in the original arrangement to give his audience a bonus for their attention.

They let the last chord ring until the sound died completely, then burst into applause the like of which the guesthouse had never heard before. Roberta Levine and Tessa Boynton even stood to give the unseen musician the ovation he deserved. Standing was too difficult for Maureen Beckman, but she applauded the loudest.

Vance put down the guitar carefully next to one of the easy chairs. He bowed.

To me.

Then he swept through the room, making sure to make contact with each of the ladies. You can feel the presence of a ghost when he wants you to, especially, and Vance wanted them to feel it. Each one, when touched, started just a little bit and smiled a special smile; the man was a born entertainer, even in death. After a lingering smile for Maureen Beckman, Vance left the library through the wall, headed in the direction of the kitchen.

"Alison!" Tessa shouted. "That was *wonderful*!"

"Yes," Maureen agreed. "How on earth did you do that?"

I shook my head. "I didn't. That was all ghost."

"But it wasn't scary at all," Roberta said. "It was lovely."

"If you like that kind of thing," Maxie said. She was up

near the ceiling, her face betraying her words. She was grinning the way a true convert does when a once-in-a . . . lifetime? performance has reached her heart.

But that was when I took a look around the library. Maxie's voice had attracted my eyes to the upper half of the room. She made her remark, no doubt to cover the tremble in her voice, and I'd looked up with an expectation that was not satisfied, and for reasons I couldn't have explained fully at the time, I felt very sad in a big hurry, like something very important and irrevocable had just happened.

Paul had left the room before the show was over. And he hadn't come back.

# Six

A thorough search of the house—well, kind of thorough, since it was just me doing the searching—did not lead to a sighting of our resident investigator ghost. This was not terribly unusual. Paul does like his privacy, values time spent alone, and let's face it, can vanish anytime he feels like it, so finding him when he's not in the mood to be found can be something of a challenge.

I gave up after fifteen minutes. The guests all told me how wonderful the performance had been, how glad they were to have chosen my guesthouse for their vacations this year and asked if there would be further musical extravaganzas at the rest of the spook shows (a question I could not begin to answer). I was still reeling from the experience myself and hadn't digested it completely.

After the show broke up, I straightened the library a bit and checked the movie room for my Blu-Ray copy of *Ghost*. I'd bought it at a local bookstore called Read 'Em and Keep, which sold video and music because far too many people wanted to read 'em and then give 'em back.

Then I stood in the movie room, for once entirely alone, and sighed. I'd put it off long enough. It was time to visit Lieutenant Anita McElone. Now I felt like I owed Vance.

Now, it's not that I was afraid of McElone; I'd gotten past that phase. It wasn't even that she intimidates me—I've gotten used to it and expect that to be the case no matter how long I know her. The thing is, the lieutenant and I had recently gone through an experience that was uncomfortable for both of us: I'd sort of saved her life and she didn't know how to handle it.

Since then, she'd clammed up on me to some extent. That had to do both with our recent adventure and the fact that the previously skeptical lieutenant now completely believed in the ghosts in my house. She was still processing the information, and right now she was uncomfortable in my presence. There was a time she wouldn't have walked into my house because she was afraid; now she wouldn't come over because she saw it as a sign of her own failure. Which wasn't true at all, but go tell McElone that.

Still, she was my best source of possible police information on Vanessa McTiernan's death, and she was the only cop I knew who treated me like an investigator, sort of. Not to mention, Phyllis had practically insisted I go see McElone, and that meant Phyllis either knew something and wanted me to go find it out for myself or didn't know something and wanted me to find out for her. That's how Phyllis operates. You eventually get what you need but you have to work for it.

Regardless, I made myself drive to the police station and McElone even let me in through the locked door to the police bullpen when the dispatcher Emily told her I was there. But she didn't look happy about it. Of course, I'm used to that; McElone has *never* looked happy when I've come to ask her about, let's say, anything.

So I started off slowly and asked if she could look for any records of a missing man named Lester from Topeka, Kansas. (I thought of it as a sort of police icebreaker.) But she just stared at me for at least a full minute, not moving a muscle, and I was unnerved enough to move on to the main event.

"A death by natural causes from four months ago?" she asked when I told her about my reason for showing up late on a Friday afternoon. "Who's your client on this one?" She stopped herself. "Wait. It's a ghosty thing, isn't it?"

"You could say that. The client is the deceased's father. Vance McTiernan."

McElone looked at her computer screen. She normally would have gone off for five straight minutes about how a private investigator shouldn't be making the police department do all her work for her, but she probably remembered how she might not have seen her husband and children again were it not for me, so we skipped that part of the ritual on this visit. No doubt it would be back next time.

The point is, she didn't react at all.

"Vance McTiernan," I said again.

"I heard you." McElone punched some keys for a while and watched her screen. "So he thinks she didn't just eat the wrong thing? Is this guy maybe a little too . . . invested . . . to allow for the possibility his precious little girl could have just died for no reason?" She punched a few more keys. "Vance? With a V?"

"You never heard of Vance McTiernan?" I asked. How was that possible?

"No. Should I have?"

"The Jingles," I said. Surely that would jog her memory.

"He writes songs for TV commercials?" Was McElone playing some sort of game only cops found amusing?

"No, the *band*. The Jingles!" *Jeez, Mom, would you get with it already? All the kids are listening to them!*

"I don't know that one," McElone said. She looked at her

screen again. "Nothing special in Vanessa McTiernan's toxicology report. She had a reaction to the soy sauce she put on her veggie lo mein. Closed up her throat and she couldn't breathe. Died of suffocation. No reason to think it was anything else."

"I'm told there was too much soy sauce in her system," I said.

McElone's eyes performed the second act of *Swan Lake*, then returned to their normal position. "You been talking to Phyllis again?"

"I'm afraid that's classified."

"Mm-hmm. Yes, the ME said there was a high concentration of the stuff in her stomach, but it was consistent with someone who might have been trying to hurt herself with a known allergen that would close her throat."

That didn't sound like information Phyllis would be anxious for me to hear. I had to dig deeper. Going back to the *Chronicle* office without new information would be admitting incompetence, and while I'm usually more than willing to do that, seeing Phyllis be smug (and *still* not tell me what I wanted to know!) would be too much.

"She knew she was allergic to soy," I told McElone. "She wouldn't have put it on her food."

She shrugged. "People make mistakes."

"Not like that. Not when they know they could die."

McElone raised an eyebrow. "Maybe she wanted to," she said.

"Oh, come on. Suicide by veggie lo mein?"

"I did the due diligence," she said with a little force. "There was no reason to think anybody did her in. *Murder* by veggie lo mein?"

Touché. "So was it ruled a suicide?"

She shook her head. "Not officially. The evidence wasn't conclusive. Could have been on purpose, could have been an accident. Either way, she died from the allergic reaction."

Time to change tactics. "Where did she die?" I asked.

"In her apartment, over on Pier Avenue. The door was unlocked," McElone answered. "The police got a call about loud music playing over and over for two days. Apparently she had a record on—regular vinyl, an LP—on an old turntable that could repeat it, so it was playing the same side endlessly."

"What record?" I asked.

"Something called *Enemy of the Mind*," McElone said, scrolling down. "By—well, what do you know!"

"The Jingles," I said. It was not a question.

"Well, that's not so unusual," McElone suggested. "You said her dad was in this band, after all. She was just kicking back with some Chinese takeout, right?"

"How about the door being unlocked? Isn't that weird?"

McElone cocked an eyebrow. "Do you lock your front door when you're in the house?"

"Look, if you're going to be logical about it I don't see how we're going to get anywhere with this," I replied. "Vance says his daughter wouldn't use soy sauce, and it makes sense to me. He says somebody killed her and he wants to know why."

The lieutenant stared at her screen. "Says here Vance McTiernan died eight years ago," she said.

"And?"

McElone closed her eyes tightly. "I'm in no position to tell you that's crazy," she admitted. "But I can't go to my captain and tell him I want to reopen a death by natural causes because the victim's dead father says his little girl wouldn't do such a thing. Can't you ask the girl herself? Since she's . . . gone?"

I shook my head. "It appears she didn't become a ghost."

McElone scowled. "That's inconvenient," she said.

"Do you have anything in there about a boyfriend?" I asked. "Bandmates? She was in a band."

The lieutenant's mouth twitched a bit, and as she punched keys she mumbled something about how she believed herself to be mentally ill for even bothering. But she did, and after a few moments her mouth twitched again.

"She was in a band. Something called Once Again. Three other members: Samantha Fine, a drummer, William Mastrovy, the bass player and lead singer, and a guy named T.B. Condon, guitars. The only one with a record was Mastrovy."

That was interesting. "A record?" I said.

"Well, he's not exactly squeaky clean but there's nothing here to indicate a history of violence," she said. "Some dealing, just weed. Nothing huge. An outstanding warrant for his arrest nobody is bothering to enforce because the paperwork would be more trouble than he is on the street. Not even a traffic ticket. But the other band members said Vanessa had just broken up with Mastrovy. So maybe that's why she went the soy sauce route."

"Mastrovy was her boyfriend and she'd just dumped him? You didn't think that was worth checking out?"

McElone put her hands flat on her desk. "You come in here months after the fact and tell me the dead father of a woman who died of an allergic reaction says she was murdered and you want to tell me how I should have done my job?" She had a point. I knew McElone was a good cop and a thorough one.

I backed off. "Is there an address for the Mastrovy guy? The other two band members? Vance would like me to find them."

McElone's eyes narrowed. "Really. This is going about as far as I'm willing to go. The dead woman's dead father wants to find people he thinks might have been involved in his little angel's death? So he can get his ghosty revenge? And you want me to provide the coordinates? I don't think so."

"It's not like that," I said, although I thought it might have been exactly like that.

"I'm not giving you the address," she said. I didn't ask again. I know that tone. And I respect McElone enough to accept her decisions on professional issues. I nodded. "Fair enough. Anything you *can* tell me?"

"Well, we talked to the kid from the restaurant but Vanessa didn't get delivery; she picked it up from Ming Garden, on Surf Boulevard," the lieutenant said without checking her screen again.

"You were at the scene," I reminded her. "You don't give up that easy most of the time."

She put on an innocent look that didn't suit her. "There was no reason to dig any deeper," she said. "The doctor did the autopsy, found the cause. The lo mein was still in her living room on the coffee table. Nothing left to ask about."

That was awfully pat. "You don't think it's fishy that a woman who knew she had the allergy ate exactly the thing that would kill her?" That was what had been bothering me. Vance had a point: Why *hadn't* McElone looked into Vanessa's death more closely?

"Not really," the lieutenant said. "The uniforms came in, saw the scene. They didn't know what killed her and she was alone, so they called me, I looked, didn't see any evidence of violence and waited for the ME's report. That sewed it up."

"Not too clean? Not like someone wanted them to find her just like that? She put on her dad's record on auto-repeat and then committed suicide via Asian food? It's just too staged."

McElone shrugged. "I've never seen you as a conspiracy theorist before," she said. "This kind of thing happens. Not all the time, but it happens. The woman was unfortunate and it's sad. I'm sorry your dead friend lost his daughter, but it doesn't have to be a murder just because he doesn't want to face it."

I wasn't listening anymore. "Who are the cops?"

"What cops?"

"The uniforms. The officers who found Vanessa's body. Who are they? I want to talk to them."

She made a "yeah, sure" face. "I don't think so."

"It's on the police report, right? That's a matter of public record, isn't it?" I stuck my hand out. "Let's have a printout, please. I'm a citizen and I'm exercising my right to know."

McElone sighed but she hit print on her screen and pointed toward the door. "You can pick it up on your way out. And I'll tell you something."

I turned back toward her. "What?"

She did not smile, did not twinkle her eye at me. In fact, she didn't make eye contact, looking at documents on her desk. "You're better at this than you used to be," she said.

There are small victories in life. You have to savor them.

# Seven

The sense of victory didn't last long. One of the cops on McElone's list had left to work in Paterson, a good hour to the north. The other told me exactly the same information that the lieutenant had. Nothing new.

He didn't know Lester, either. I was now asking everyone I met. The mental image of that forlorn ghost dragging an empty wagon and looking for Lester had gotten to me.

And I sneezed again the second I walked back into the guesthouse. This was getting tedious.

Before any of the guests could spot me (as my eyes got puffy and red), I made my way to my bathroom upstairs, opened the medicine cabinet and looked for the antihistamine.

It wasn't there. It had been so long since my last allergy attack that I'd forgotten to replenish my supply. Drag. Since I didn't want to be sneezing and wheezing tonight or on Sunday, I would have to get back out to a drugstore and pick up the proper medication. But for now, a hot shower would clear out the sinuses and besides, I needed one.

Before I did that, though, I did a quick round of the downstairs to make sure none of my guests needed anything. Just when I thought I'd gotten a free pass to the shower, I ran into Berthe Englund walking in from the beach into the den. The glass doors in the back open right into my backyard, which leads to my beach (which technically belongs to the town of Harbor Haven, which means I have to buy beach passes for myself, my daughter and my guests every summer to go out onto property right behind my house. Welcome to New Jersey).

"Alison," Berthe called as she walked in after wiping the sand off her feet. "Do you have a minute?"

"Sure, Berthe. How can I help?" The ancient rime of the innkeeper.

Berthe, a larger woman with a friendly smile and a lovely island lilt to her speech, walked over and met me near the door from the den to the front room. "I missed the morning ghost show and I hear there was a wonderful musical performance. Is it going to be repeated this afternoon?"

"You'll just have to come and see," I said. The ancient rime of someone who really didn't know the answer to the question.

"I'm so sorry I missed it," she said, shaking her head.

Great. Now having Vance McTiernan play instrumental versions (as far as the guests could tell) of his greatest hits was going to become an expected feature of my spook shows. That would be amazing—if I could guarantee it would happen.

"I'll see what I can do," I said. Maybe I'd ask Maxie to get Everett here as a backup should Paul, Vance or both decided not to play the gig.

*The gig?* Now I was talking like a musician.

Berthe then asked me for a recommendation for a surf shop; it turned out that in her youth in Bermuda, she'd been an accomplished surfer before relocating to Highland Park to be with her (now late) husband, a professor at Rutgers University. Berthe wanted to see if she could take up the sport again now after "an interval of some years."

I directed her to Cut Bait and Run, a local surf and deep sea fishing business that also sold athletic shoes. Ted Iacobuzio, who runs the place, was a few years behind me in high school, which is annoying. He'll always be younger than me, no matter what.

Berthe thanked me and headed to her room to change. I decided to do the same while I had the opportunity; the next spook show would be in about two hours and I had to see who would be in my lineup for the afternoon.

I took the quickest shower in recorded history and had just managed to get myself fully clothed again when Vance McTiernan emerged through the floor and asked, "So is there any progress on finding Vanessa's killer, love?"

After a very deep and not necessarily voluntary breath, I gasped, "Vance! I asked you just yesterday *not* to come into this room unannounced, right? I just came out of the shower."

Vance, doing his "I'm-so-naughty-but-aren't-I-charming" face, put up his hands in a defensive position. "Okay, okay," he said. "I'm not really all that dirty an old man, you know. It's just what's expected of one in my business." He started to float backward toward the door.

"Hang on. Since you're here anyway, I wanted to ask if you might keep playing at the spook shows maybe once a day while you're here. The guests really enjoyed it."

He cocked an eyebrow. "The guests? Not you?"

"You're fishing for compliments, aren't you? It was the highlight of my year. You know I'm a big fan." He looked at me with the look that no doubt afforded him much success back in the day. "Of your *music*."

"Killjoy."

"So you'll play the gig?" I asked.

"For you, love, anything. Now, how about some suspects and their addresses?"

I sidestepped the question. "I'll tell you what I've been thinking: Doesn't it make more sense to look for Vanessa's mother, Claudia?"

It's not possible for ghosts to turn white—they're already pale enough, wispy and semi-transparent. But Vance Mc-Tiernan's reaction screamed for the ability to look ashen. His eyes bulged, his Adam's apple took a trip up and down his neck and his lips quivered.

For reasons I couldn't begin to imagine, what I'd said had scared him.

"Claudia?" Was that the best he could do?

"Yes. She might have some ideas about what happened to your daughter, no?"

Vance's tongue did a lap around his lips. "Yeah, see, the thing about that, love, is that Claud and I didn't exactly get on great in life, you know? I don't think she'd want to hear from me."

"She wouldn't be hearing from you—you're dead. She'd be hearing from *me*."

He shook his head. "No, no," he said. "You're barking up the wrong tree there, I think. Just do your detective stuff without Claud, right?"

"This is 'detective stuff.'" From the wall I heard Paul's voice, and I turned to see his lips—just his lips—protruding through the plaster. "I thought you'd asked Alison to find out what happened to your daughter. Are you sure you want her to do that?" Paul floated all the way into my room, something that—unlike Vance—he almost never did unless asked in specifically.

"Jeez, I should sell tickets today," I said. "Everybody's coming through here. Where's Maxie?"

"She'll be here soon. Something about finding the right

shirt to wear." Paul turned his attention back to Vance. "You don't seem that interested in finding the truth as much as punishing those involved. So is this about justice, or revenge?"

"What's the difference?"

I interrupted to change the subject in a hurry. "Paul, I've asked Vance if, while he's here, he might continue to play songs during some of the spook shows. I hope that won't be a problem," I said. Note that I did not ask if that was all right with him; it's my guesthouse. Paul's just the guy who haunts it.

I couldn't read his face. It's not that easy most of the time—the ghosts' faces, like the rest of them, are largely transparent. His teeth clenched but he did not look shocked. "I don't see why it would be," he managed to spit out.

"All right!" Vance butted in. "We're playing on the same bill, mate!" He clapped Paul on the shoulder and Paul looked like he was considering decking Vance. That probably wouldn't help things much, so quickly I turned toward Vance. "As for progress in the *investigation*, I have gotten some information, but nothing I can report back to you yet. I will when I know more. Now both of you get out of my bedroom and don't come back unless invited."

I'm sure Paul would have blushed if it had been possible. He stammered a bit, opened and closed his mouth to no coherent effect, and dropped down through the floor.

Vance, on the other hand, just shook his head and chuckled. "As you wish, madame," he said, then simply evaporated, slowly. His eyes were the last feature to disappear. The rock star as Cheshire Cat. He was clearly going to require some supervision during his stay.

And that was why I wasn't at all disappointed when Maxie came floating down from the ceiling. She spends a lot of time on the roof and in Melissa's attic bedroom, so I can expect her to descend. Paul tends to ascend. It provides, I don't know, symmetry or something.

"Did I miss it?" she asked once in the room.

"Miss what?"

Wearing her trademark skintight jeans and a black T-shirt (this one bearing the legend "Danger, Will Robinson!", which frankly didn't seem to have merited extra time to select), she hovered in the area of my dresser, surveying my outfit and choosing, against her usual nature, not to comment on it. "It sounded like there was gonna be a showdown between Paul and the British singer. I thought maybe they'd get in a fight." She sounded enthused about that last part. "Did I miss it?"

"There was nothing to miss," I told her. "We had a brief discussion about Vance playing some songs during one of the shows every day, and Paul wasn't happy about it but he didn't get mad."

Maxie looked disappointed. "Really? He doesn't like that guy."

"He doesn't like a lot of guys I meet," I reminded her. Paul has an odd jealous streak and sometimes reacts badly to men in whom I show an interest. The fact that Josh had hung in for a year now was no small thing. Paul didn't exactly welcome him, but he didn't seem to dislike Josh, either. It's hard to dislike Josh, and Paul's not the type to put in the effort. "There's something I want to talk to you about."

Maxie straightened up a little. "Whatever it is, I didn't do it," she said.

"Nobody thinks you did anything. I need your help on something."

Maxie floated a little closer to the ceiling. "Me? Not Paul?"

"Given Paul's mood, I think I'm better off with you."

Maxie's hand went to her mouth, I think to suppress a laugh. "You're kidding," she managed. Maxie thinks I hold a grudge because she dropped a bucket of wall compound on my head and started me seeing ghosts. She's not entirely wrong.

"Not even close to kidding. I want someone to keep an

eye on Vance, someone who can follow him wherever he goes."

Maxie made a show of "getting it": She turned her mouth into an O and nodded. "Okay. So what am I looking for?"

"I'm not sure. I just want to know if I can trust Vance or not. Can you just keep an eye on him without him knowing it?"

She gave me the "okay" sign. "Sure. Discretion is my middle name." And she zoomed into the ceiling.

So things were looking great already. And, no, I didn't mean that sincerely.

I turned to my laptop, which was, in computer years, about three hundred years old. And it wasn't state-of-the-art back when I bought it, when I was still married to The Swine. It operated, mostly, but could not be called lightning fast. Or even disabled-snail fast.

It was slow, is what I'm saying.

Still, it was marginally better than nothing, so I figured that with a few minutes to spare, I might as well run a search for any missing men named Lester from Topeka, Kansas. (It was a distraction from what I really should have been doing, which seemed attractive at the time.) But the Internet, amazing tool that it has become, still came up dry on that one. I looked for obituaries of men named Lester (one first name, one last) in the *Capital-Journal* and found two, both from 2003. Neither was blond, either, based on the pictures, so probably not my guy.

Next, I looked up Vanessa's bandmates in Once Again. The only Samantha Fine I found in New Jersey worked in an investment firm in Red Bank, so that was no help. T. B. Condon could have been one of thirty-eight people in the New York/New Jersey/Pennsylvania tristate area, none of whom at first glance was in a band or mentioned Vanessa McTiernan. William Mastrovy, the boyfriend, I saved for last. Just because McElone wouldn't give me his address didn't mean I couldn't find it myself and then decide how much information I wanted to give to Vance, if any. The man wrote beautiful songs, but I reminded myself that he could still be dangerous. The Marquis de Sade was considered a really good writer in his day. One thing doesn't necessarily assume the other.

Since *Mastrovy* wasn't the most common name in central Jersey (or anywhere else outside of Pinsk, apparently), even someone with my level of computer "skills" could zero in on him fairly quickly. There were only two Mastrovys within a two-hundred-mile radius and one of them was named Stanislav and lived in Delaware.

The other was William. Or at least W. He lived in Asbury Park, not far from where I was sitting, although no street address was offered. But he wouldn't be hard to find. Probably. If I wanted to.

The Internet also told me that William Mastrovy was the front man for a cover band called Once Again that played local bars and clubs on the Shore. Once Again covered older groups like the Zombies, the Animals, Duran Duran and, yes, you guessed it:

The Jingles.

Once Again had an upcoming booking at the Last Resort, a small, seedy club in Manalapan on Route 9, the very next night. I considered going to see them, talking to Mastrovy and getting a gut reaction regarding whether or not he was a killer.

In retrospect, I probably should have looked up the band first.

The problem with my plan, of course, was that unlike Paul, Vance McTiernan was a mobile ghost who could easily follow me to the Last Resort by hiding in my car, and at this point in the investigation, I really wanted to keep Vance away from Mastrovy.

I wondered if I could actually ask Paul for advice on this. He was not usually so petty, but would he hold a grudge about what was said the night before, or the fact that I'd asked Vance to join in the spook shows, and refuse to participate in the investigation at all?

I decided that the only thing to do would be to gauge Paul's mood later at the afternoon spook show. I'd play it by ear, and that was usually a reminder that I am essentially tone-deaf under such circumstances.

So I got out my phone and dialed Josh. "How'd you like to take me to a dive bar called the Last Resort to listen to a band that's probably not very good destroy some songs you've loved all your life?" I asked.

"Sounds great! When?" The perfect boyfriend.

"Tomorrow night. Dress grungy, and I don't mean Seattle Grunge, okay?"

"Is this a detective thing?"

"Yeah, but we're keeping that quiet, okay? I don't want Vance to hear anything about us going." I made sure I said that quietly and looked around the room for any wayward shreds of ghost that might be visible in the walls, floor or ceiling. There was nothing.

"Got it. I'm still seeing you tonight, right?" he asked. "You're not canceling on me, are you?"

"No, of course not. Dinner's like always on a Mom night."

"Good," Josh said. "So what's our cover story?"

"Ooh, something exotic. We're going to the movies."

"Nah," Josh said. "We're watching a movie at your house the next night."

*Oh, yeah. "Ghost,"* I groaned.

"Don't be a sore loser."

"It's okay. But we're getting to *Lawrence of Arabia* some-time. I want to see it on that screen." Okay, we needed a cover story to tell everyone, not just Vance. That would make it less likely a slip would occur.

"I've got it," Josh said. "We're going to see friends of mine and you're meeting them for the first time."

"Nobody will believe that," I teased. "You don't have any friends."

"Their names are A.J. and Liz and we're meeting them after dinner."

There was something in his voice. "Are these real people?" I asked.

"You'll find out tomorrow." And he hung up.

So Josh wanted to have his fun. He deserved it. Not many boyfriends are willing to put up with a single mom who has two ghosts in her house. You have to be a little flexible about things when you find one who doesn't consider that odd.

I went downstairs, put out a couple of very minor fires for Tessa and Roberta (who seemed to be developing a friendship) and looked for Paul, who was not around.

Phyllis called while I was in the den. "You sitting down?" she asked.

"No. Should I be?"

"Your choice. It's more of an expression. I've got some information for you, which you can have if you tell me something useful."

"Spill," I said. "Tell me what you've got, and I'll let you know what it's worth." Phyllis brings out the tough-as-nails dame in me.

"Who are you, Barbara Stanwyck?" She didn't wait for a reply but I considered myself more a Jean Arthur kind of girl. "I talked to my friend at the medical examiner's office. It took a little convincing, but he went back over the report on your pal Vanessa McTiernan. And there is something a little strange about it."

That was promising. "What?" I asked.

"First, you gotta give me something." Ah, Phyllis. The mistress of quid pro quo.

"Okay. Look for a guy named Lester who vanished from Topeka, Kansas."

"Why?"

"I don't really know," I said.

Phyllis's tone, usually businesslike with a tinge of humor, was now just businesslike. "Something I want, please."

"What is it you want?" Okay, so I was stalling. I didn't have any information Phyllis could use. I didn't have information Phyllis didn't already have.

Let's face it: I didn't have any information.

"You know what I want. Give me something that helps me with the story."

"I thought you didn't think there was a story," I reminded her.

Maureen Beckman came into the den with her walker, inching her way toward what must have been the Promised Land: an overstuffed easy chair. She nodded at me as she entered, and I nodded back.

"So you need to tell me something that convinces me there could be," Phyllis replied.

Well, I wasn't going to make something up. "I've got Vanessa's ex-boyfriend playing a gig with her old band in Manalapan tomorrow night," I said, lowering my voice a bit. The den is a large room, and even if Maureen could hear what I was saying, it probably wouldn't mean much to her. But why take chances?

"That's it?"

I looked at the phone as if Phyllis could see my expression. "Am I mistaken, or are you the one who called me? Since when am I supposed to be the source of all crime information?"

"Jeez," she said. "Somebody got up on the wrong side of the bed of nails. What are you so cranky about?"

"I have to figure out who killed Vance McTiernan's daughter four months ago, and one of my best friends is refusing to tell me something based on some strange journalistic barter system. That's what I'm cranky about." I looked up to see if Maureen had overheard me, but there was not a flicker, not a blink from her. I wondered if she had hearing problems, which would be unusual but not (no pun intended) unheard of in someone of her relative youth. More likely, she'd just tuned me out.

"Okay, okay. Obviously you don't know when someone's just having fun with you." Phyllis's voice betrayed her words—she really did sound a little concerned that she'd hurt my feelings. I'd found a way to get to her and I wasn't even looking for one (that was something to file away for future use). "Here's the thing: There was soy sauce in her stomach."

I waited. I wasn't going to give Phyllis the straight line she was waiting for. But she didn't say anything else. She was holding out.

"We knew that," I muttered, giving in. I needed to hear the rest, and Phyllis obliged.

"That's just the thing. There was soy sauce. There wasn't anything else."

How did that make sense? "What does that mean, there wasn't anything else?" I asked.

"No vegetables, no noodles. Just the soy. And going down pure, as it were, probably sped up the allergic reaction she had; there was nothing to absorb it."

"You're saying she chug-a-lugged soy sauce?"

"Do you want to hear this or not?" Phyllis demanded. The hurt-feelings thing had clearly worn off and we were back to standard operating practices.

"Sorry. Go on."

"Anyway, the contents of what she'd eaten included her lunch, which wasn't completely digested, but nothing else." Phyllis was back in reporter mode.

"Except soy sauce."

"Precisely. And people think it's the salt in that stuff that kills you."

That was weird. Who drinks soy sauce, without a chaser or anything?

"Why didn't the cops investigate further?" I asked, mostly to myself. "Did the ME sign off on an accidental allergic reaction?"

Sometimes you can hear in a person's voice when she's smiling and Phyllis was clearly grinning from ear to ear. "That's my girl," she said. Phyllis thinks I have the makings to be a great reporter. It's one of the many things she's deluded about. "No. The coroner didn't declare it accidental."

"Then what was it?" I asked.

"Well, he didn't rule it a suicide, but he didn't say it wasn't," she answered.

"No reason to think it was murder?"

"Ask the cops. Maybe they did," Phyllis said. "Another good question for our Lieutenant McElone."

"I did ask, and she said no."

"McElone's good, but she's not infallible. Go back and follow up."

Oy. My first inquiry with McElone had been awkward, and now Phyllis was suggesting I go back and ask why the Harbor Haven Police Department hadn't done its job adequately? *That* was going to go over real well, I was sure.

I looked over at Maureen, who had pulled an e-reader/tablet out of her purse and looked deeply engrossed in the screen, which I could not see from here.

"I have an idea," I told Phyllis. "Why don't *you* ask McElone all about it and then tell me what she says?"

"Because I have a newspaper to run, and because you're the reporter on the story."

"No, I'm not. I'm the source on the story. You ask me stuff, I answer, and then you write it up for the newspaper you run. And by the way, I have a business to run, too, and might not have the time to go ask the lieutenant all those questions you want answered right away."

Phyllis laughed. "Coward," she said, and hung up.

I'd had better days than this one, and it wasn't even three in the afternoon yet.

Speaking of which, I had to go pick Melissa up from school. As I passed Maureen on the way out of the den, I caught a sneaky glance at the screen on her tablet. I was right; she did want everyone to know how smart she was.

She was playing *Jeopardy!*

# Eight

Melissa was running her teeth over her lower lip, a practice she calls "scratching," which is an indication she is thinking hard.

Against my advice, Melissa had quit the tech club, so she was coming home at her regular time. I was trying to find a way to suggest, once again, that she might have been hasty, but she had launched directly into a discussion of what she referred to as "*our* investigation."

"So it was a straight ingestion of soy sauce that killed Vanessa," she said. Melissa had left much of sixth grade behind her when she'd gotten into my Volvo wagon and was now in her best Encyclopedia Brown mode, where she took all the facts I gave her and told me what they meant in relation to the case I was working. "So if Vance is right and someone did murder her, it's possible that her killer forced Vanessa to drink the soy sauce, right?"

I know; you're going to say that most eleven-year-old girls don't talk like that to their mothers. I'm very proud.

"Or it's possible she drank it because she was depressed and didn't want to live anymore," I said. "We can't be sure. We don't know anything yet. We can't get in touch with Vanessa to ask her, and as far as we know, nobody was there when she died."

Liss, I could tell even while driving, gave me a sideways look. "You realize this would be a lot easier if Paul was involved."

"Yeah," came a voice from the backseat. I drew a sharp intake of breath and managed—valiantly, I believe—not to drive into the next lane and cause a six-car pileup.

"Maxie!" I hadn't known she was there. Maxie loves to hitch a ride in the car, not make her presence known (often by riding on the roof or hiding in the trunk or the engine block) and then pop out at an inopportune time, like ever. "Don't do that!"

"Sorry, sorry," she drawled, not sounding the least bit sorry at all. "Who knew you were so excitable?"

"You should, from the seventy-five times you've done this to me before. What are you doing here?"

"I can't take a ride in the car?"

I was going to respond, knowing fully that wasn't why Maxie had secreted herself in my Volvo, but Melissa gave me a warning look that said my reaction wouldn't help, which it wouldn't.

"*Anyway*," my resident poltergeist went on (as if I had rudely interrupted her thought), "I agree with Melissa. This is the kind of thing Paul loves to do and he'd be a big help."

I stifled a groan. "May I remind both of you that it wasn't my idea for Paul to stay away from this investigation? He was the one who didn't want to help Vance, for reasons I can't begin to explain."

There was an uncomfortable silence. You know when

you say something and no one responds . . . and you get the distinct impression it's because what you just said was so self-delusional they're trying to figure out how you could possibly be that blind and still drive a car?

"What?"

Melissa cleared her throat, which I would bet cash money didn't need clearing. "Well, you know, um . . ." That definitely wasn't helping.

"You told Paul you didn't want him on the case," Maxie blurted.

"What? I did not."

"Yeah, you did. You told him that if he didn't want to be on the case, you'd just do it yourself, and then you walked out of the room without even giving him a chance to talk." Maxie didn't even sound as gleeful as I would have anticipated. Which was troublesome, because it meant she was being sincere.

"That's not the way it was," I insisted.

Melissa made another very uncomfortable sound. "Yes it was, Mom," she said. "I'm sorry," she quickly added.

Was that true? Had I actually ordered Paul to stay away from Vanessa McTiernan's death just because I felt disrespected?

"But he said I was a bad detective and I didn't know what I was doing," I tried.

"No he didn't," Liss told me gently. "He said he didn't think Vance was telling us the truth and he didn't trust him. He said it was dangerous to get involved with a case when you didn't know the facts and you couldn't depend on your client."

"It went further than that," I told her.

"Yeah," Maxie—of all people—agreed. "But both of you pushed it there; it wasn't just Paul."

My head was swimming a little. I actually considered pulling over to the side of the road, but I got my second wind and soldiered on (it helped that we were pulling into the driveway). "I'm gonna have to think about this," I said.

"You can just ask him," Liss suggested. "He's, like, really good at this detective stuff." She sounded like she was worried about my progress if I didn't have Paul's guiding hand behind me.

And that reminded me of my argument with Paul to begin with. "Are you saying I'm *not* any good at it?" I asked. I didn't mean to sound angry with Melissa but my voice was not performing as I was requesting.

"That's not it," my daughter was quick to answer. We got out of the car and walked toward the back door, Maxie floating alongside us. "I'm saying it's better to have two people working on something than just one. In school when we do group projects, you have to let other people do stuff, too."

"Like how I do all the research," Maxie helpfully chimed in. She doesn't do *all* the research but she has a need for validation that she exercises more frequently than I do my triceps.

I opened the back door and walked into my kitchen. Vance McTiernan was there, hovering by the refrigerator as if he was about to get some food, though he was, of course, far beyond the need for nourishment. At least physically.

It had gotten to the point now where I sort of expected to see Vance; you can get used to anything. It's like when you get a new sofa and you can't help but admire it whenever you walk into the room, but eventually it's just the thing you sit on.

Maybe Maxie and Liss were right: maybe I *should* just swallow my allegedly misguided pride and ask Paul for help. He wasn't the type to lord it over me and I would feel better if things could be at least closer to the way they usually were when I pretended I was a detective. I'd seek him out shortly and get him on board.

"What's going on, Vance?" I asked when we were all inside the kitchen. I put my car keys on the hook next to the kitchen door. See how casual I was about having *Vance McTiernan* in my very own kitchen? I'm so professional.

"Where have you been?" He sounded insistent, which caught me off guard.

"I was doing some work on your case," I said. It is slightly possible I had the smallest touch of defensiveness in my voice. It is also possible I was lying, since technically I had been out collecting my daughter from school.

Then I sneezed, just to remind me of what I *hadn't* done, which was getting some allergy medicine from the drugstore. Absolutely next on my agenda after the impending spook show.

"Have you been crying?" Vance asked.

Maxie, floating near the ceiling (Vance was lower, more on eye level with me), snorted.

"No, I haven't been crying. I have allergies."

Melissa, normally interested in such things, hustled through the kitchen and toward the stairs to her room without stopping. Odd, but she's eleven.

"Well, if you need something for it, I know a good pharmacist in almost every town in the world," Vance said. Suddenly I was glad Melissa had left the room.

"Maybe another time, Vance. I think with this one I'll go for the over-the-counter stuff."

"Your choice, love. I wanted to tell you there's someone I think you should be looking for. Friends in the business, who only just passed on recently, tell me she had a big album on the way from Vinyl Records. Maybe that's why somebody wanted her dead. Jealousy, or greed or something."

Now, please keep in mind that I worshipped Vance McTiernan's music. I'd spent much of my life identifying with him and wondering what it would be like to have him as a friend. Before I went to college, I spent a week in my room playing Jingles albums to get me past my anxiety about leaving home (don't tell my mother, okay?).

But I knew a line when I heard it. And I was hearing it.

Maxie was faster than me, though. "Oh, gimme a break," she howled from the ceiling. "These days anybody who wants to can have an album. Why would somebody kill your daughter because of hers?" She pointed at me. "You're gonna have to do better. She's not as stupid as you might think."

"Don't help me," I told her. She looked a little surprised. Makes you wonder.

"I've simply realized the error in my ways," Vance said, his accent getting just a little less Ringo Starr and a little more Kenneth Branagh. "You were right, Alison. I wasn't thinking straight. I was so upset with my grief that I wasn't helping you find Nessa's killer. I want to help now. You got through to me and I want to thank you for it."

He floated over toward me and put his hands over mine. It's not true that the ghosts can't touch us at all; they can. In fact, Maxie and Paul have been capable of carrying Melissa through the "flying girl" sections of the spook shows—something all parties concerned who aren't me enjoy immensely—and Maxie once carried me out a window.

Vance McTiernan's hands on mine felt neutral and unresponsive. It was like having an object touch me. It wasn't scary or threatening; it had no sensation attached to it other than a sort of inanimate contact. I was at once surprised and disappointed: The idol of my adolescence had just touched me and he might as well have been a block of wood.

"You helped me see the error in my ways," he said. "You did it through the way you think and the way you talk. I can't possibly thank you enough."

This tactic should have worked. Vance was a consummate showman who knew how to put over an act to an audience. But he had miscalculated in one crucial area. He had not considered my past (which was not his fault because he knew nothing of my past). If he had, he would have known that was exactly the kind of line The Swine had used on me a hundred times, and he would have realized that I could spot that hog-wash seventeen miles away.

"Nice try, Vance," I said. "Now tell me what's *really* going on."

Vance actually looked hurt. How could I not have simply swallowed his insincere praise and utterly false declarations of change when he was pretending to mean them so deeply?

"What I said," he tried.

"I don't think so. You have an agenda. You're a man who's used to getting what he wants. And now you want me to believe your daughter was murdered, and to some extent I do. But if you really think I'm going to do what you ask, you'll have to tell me the truth. So I'll ask again: What's really going on?"

"I read about the album in *Billboard*, in the back section that lists new signings. Nobody I know told me about it. I made that up." His voice was raspy and forced.

"Why?"

"It's part of my charm," he said. And then he was gone.

Maxie made a noise with her lips that I can confidently report was not meant to be respectful. "Something's definitely going on with him," she said.

"Ya think?"

I walked out of the kitchen and into the den, where once again Maureen Beckman was sitting, this time with a long scarf she was crocheting. "How's it going, Maureen?" I asked as I passed by.

She looked up as if I'd startled her from a light nap. "Oh, I didn't hear you there, Alison. I'm doing just fine; how about you?"

"Pretty much the usual," I said truthfully, and smiled. She didn't need to know what my "usual" was.

The scene with Vance might have given me more resolve. It might have convinced me that I was definitely on the right track, because you can be sure that you're doing something right when a person without a lot of credibility tells you to do something else. It might even have made me feel empowered and fierce, as if I should go out and start snooping on Once Again immediately, but I had that planned for tomorrow.

Instead, I had a sneezing attack in my front room just as I heard my mother call from the kitchen on the other side of the house. "We're . . . I'm here!" she shouted. "And I could use some help with the groceries!"

Knowing it wasn't a dire emergency, I didn't break land speed records getting back to the kitchen. Maxie had vacated the premises, probably in favor of the roof. Once there, I saw Mom unpacking the child's backpack she uses in place of a purse ("It's easier on my arms") with what appeared to be enough food for seventeen people.

"Did you invite the 101st Airborne Division without telling me?" I asked, grabbing eight ears of corn from her hands and putting them on the counter. "There's only four of us who'll be eating dinner." Sure, there would probably be three or four other people in the room while we ate, but being dead apparently cuts back one's appetite pretty severely.

"I get what's on sale," Mom said. "Don't be a wise guy."

"I'm not criticizing what you bought. It's how much of it you bought."

"How do I know how hungry Josh will be?" Mom still acts like it's a novelty when Josh shows up for dinner. She pretends this hasn't happened at least twice a week for the past year. "He works hard all day."

I would like to explain right here that my mother was not taking a dig at me, not implying that I *don't* work hard all day. My mother believes everything I do is astonishingly wonderful. Yeah, you think it sounds good, but believe me it gets to be a real pain after thirty years or so.

My father, who was removing an uncooked beef brisket the size of the Battleship Missouri from Mom's backpack, floated over to the fridge and put it inside by hiding it in his jacket (which was a very large jacket), walking into the fridge, and then emerging sans brisket. It's a system, and it works for him. "Hey, baby girl," he said.

To this day I get the urge to hug Dad when he calls me that, but since that wasn't going to be a rewarding experience, I gave him my best grin and said, "Hi, Daddy." He loves it when I call him that. "I'm glad you're here."

My father looked over, eyebrow raised. "What needs fixing?" He knows about six times more about home maintenance than I do.

"Nothing, for a change." Dad looked disappointed, so I added, "But the handle on the toilet upstairs is a little wobbly."

He gave me a satisfied nod. "I'm on the job." And off to the basement—where I keep my tools—he sank.

Mom and I finished unpacking the ingredients for our dinner. My mother can take something the size of a backpack and pretty much fit an entire restaurant kitchen's cooking equipment into it. The woman can pack.

"Is Mr. McTiernan still here?" she asked casually.

"Yeah, and I'm really sort of conflicted about it." I updated Mom on the situation and told her how Vance had lied to my face only minutes ago under circumstances I didn't especially love.

Mom listened carefully, wiping down a counter I thought was already clean, and sort of puckered her face, which indicated that she was thinking. "You're reacting differently to this than to anything before," she said finally. "You really want to help this man because of the music you listened to when you were young."

"Well, yeah, but also because it really does seem like something crazy happened to his daughter, Vanessa, and nobody's done anything about it," I said. "Isn't that a good reason?"

Mom's face twitched the way someone's does when they're worried that what they're about to say will offend or anger the other person. "Yes it is, but that's never really driven you before. Anytime one of these investigations came up, you did all you could to get out of it." Then she actually took a step back as if I was in danger of exploding and she wanted to shield herself from the fallout.

"This is different," I said, doing my very best to exude calm because I didn't want Mom to think she'd crossed a line she shouldn't. "This is one I took on myself, and, yes, it was because of the Jingles and what they mean to me. But now . . . now I don't know."

"The way you talked to Paul last night," Mom said. "That wasn't like you."

*That again.* "I have to apologize to him. I just got unnerved when he told me not to trust Vance, and then I thought he was telling me I was a bad detective and I got mad."

"I *was* telling you that," came the voice from behind me. "I think you're in over your head and you should stop investigating immediately."

I turned around to see Paul, his goatee looking more unkempt than usual and his hair mussed, which frankly shouldn't be possible, hovering near the kitchen door. It took me a moment to digest what I'd just heard.

"Don't pull your punches," I told him. "Tell me what you *really* think."

"I just did." Paul is from Canada. Sarcasm just doesn't come naturally to him. It's more of a Jersey thing.

"Alison." He floated over and tried to soften his expression. "I have been concerned about you since Vance showed up yesterday. You are not thinking rationally. You are acting like an overenthusiastic teenager when he is around. Whatever this connection is that you have to Vance, it clouds your judgment. You're getting yourself into a situation you would never allow under normal circumstances."

"The part I can't get past is where you're saying I'm a bad investigator," I told him. "That's what's hurting me."

Paul looked away. That isn't ever a good sign, in case you're wondering.

"So deep down that really is what you think," I said. "Even when you told me I was improving, you meant that I was marginally less awful than before, is that it?"

"No." But he still wouldn't look at me. "I really do think you have potential, and that you are progressing." Then his eyes narrowed and he did face me. "I thought you never cared about this before. I thought it was a question of commitment."

So that was it. Paul had been harboring resentment because I hadn't been taking his "detective agency" seriously enough. Well, I do believe that he tends to see it as something more than it is—namely, a real detective agency—and that tends to lead to some less than reverential remarks on my part. That, too, is a Jersey thing.

"I'm sorry if I made you feel that way," I said. From the corner of my eye I could see Mom beaming at me. She loves it when I'm reasonable, if only because she doesn't get to see it very often. "I act like that because I'm insecure about it." Jeez, I hadn't opened up this much to the therapist I saw when The Swine left for sunnier climes. "I didn't mean to give you that impression."

Naturally, the next thing I'd hear would be Paul apologizing for the way he had made me feel and I could be incredibly gracious about it. Then we'd be back on equal footing, he could tell me what the heck to do about Vance and the Vanessa investigation and I could breathe out for the first time today.

"Very well, then," he said.

I waited. *One Mississippi, two Mississippi* . . . Nothing.

"That's it?" I said. "I apologize for something and open up like that and all I get back is, 'very well, then'?"

Paul looked surprised. "I don't understand. What were you expecting?"

"Don't you want to apologize for making me feel like

you thought I was a bad detective? And then help me figure out Vanessa's death?"

I wouldn't swear to it in a court of law, but I'm pretty sure I saw Mom wince.

Paul gave me the same look he would undoubtedly give someone who told him the aliens were coming for her and she knew because of the signals coming from her tinfoil hat. "I'm sorry," he said in a tone so unconvincing I doubted Melissa would have believed him. When she was two.

"No, I can tell you aren't."

He spread his hands and looked toward the ceiling, no doubt for guidance in dealing with someone irrational. Which would be the place to look, because Maxie was probably up there somewhere. "I honestly don't know what you want," he said. "I warned you from the very first that I thought taking on Vance McTiernan's investigation was a mistake, yet you decided to go ahead. That's your prerogative, but I don't see why my opinion on the subject should change."

Mom was filling the teapot with water. It was much too early to start cooking dinner and she's uncomfortable in a kitchen unless she's making *something*. "I think Alison is trying to ask you for help," she said to Paul. Then she glanced toward me. "Isn't that right, honey?"

I didn't know how to answer. Paul clearly wanted to make some kind of nutty point about how he was right and I should have listened to him all along, and I wanted him to validate my efforts and help me with something I thought was becoming too difficult for me to handle alone.

If I'd wanted to have this kind of problem, I could have stayed married to The Swine.

It didn't matter anyway, because Paul looked at Mom and answered, "I don't see how I can help with an investigation that is based on the statement of an unreliable client."

There were sixteen different ways I could have argued with that. I could have pointed out that we'd had clients who had been less than completely truthful before and Paul hadn't minded. I could say there was evidence—Paul's favorite thing—beyond just what Vance had told us. That there was some strange data in the medical examiner's report. That it was weird Vance had ordered me off the case as soon as I'd found something to investigate. Four or five other tactics might have come to mind.

Instead I said, "This is because I asked him to play during the spook shows, isn't it?"

Paul stared at me, opened his mouth, made no sound, and sunk down through the kitchen floor.

"That didn't go so well, did it," I said to Mom.

"No dear, it didn't," she answered. "Would you like some cocoa?"

# Nine

The ghost with the wagon was outside the house when I went to pick up the newspapers from the curb the next morning.

"Have you seen Lester?" she demanded as soon as I walked out the front door.

"Not yet," I said. I don't have many neighbors but I do usually wear an unconnected Bluetooth device in my ear when I'm outside, just to cover any talking I might do to people who "aren't there." I didn't have it on now, just to retrieve the papers, but on the other hand, my building does have a sign on it that says *Haunted Guesthouse*. Passersby would just have to cope.

"I've been asking around, but I haven't gotten much response. Can you give me a more detailed description?" I asked as I bent to pick up the *New York Times*. We are a classy establishment.

"Not very big. Light hair. Big brown eyes. Not too bright." This was essentially a reiteration of her last description.

I also picked up the *Asbury Park Press*. Got to have the local news and Phyllis only puts out the *Chronicle* once a week. "How did you two get separated?" I asked the ghost.

She had clearly not been very lucky when she was alive; her clothes were a tick or two short of ragged and her hair was straggly and unwashed. She had not regenerated, as Everett had done, into a younger, happier, stronger version of herself when she'd died.

"He just wandered off," she said. "Lester does that."

Finally, I picked up the *New York Post*. Not all my guests are that classy. "It would help if I knew Lester's last name," I told the woman.

"He doesn't have one," she said with a why-don't-you-know-that tone, and vanished, wagon and all.

Well, that was helpful. Now I had to deal with a prickly Paul and a quest for Lester with no road map for either. That didn't even include Vanessa and Vance McTiernan and what I was supposedly doing for them, with even less help than usual.

Given all that, it still would have been so much better if Paul had not shown up for the Saturday afternoon spook show.

All of the guests were present for this one except Roberta and Stan Levine, who'd told me that they were taking a day trip to Atlantic City (while there still is an Atlantic City) and expected to be home quite late. With Melissa here to do her "flying girl" extravaganza, it should have been a rousing performance, giving the assemblage their money's worth for choosing to stay in an establishment that proudly displayed said "Haunted Guesthouse" sign to the left of its front door.

But Paul, although gamely going through the motions (even though only Liss, Mom and I could see them) was barely entertaining enough to get a kid to hand over a quarter. And the more the guests asked if "that musical ghost" was going to come and play for them again (a question for which I had no answer), the more Paul seemed disinterested and tired. He didn't even try to pull the tablecloth out from under the extremely cheap (and hopefully unbreakable) knickknacks I had especially displayed on the den's side table, something that always presented a welcome challenge to Paul. He had never successfully accomplished the feat but had always seemed determined to improve to the point where he would do it.

Until now.

Maxie, rustling the curtains and "flying" an apple around the room, looked at her partner and demanded, "Are you going to pull your weight, or what?"

Paul, brows low, turned toward her and put down the orange he'd been . . . holding. "I don't understand," he said.

"You're making me work too hard," Maxie said, shaking the light fixture in the center of the room (I hesitate to call it a chandelier for fear of making it sound too grand). "Get in the game."

"I'm doing what I always do," he answered. Except he had forgotten to "fly" Melissa down the stairs and she was no doubt waiting on the second floor as we spoke for her cue.

I was trying not to get involved in the argument because the guests were present and needed to feel that the "entertainment" going on was wholehearted and enthusiastic, for their benefit. Mom was off in the kitchen doing something, as she prefers not to attend the spook shows. She always worries that something's going to get broken.

"Are there any questions for the spirits?" I asked. If the guests feel like they're in contact with Paul and Maxie, they can tell their friends at home about the direct interaction they had with ghosts. You can laugh if you want to, but I've gotten guests on referral this way.

"Yes," Berthe Englund piped up, raising her hand like a second-grader. "Can they communicate with my late husband?"

This is not an unusual question. Paul can do his Ghoster-net thing and try to find some dead people but since the system is so random—some people (like Vanessa) don't show up as ghosts, others don't communicate the way Paul does and there is a percentage that legitimately don't want to talk to the living anymore—we don't advertise that fact. Not to mention it would tie up all of Paul's time and he considers the Ghosternet stuff personal.

"It doesn't really work that way," I told Berthe. "Otherwise, I would have checked in on Abraham Lincoln by now." That's my prepared answer for such questions and it got the chuckle it often does. Truth be told, I had once asked Paul to see if he could link minds with the Great Emancipator but Paul apparently didn't have Abe's area code because there was no answer. The president was probably trying to find a revival of *Our American Cousin* so he could see how the play ended.

"Oh," Berthe looked disappointed. Some people sign up for a trip to the guesthouse just for such purposes, although I've asked Senior Plus Tours to be clear that I'm not a medium, so much as I mainly just communicate with the two ghosts already not-living in the house.

"I'm sorry about that, Berthe. Any other questions?" Got to keep the show moving. Maxie picked up a pair of scissors from the table and pretended to cut Tessa's hair without actually doing so. But she was glaring at Paul, who simply watched the whole time. Tessa didn't seem to notice, but the other guests had a chuckle when it was clear no hair was being removed.

"Yeah." Jesse Renfield stood up, apparently believing he wouldn't be heard if he were sitting. "Is it scary being dead? I mean, should we be afraid of it?" It was a reasonable question, and would have been a better indicator of Jesse's deep thinking if he hadn't been wearing a Speedo and a T-shirt that read, "Jersey Girls Don't Pump Gas." I mean, we don't—gas stations in New Jersey are all full-service by law—but why would a man wear that shirt?

"Answer number twelve," Maxie said after waiting for Paul to reply and seeing him stare, glassy-eyed, toward the kitchen door.

"Maxie says it's not something she's glad happened, but it's not the terrifying existential void some believe it to be." That was close to the standard answer Paul traditionally gave, which was, "We're not happy about it but we like being here for you." I embellish a little.

"Is there a heaven?" Maureen Beckman asked as Maxie threw an orange at Paul, who reflexively caught it.

I pretended to wait for an answer. "Paul says he doesn't know," I told Maureen. "Since he died, he's only been here."

"I didn't say that," Paul informed me, as if I wasn't aware. "And I do hope to move on someday." I knew that, and hadn't intended the comment as a dig at his inability to leave the premises, which Paul's touchy about.

"How about a hell?"

Maxie and I turned to see Vance McTiernan, acoustic guitar in hand, hovering in the kitchen doorway.

Paul didn't have to turn. Vance was right where Paul had been staring all along. He'd been waiting for Vance.

Seeing me turn, Tessa followed my eyes and saw the guitar suspended in midair. "Oh, the musician is back!" she said, and actually clapped her hands.

Berthe and Maureen joined her. Jesse, who had not been at the first performance Vance had delivered, held back his adulation. He was a show-me kind of guy. Or he had no idea why they were clapping. Either way.

"Vance," I said under my breath. "Thank goodness."

Paul's eyes darkened. He didn't evaporate, but he folded his arms defensively and faded—literally—back into the wall. Only his face remained in the den.

I stepped forward. "Ladies and gentlemen," I announced, "Vance McTiernan!" There was not a flicker of recognition in the crowd, but they did offer light applause.

Vance began to play, quietly at first and then with more conviction. I immediately recognized the tune, from the Jingles first album. It was *Sunflower*, a simple, heartbreaking remembrance of first love. Again, Vance was aware that most of his audience couldn't hear his vocal, so he concentrated on the acoustic guitar. But for Maxie, Paul and me (well, maybe not for Paul), he sang:

> *Sunflower/*
> *You gave a lonely boy/*
> *a taste of power/*
> *Then you took it away . . .*

It was an adolescent's point of view but when I'd first heard it, I *was* an adolescent, so it continued to resonate and evoke nostalgia in me. While he was singing, I forgave Vance for manipulating me, for confusing me, for making me question my friendship with Paul. Music is not a benign tool—it can save your sensibility or talk you into some terrible mistakes. I didn't know which it was doing now.

Vance finished the song and got the rousing round of applause—even from Jesse—that he'd known he would. He even bowed, probably out of habit.

Then he turned toward me. "That was my way of apologizing," he said. I didn't have to ask what he thought he'd done to warrant an apology.

"Accepted," I said, quietly so the guests couldn't hear. It wasn't that they needed to be left out of the conversation so much as the time it would take to explain it.

Paul rolled his eyes at the scene. His mind is tuned to logic and fact. He makes his decisions based on things he can prove. Music is a pleasant distraction to Paul, but actually letting it dictate one's actions is absolutely unimaginable to him. I understood, and did not take him to task for his obvious distaste at what I'd thought was a tender moment.

Maxie put her fingers in her teeth and whistled. Maxie is the very embodiment (if she had a body) of class.

The guests, assuming Vance's performance was the finale for the afternoon show, started to gather what few things they had brought and stood to leave. Paul was at least not so delusional to think he could top what had just gone on but he did look somewhat offended by their total indifference to him as he waved a napkin in the air. Nobody looked.

He gave a glance toward the side table, considering the tablecloth trick, then probably remembered the times it hadn't worked (all of them) and sighed a bit. He sunk through the floor to go lick his wounds, I assumed.

Vance stashed his guitar behind the sofa and watched Paul leave without comment. Maxie, who usually clocked out like an hourly employee after the spook show, floated down and "sat" on an armchair, watching Vance with a kind of interest I couldn't read from her face.

"You always played music?" she asked. I had to squint to make sure it *was* Maxie, since I'd never heard her evince interest in anyone who wasn't her or, lately, Everett. But mostly her.

"Saved me," Vance said. "Me mates and I, well, we heard the records coming over from America and we wanted to be those guys. Otherwise, I probably would have ended up a hooligan, you know, kicking people's heads in after a bucket of beer for absolutely no reason at all. I wasn't any good at school, but I could play me some guitar." I got the feeling this was a rehearsed response, something he'd used in the countless interviews he'd done during his life. Parts of it—the phrase "bucket of beer" especially—I thought I remembered from an article in *Rolling Stone*.

Now, *this* was the sort of exclusive interview Phyllis would die for, except that she'd actually have to be dead to get it. So I gave up the idea.

"I wish I'd been good at something," Maxie said.

"What are you talking about?" I asked as Maxie frowned.

"You were an up-and-coming interior designer before you got poisoned." All right, so I should have stopped before the part about the poison. I admit it. I had gotten Maxie annoyed now, and that was not a good idea.

"Do you think you could teach me guitar?" she asked Vance, completely ignoring what I'd said.

"I would be tickled to try," he said.

Maxie giggled. No, really. "You can't play guitar while you're being tickled," she crooned.

His face brightened; he'd seen this before. I had, too, but never from Maxie—she was *flirting*. I didn't think such a thing was possible. It was disgusting.

"So how's Everett?" I asked her. "Are you seeing your *boyfriend* tonight?"

Luckily, my mother exercised her gift for perfect timing at that exact moment and emerged from the kitchen, wiping her hands on a dish towel. "I've been making cookies," she announced out of the blue. "Anyone want one?"

Maxie and Vance, who after all don't eat, shook their heads out of politeness. "I think I'll be off to do some exploring," Vance said. He looked at Maxie. "Do you know the area?"

"I'd love to show you around," Maxie said to Vance. She didn't extend her arm for him to loop his own through but he did so anyway and they phased through the den's outer wall toward Seafront Avenue.

For some reason, this annoyed me. Maxie and Everett hadn't been together long (and they were dead, of course), but her cavalier attitude toward that relationship was worrisome at best. Yeah, I'd asked her to keep an eye on Vance, but this looked like more than an eye. Everett had been a really good influence on Maxie these past weeks, with his military discipline and sensible attitude. Was she really going to jeopardize that for this flaky British musician? (That's how concerned I was, to think of Vance McTiernan as a flaky British musician.)

"I'll get Liss," I told Mom, mostly because I couldn't

think of anything to do other than ask Paul to Ghost-mail Everett and warn him about what was going on behind his back. That probably wouldn't have helped and Paul might not have agreed, given the mood he was in.

"What's with them?" Mom asked. "I thought she was with Everett."

"Apparently Maxie is easily distracted," I said. I think a drop of acid may have fallen off that last word and burned a hole in one of my floorboards.

Mom considered my face carefully. "I'll get Melissa," she said. "You go in the kitchen and have a cookie. There's cold milk in the fridge." There are times we both forget whose house this is. Mom walked off toward the stairs toward Liss's attic room. She'd probably just get to the first landing and text; Mom's knees aren't what they used to be but she seemed to want to give me a moment alone.

I took it: I went into the kitchen because, hey, there were freshly baked cookies. I was sitting there idly munching on one of them when Paul raised himself up through the floor, at least up to his belt.

"I think I just got a message from Vanessa McTiernan," he said.

# Ten

"What does that mean?" Melissa asked. "You *think* you got a message from Vanessa? How come you don't know?"

She chewed on one of Mom's chocolate chip coconut cookies, which she had whipped up with no prior preparation, having simply brought the ingredients for them by chance. That was Mom's story and she was sticking to it.

Melissa had a glass of milk in front of her. I had finished my cookie before she and Mom had come down from upstairs and was considering taking another because neither of them had seen me eat the first one. Paul had, but he doesn't care about such things and wouldn't rat me out. For the record, Mom and Melissa wouldn't care, either, but in my guilty mind they would judge me and that was keeping me from taking the second cookie.

For now.

"It's not an exact experience," Paul explained. He was gracious enough not to affect a weary tone despite having explained his ghost telepathy to us more than once before. "I receive impulses, feelings. It doesn't take the form of words all the time. This one was a very strong sense of regret and she seemed to be trying to tell me she was Vance Mc-Tiernan's daughter."

"So she *has* come back as a ghost," Mom said. Mom was eschewing the cookies entirely but she didn't fool me; she'd probably eaten some of the dough while she was baking them and maybe had a "test" cookie when they came out, too. There is an advantage to having grown up in her house. "I was sure you wouldn't hear from her."

"I'm not completely sure I did," Paul reminded her. "People don't generally materialize in this state after four months. This is highly unusual."

"What did she say?" I asked. I took a step away from the cookies, which were on a white plate ringed with yellow on my center island. I was being a responsible adult. It was new to me, but I believed I liked it.

Paul refrained from once again mentioning that these messages weren't literal. "She was concerned about her father," he said. "She seemed to think he was engaged in a campaign of revenge and she didn't want that."

This sounded suspiciously like Paul conjuring up a fictional conversation with Vanessa to convince me I should quit her case. The idea that Vance was unstable and irrational was awfully convenient, especially given that this revelation had come to him right after the spook show when Vance had stomped all over Paul's turf.

"Uh-huh," I said. "Did she want you to do anything?"

"She wasn't that direct. But she said something about finding her band, that they could be the key to her death."

Curiouser and curiouser, Alice would say. "Doesn't she know what happened?" Mom asked.

"She wasn't clear about that."

This seemed fishy. "She's saying exactly what Vance said

to me before," I said. "Doesn't that seem like too big a coincidence? Who in the band does she want me to talk to?" (I was going to see the band that night anyway, but Vance, significantly, didn't know that.)

"She didn't say." Paul stroked his goatee. I'd been waiting for that; it was a sign he was thinking about the case as a case.

"Interesting," I said. If I let Paul stew in his own juices, he might come back to being an investigator without my prodding. I wanted him back on the case but I didn't want to have to swallow my pride any further to get him there. Does that make sense? I'd have to gently nudge him here— *very* gently. "What do you think it means?"

Paul's head snapped up like he'd been challenged to a duel. "Means?" he asked. "It means she wants you to talk to her band. Why? Have you told Vance something you shouldn't?"

Aha! So this was a reconnaissance mission! Paul was trying to determine what I had or hadn't done, to make sure he was in charge without actually having to say he was on the case.

"No I haven't," I said. "But I think your 'Vanessa' is some ghost pal of Vance's he convinced to get in touch with you because I'm not doing what he wants me to fast enough. I love Vance's music, but the man himself is more devious than I would have thought."

"So you see what I see," Paul said. "He can't be trusted."

"Doesn't mean we shouldn't see about his daughter's death," I told him. I'd said "we" to see if it got a rise out of him; he hadn't reacted at all.

"What about Maxie?" Melissa said. "Mom told me she and Vance went off together. If Vance is all unstable like you said, Paul, is Maxie in trouble?" Liss will avoid the point of the conversation only if she wants to, and in this case she wanted to. She was more concerned about Maxie than Vanessa because she knew Maxie. She could be concerned about Vanessa later.

Paul considered that. "I doubt it. There isn't much that can happen to Maxie."

"What about messing up her relationship with Everett?" I suggested. "That would be a problem."

Melissa nodded but Paul shrugged. "I don't think that will be an issue," he said.

I didn't get to ask him why he thought that because Berthe Englund stuck her head through the kitchen door. "Am I interrupting?" she asked.

I shook my head. "What can I do for you, Mrs. Englund?" Berthe preferred the title even though her husband was long gone. Maybe I *would* ask Paul to look him up, just to give Berthe some closure.

"I'm just wondering if there's going to be a whole concert now," she said.

"A concert? I'm afraid I don't understand."

She pointed behind her, toward the den. "In the movie room," she said. "The instruments there are playing now." And my first reaction: *There are instruments in the movie room?*

Melissa was up and out the door before I could react. "I wasn't aware of it, Mrs. Englund, but if you'd like to sit and listen awhile, I see no reason you shouldn't."

Berthe smiled. "Thank you," she said. "I just wanted to make sure it was on the agenda." And she was gone.

Paul looked at me. "If it's Vance, this would be a good time to confront him," he said.

"Does this mean you're back on the case?" I asked.

"What case?"

I ignored him. We went—Mom and me by foot, Paul by whatever that bizarre method of propulsion it is that he uses—to the movie room. But you could hear the music coming from there long before we made it to the door. And even before we got there, I could tell something really special was going on. What we saw, and heard, there absolutely floored me. I stopped dead—pardon the expression—in my tracks and stared.

At the front of my movie room, just under the ginormous TV I'd installed on the wall, stood—floated—Clarence Clemons, saxophone in hand, wailing away at a rendition of "Baker Street" that completely blew away Gerry Rafferty's recorded version. But the band that was backing up the former E Street Band's legendary saxophonist almost upstaged the Big Man himself.

Phil Ochs and Harry Chapin were on acoustic rhythm guitars. Sid Vicious was on bass. Clemons's former band-mate Danny Federici was on keyboards, Rick Danko was on electric lead (alongside—get this—*Les Paul*), and the drummer (playing a set of bongos and some folding chairs) was Levon Helm. Singing backup were Luther Vandross, Tammi Terrell and Phoebe Snow. For this ensemble, Vance McTiernan was reduced to playing percussion.

Leading the band and singing (which only half of the living people in the room—which included Mom, Melissa, and me along with Tessa, Jesse, and Berthe—could hear) along with his electric rhythm guitar was John Lennon.

I couldn't move. I'm not even sure I wanted to move. This was the most amazing group of musicians I'd ever seen. It was probably more amazing than anyone else had ever seen, either, and not one of them was alive. The music they were making, apparently impromptu, was astonishing, each member of the band contributing without having to overshadow the others. They were complete professionals, they were collaborating, and each one had a huge smile that indicated they'd never had such fun in their lives.

Literally.

The song lasted another few minutes and when it was over, the assemblage—which now included Paul, Maxie and Dad, who hovered over the musicians, and Josh, who must have appeared when I was busy being mesmerized—broke into a tremendous round of applause.

"I hope you don't mind that I invited a few friends over to jam," Vance said, grinning at me.

"It's . . . fine," I managed to choke out.

"One more, lads!" Lennon called out. The others looked to him. He raised an eyebrow. "Vance?"

Vance didn't miss a beat. "'Born to Run,'" he said. "This is New Jersey, John."

The ex-Beatle beamed. "Always know your audience, don't you?" He nodded to Clarence and Danny. "We'll defer to you two on this one, right? Count us in."

The big sax player acknowledged Lennon with a nod and shouted, "One, two, three *four*!" And they were off.

It was the most exhilarating moment of my life. (I'm sorry, Liss, but I was so tired after thirty-two hours of labor when you were finally born that "exhilarating" doesn't accurately describe it.)

They played on, and I was aware of Josh sidling up to my side. "You booked a ghost band?" he asked. "They're good."

"They oughta be," I said into his ear. "Just listen. I'll tell you who they are later." He smiled; he's used to this sort of thing.

The music was over far too soon. The band played only about fifteen minutes in total until Levon mentioned he had a gig in the city later that night, so he'd better find a car heading in that direction. Tammi asked if she could ride along. Phoebe was going to visit relatives in Teaneck. Everyone went his or her own separate way, rising, sinking, exiting through walls. Federici folded up the electronic keyboard and hid it inside a long peacoat he was suddenly wearing, saying he'd better get it back to the family restaurant in Freehold before it was missed.

My guests, thrilled with the music but unaware of the miracle they'd just witnessed, thanked me for the show on the way out of the movie room and asked if there'd be another soon. I said I doubted there would be another one like that, but nothing was impossible at the haunted guesthouse.

Because all of a sudden that seemed to be true.

The topper for me came when, after all the guests had shuffled out, John Lennon swooped down, smiled at me and asked if he could come play here again because he liked the room's acoustics. I told him he was always welcome and couldn't help wondering aloud why he was still bound to Earth.

He laughed. "'Imagine there's no heaven,'" he said. "Apparently someone is taking that personally." Then he gave Vance a departing nod, said something about going to haunt Yoko and flew out the back wall.

"That was so bitchin'!" Maxie yelled from the rafters. "I might have to start listening to those oldies you like. Who was that guy doing the singing? I liked him."

I sat down heavily in one of the chairs I'd laid out for the Sunday night movie, which was now definitely going to be a major disappointment, and shook my head. Had I really just seen and heard all that? Josh sat down next to me.

"I've never seen you look like that before," he said. "Are you okay?"

I blinked. Three times. "I am so much better than okay," I said. I looked at Melissa. "Did you know who any of those people were?" I asked.

"I knew some, but Grandma knew almost everybody," she said. "Wow."

"Wow indeed," Vance said, crossing his arms in a casual expression of smugness and floating just above my eye level, so I had to look up at him. "Not bad, huh?"

"That was . . . spectacular," I said. "Thank you so much." From the side of my eye I caught Paul looking displeased in the corner near the ceiling. Men are so competitive.

"Don't mention it," Vance said.

"No, really," I gushed. "Nobody's ever done anything like that for me before. I mean, nobody possibly could." Now Josh looked displeased, which proved he had a male ego, too. "I wish I could do something for you."

"Well . . ." Vance stroked his chin. I looked up. Paul was stroking his goatee. They looked like they were doing impressions of each other. "Maybe you can."

Paul's eyes almost closed; he was staring at Vance through slits. Even Maxie, ecstatic a minute ago, looked suspicious.

"Name it," I said.

"Stop investigating about Nessa," he fired back much too quickly.

That was too much. "Why?" I exploded. "Aren't you the guy who wanted me to dive into this with both feet, like, an hour ago? Why can't you make up your mind?"

"I don't want to know. If I was a bad dad—and I was— maybe that led to her wanting to do this, and it would make me feel horrible. Her death left a hole in me. I don't want another one." Given that I could literally see through him, the metaphor was a little less effective than he might have hoped.

Paul, no doubt realizing he could do little good now, did not speak.

But my father did. "Vance, I have only one daughter," he said. "And I would be absolutely devastated if anything happened to her. I'd never be able to think straight if I didn't do something about it."

Vance didn't acknowledge Dad; he just stared straight at me. "You asked if there was something you could do for me," he said urgently. "There is, and I'm asking. Please. Stop looking and let me move on."

Paul looked at me and shook his head. It was a test. For me.

I knew Vance was trying to charm me, and to intimidate me into doing what he wanted. I knew he was counting on my weakness, my admiration (okay, bordering on idol worship) for him and his music, to convince me that I should do something I thought was wrong. If someone willfully exposed Vanessa to something they knew would kill her, they had to pay. And I knew that the least I should get out of him before agreeing to something so ludicrous was a sincere explanation of his desire to keep me off the investigation I was conducting, solo, supposedly on his behalf.

There was also the weird alpha-male vibe going on between Paul and Vance that was coloring the discussion. To agree with Vance would be to somehow reject Paul, who had been my friend and confidant for years, and who knew infinitely more about investigation than I did. To refuse Vance would be to turn my back on the great warmth and emotional support he'd offered, even without knowing it, when I'd been badly in need of it.

"Alison," Vance said. "Please."

There was only one thing to do. I took a deep breath, let it out and then turned my gaze away from Paul and into Vance's pleading eyes.

"Okay," I said.

Paul actually smote himself in the forehead and fell, backward, through the wall and out of the house.

"Ooh," Maxie said.

# Eleven

"Get Paul," I said to Maxie.

Dinner had been a somewhat tense affair. I'm understating it.

The kitchen, where Melissa, Mom, Josh and I ate, was divided into two camps: On the one side were all those who believed that I'd disrespected Paul's experience and judgment by agreeing to give up the investigation. Which sounds weird, since Paul hadn't wanted to take the case. But when Vance had suggested we stop, Paul had shook his head to indicate I should refuse. So now one camp thought I had done badly by Paul. That camp consisted of Mom and Dad, Maxie (of course), Josh and even Melissa.

The other camp, which believed I had done the only rational thing available under the circumstances, consisted of me. So it was a pretty evenly divided gathering.

Liss, to be fair, had not chided me for the scene in the

movie room, but her expression clearly showed she thought I was being mean to her ghostly friend. And the cacophony from the others (okay, mostly Maxie) had drowned out any questions even after she and Mom had cooked the brisket, some roasted potatoes and carrots and made a side salad. Josh's perceived disapproval was based mostly on his somewhat nebulous knowledge of Paul, whom he couldn't see or hear but knew was a decent guy. He wanted to side with me but was already not all that crazy about Vance.

Maxie had ranted on for the whole time—even when guests were asking about nearby restaurants or thanking me again for the concert they thought I had organized—about my insensitivity and disloyal insubordination (she used other words) that I couldn't get my thoughts out completely. After a while I realized voicing my defense would make no difference unless Paul was in the room, anyway.

First, I had to wait for Vance to leave, but that didn't take long. He had been invited to jam with Clarence and Luther at a "very pre-Halloween gig in Red Bank" and was already late. Maxie had stared after him as he left as if expecting to be asked to come along, but she wasn't.

I was going to have to get in touch with Everett and tell him his new girlfriend was looking at other boys. Because life never progresses beyond seventh grade, even after you're dead.

"What do you mean, 'get Paul'?" Maxie asked me now.

"Is that a complex sentence? I need to talk to Paul and he's not going to answer me if I call him now." I was rinsing off some dishes in the sink before putting them in the dishwasher as Josh and Liss cleared the table. Mom was repacking her backpack with those few items she'd determined I would not be able to reheat or in some way convert into another meal.

"What do you want Paul for?" Maxie's voice, unsurprisingly,

had a combative tone. "All you did was ask him to come back and then tell Vance you'd stop the investigation. You threw Paul under the bus."

"I could throw him under a real bus and it wouldn't hurt him now," I pointed out. "Please just find him."

"I'll do it," Melissa said. "He'll talk to me."

"Thanks, baby."

Liss, probably grateful for the break from KP duty, headed for the basement door and vanished down the stairwell; it's always a decent bet to find Paul in the basement.

Maxie continued on her rant about how I'd betrayed my "best friend in the world" (Jeannie Rogers is actually my best friend, but that was the least of the points worth arguing and I wasn't even arguing) for the sake of "sucking up to a famous guy" that Maxie had "never even heard of three days ago."

"Don't be so hard on Alison," my mother told Maxie. I can always count on her when I need defending. "She made a mistake. Everybody makes mistakes." Everybody has days like this one, too. I just tend to have them four times a week.

Thankfully, Paul finally rose up through the kitchen floor, face impassive. "Melissa said you were asking for me," he said with as much inflection as a goldfish.

"Yes." I dried my hands on a dish towel. "About what happened before in the movie room—"

I couldn't even get a whole sentence out of my mouth. "I understand what happened," Paul said.

"I don't think you do," I said.

"Of course I do. You were given a choice and you decided that Vance McTiernan was the more trustworthy person in the conversation." Paul is often wise and almost always logical. It is rare to hear him be neither at the same time, but now he was sounding like a jilted sixteen-year-old.

"Paul," I said.

"It was clear enough," Maxie joined in without the benefit

of anyone indicating she should. "He got all these famous musicians to come to your house, so you sided with the guy who brought them here. It's a little sad, really." She lay back, hands intertwined behind her head, floating in a pool that wasn't there. "I would have thought you'd be more loyal."

"That's not the point," Paul told her. "What hurt was the fact that you didn't trust my judgment, Alison. You didn't believe after all we've been through together that my advice might be of some value."

"Pardon me, Paul, but isn't that what Alison was saying to you yesterday?" This time Mom really was coming to my defense. (Josh probably would have, too, but he hadn't heard a word Paul or Maxie had said. Besides, he was engrossed in wiping down the center island.) "That you should have trusted her a little bit more with the case Vance was asking you to take?"

Paul blinked and looked away; he was thinking.

Maxie was still floating on her nonexistent barge and thinking is something she tries to avoid whenever possible. "Is that what this was about?" she asked, presumably, me. "A way to get back at Paul for the way he talked to you? Wow. That's petty." *Hello, Pot? Kettle has a message for you.*

"Is everybody done telling me what I did and why I did it?" I asked. "Because I'd like to say a little something about the case."

Paul, newly attentive, turned toward me. "You promised Vance you'd stop the investigation," he said. "He asked you to stop looking into his daughter's death. What is left of the case?"

"Paul." I almost told him to take a deep breath, but that would have been inappropriate. "I lied to Vance. I told him I'd stop looking for Vanessa's killer because it was the easiest way to placate him. I'm not giving up the case and I'm not about to drop the only leads I have."

"You're not," Paul said. It wasn't a question. A small smile was attempting to break out of the prison his lips had built for it.

"No, I'm not. But I am feeling a little over my head on this and I really need your help. Will you please guide me through this investigation?"

Paul dropped down a little to my eye level. Josh looked over at me, half-grinning, and touched my hand. His fingers were still cold from the kitchen wipe he'd been using but I appreciated the gesture.

"Are you sure you need me?" Paul said.

"I'm sure," I answered. "I'm very, very sure."

Paul's smile got a millimeter broader. "All right, then. Since you begged."

I let it go.

Maxie, realizing the "fight" between Paul and me was over, suddenly lost interest in the conversation. "I have a date with Everett," she said, and shot up through the roof. Really.

"All right," Paul said, immediately getting down to business. "First, I think you are right in trying to find the other members of Once Again. But I've been confused as to why you haven't yet searched for Jeremy Bensinger, the half brother the obituary mentioned, or for their mother, Claudia Rabinowitz."

Damn. He was right.

"See, this is why I need your help," I said. Paul smiled. And I started to feel a little better.

I didn't tell him about my plan to go see the members of Vanessa's old band in Asbury Park tonight for the very reasons I'd suggested to Josh (even with Vance supposedly out of the house, I couldn't be sure he was where he said he'd be). I'd see about getting Paul by himself after Josh and I got back from the club and I'd tell him then.

But first, there was some searching to do for Vanessa McTiernan's mother, Claudia Rabinowitz. Since Maxie was now unavailable, Melissa volunteered to girl the laptop (well, she couldn't *man* the laptop) and do some searches for the name.

"Google lists more than two million hits for 'Claudia Rabinowitz,'" she reported in a few seconds. "I'll narrow it down." I thought that was a good plan.

We moved out into the den so I could keep an eye out for guests. Nobody was in the room when we entered—they were probably all out to dinner in nearby restaurants—but as the innkeeper, I needed to be available.

Mom had already agreed to stay with Liss while Josh and I were out "meeting his friends A.J. and Liz," and Dad was staying with her because, well, that's what they do.

Josh sat down beside me on the sofa. Since the all-star concert earlier today, he'd made a point of being close to me whenever he could. I'd never seen a jealous side of him before and it was interesting—did he think I was going to throw him over for a man who wasn't just decades older than I was, but had also been dead for eight years?

I was about to ask if he was all right when Liss announced, "I can't find any Claudia Rabinowitzes listed in New Jersey. It's like searching for an answer when I'm doing history homework."

My face scrunched up. "Are you allowed to do that?" I asked.

Melissa gave me her "oh, mother" face and nodded. "We're *supposed* to. But that's not the point. Maybe Claudia moved out of the state."

"Maybe she got remarried," Josh suggested.

But Paul was already holding up his hand, which made no difference to Josh, of course. "See if there is a 'C Rabinowitz' listed," he said to Melissa. "Also, the obituary said Vanessa had a half brother whose last name was Bensinger. Claudia might have changed her name. Maybe the brother is the place to start looking."

It was good to have Paul back on board. Someday when I was very old I'd be sure to say that to him.

"Jeremy's living in Marlboro, if I recall correctly," I said. It was necessary to get back some of my own. Although I didn't recall giving any away.

"That's right," Paul said. "Melissa, can you . . ."

"I've already got him," Liss said. Josh nodded, no doubt thinking she was answering me. "I can print you out an address and MapQuest it if you want, Mom."

"How about a phone number?" I asked. I'd rather call Jeremy than go see him if I could. Quicker, and I didn't have to worry that Jeremy might himself be a murderer. So few gruesome killings happen over the phone.

But Liss shook her head. "Sorry. If we want to sign up for one of the pay sites, maybe we could find it." I didn't own a Marlboro-area phone book.

However, I could still dial a phone. I picked up mine and punched up Information. There was no listing for Jeremy Bensinger in Marlboro, which is not terribly unusual. Most people operate with just a cell phone these days, and those are not listed.

"Looks like I'll be visiting Jeremy Bensinger tomorrow after the morning show," I said. "Do you think that was really Vanessa who got in touch with you?" I asked Paul.

"Actually, I don't," he said. I'd suspected as much—he had been trying to get me to tell Vance the investigation was over (something Vance was now suggesting on his own; the world is an ironic place). "She was too vague and didn't seem to know any details. I'm not sure she really knew anything about Vanessa or Vance. It might have been someone just answering my message generally, hoping for some attention. That happens every now and again."

"That's so sad," Melissa said.

"It might also have been Vance trying to play us," I said. "See if you can get her to admit to anything."

Josh looked over at me and then glanced at his watch. "We should go if we're going to meet A.J. and Liz," he said.

I saw the time and agreed. "I'll talk to you later," I told Paul. "I should have something to report."

"I imagine so." Paul sank into the floor.

It was nice to be back in our traditional roles.

# Twelve

"What?"

It had become my signature line since we'd entered the Last Resort, which lived up to its name in every way except that it was not at all a resort. The music, which at the moment was coming from a band named Whatever, was loud, mostly bass and repetitive to the edge of madness. But at the moment I was trying to determine what Liz Seger had just said to me.

It turned out Josh really *did* have friends named A.J. and Liz, and they really *were* coming along with us on my reconnaissance mission to find and question Bill Mastrovy and the other members of Once Again. A.J. Merrill was an English professor at Monmouth University, specializing in humor and the Edwardian period, of which I knew nothing. Liz, who was now to my left at a round table the circumference of a quarter, worked in a business I could not begin to understand even after having it explained to me in very clear language (which had happened before we'd entered the club, so I'd actually heard it).

Josh and A.J. were sitting, respectively, to my right and Liz's left at the table, each holding a bottle of beer (I'd agreed to drive because I wanted to be completely sober when Mastrovy and his cover band hit the stage), and even at a table this small, that was far enough in this din to keep them completely shut out of our talk. They didn't seem the least bit concerned about it and were probably talking (screaming) about baseball—Josh doesn't like other sports much—or movies. Guy stuff.

"What?" I repeated.

"I said I'm glad we finally arranged this," Liz shouted directly into my ear. "Josh has been talking about you for a long time."

Now I felt guilty, generally my baseline emotion. "It's my fault," I said. "We've been together for months, but because I run the guesthouse I can't get out much at night, or even during the day. How about you guys come over for dinner one night?"

"What?" Liz shouted.

(In the interest of time, just assume that everything either of us said while the band was playing had to be repeated at least once. Okay? It'll just simplify this whole process tremendously.)

After I restated my case, Liz laughed and shook her head. "No, I don't mean just the last few months. Josh has been talking about you since I met him, and that's got to be seven or eight years."

Since Josh and I had only recently reconnected after not having seen each other since middle school, that was something of a shock. "What do you mean?" I said. "We were out of touch for years."

"Yeah, but he always mentioned your name. He would tell us what he heard about you from your dad, until he passed away." Liz clearly hadn't been told that Dad was still available for opinions and updates, which was something of a relief. I don't hide the haunted aspect of the guesthouse, but neither do I go around telling people that I consult with deceased family members on a regular basis.

"That's sweet," I said. "A little creepy, but sweet."

"Creepy?"

"Well, we weren't in touch. The idea that Josh was obsessed with me all those years is a little . . ." I trailed off when I saw the look on Liz's face.

"Obsessed?" She laughed. "I wouldn't go that far. He mentioned you once in a while." The fact that, during those years, I probably would have had a slightly difficult time recalling Josh's name was probably not the best thing to mention.

There was an extremely welcome break as the bandleader of Whatever, who looked just as engaged as his band name would indicate, leaned into the mic after the song and mumbled something about us being a great crowd and walked off without a look back. We in the crowd (although "crowd" was a pretty serious overstatement) had been great in context, mostly because we hadn't run for cover and left the room empty six notes into the band's first song. The second the live band left the stage, recorded music started to play over the club's sound system, thankfully at a much lower volume.

"That's a relief," I said.

Liz regarded me with something that resembled judgment. "I wouldn't think a guy thinking fondly of you would be a problem."

Huh? Oh. "No, I meant the music stopping. That was the relief."

The pictures on the website hadn't given me much of an idea what William Mastrovy looked like, so I'd have to wait until Once Again took the stage. He'd be the lead singer and Maxie had said he played bass. After their set, which I could only hope would be at a lower decibel level than Whatever's, I'd do my investigator thing.

Liz was still scrutinizing me carefully and I worried that she might be considering whether to bring me back for a size that fit better. "How are things with the two of you?" she asked in a regular tone of voice, but quietly enough that Josh and A.J. (who seemed to be engrossed in a deep discussion about . . . some guy thing) couldn't hear.

"We're fine," I answered, wondering how you measure such a thing. "Josh seems happy with the way things are, and I certainly am."

"Did I hear my name mentioned?" Josh looked over suddenly, and I was greatly relieved. "Are you saying nice things about me?"

"Always," I breathed. Josh always rescues me, and that's one of the best things about him—I know I can depend on him.

Liz looked skeptical. I was starting to worry about Liz. But she didn't add anything, and that at least was a positive sign. Luckily Josh would be riding home with me so he wouldn't hear the postmortem from his friends.

"So the deal is what?" Josh asked. "We wait for the next band to play and then you just go and accost the front man? Is that about right?"

"Pretty much." I leaned into him a little bit to better demonstrate some affection. I couldn't see if Liz took notice.

Josh told me he'd mentioned my private investigator status to his friends, leaving out the rather difficult-to-explain aspect of collaborating with ghosts. It tends to smooth out a conversation when you don't have to mention that your business partners (as if we ever got paid!) are dead but continuing to participate.

"What's this guy supposed to have done?" A.J. wanted to know. I guess Josh hadn't filled them in *that* much. "Deadbeat dad? Cheating husband? Something like that?" People you meet all think they know what investigations are like. I'm not that sure I know, but I can tell you that most of them definitely don't.

Well, I was about to throw a grenade into A.J.'s expectations. "Um . . . he's not necessarily a suspect, but he probably has some information about a woman's death." That was about as straightforward as I could be while sounding matter-of-fact.

"A death?" Liz said. Suddenly she was all attention and appeared to be intrigued. "You mean he might've killed her?"

"Well, I don't know. She might have died of natural causes, or someone might have helped her along. All I'm doing is trying to find out if he was there and what he knows about it."

"Wow," Liz said. "How do you do that?" Her demeanor had completely shifted from skeptical and a little frosty to engrossed and oddly delighted. I wasn't sure if it was a good change or a bad one.

"I ask him." That seemed obvious. To me.

A.J. smiled. "That's it?" he asked.

"Yeah, pretty much. You can't find out what somebody knows until you ask them." Duh.

Liz crinkled her brow. "What if he lies?"

Josh put an arm around my shoulder. "Alison's pretty good at figuring that out," he said. "But let's talk about something else." He looked over at A.J. "Have you heard from anybody? I didn't go to the reunion last year, but . . ."

Liz cut him off. "No, I really want to hear about this detective stuff. How can you tell if somebody's lying?"

I debated getting into Paul's theories of "tells" that can indicate a person is uncomfortable with the line of questioning, even if they're not perfect predictors of guilt. I also tape all my interviews with a voice recorder so I can play the interviews back for Paul after I get home and he can tell me all the things I missed. He's better at deciphering these things.

It's a functional professional relationship, but one that would be really difficult to explain to Liz.

And then Bill Mastrovy himself bailed me out.

I'd like to say the lights dimmed, but they were never exactly what you'd call bright to begin with, so it was really more a question of two guys (clearly a new band member had taken Vanessa's place) and one woman trudging—there is no other word for what they did—up to the stage and plugging into the amplifiers. Apparently, management had not noticed this was a relatively small room and people in the back could have heard the musicians using two tin cans and a string if necessary.

The difference between Whatever and Once Again was obvious immediately. As soon as they were onstage, the Once Again musicians became animated (no, they weren't cartoons—very funny), looked the audience in the eye and actually—you'll find this amazing—*smiled*. After the lavish show of indifference the previous performers had cultivated, this was positively refreshing.

There was no introduction. The lead singer, presumably William Mastrovy, just waited until his bandmates had tuned up and plugged in, and then leaned into his microphone at center stage.

"Once Again," he said simply. Then the drummer—the tattooed, pink-haired woman with the piercings who must have been Samantha Fine—counted them in.

The music was familiar, and played professionally. Each song was a bygone hit, an "oldie," and could be identified within the first four notes. No surprises, no amazingly fresh or original arrangements. This was not the superstar jam session I'd seen in my house earlier today; nothing else could be. But what they did, they did well, and they knew they were playing for an audience.

The problem was, much of the audience had come to see Whatever and were expecting more of the earsplitting same.

They were restless at the beginning of the set and looks among the band members showed some notice of that.

They simply played harder. Bill Mastrovy (he confirmed his name when introducing every player in the group after four songs) talked to members of the audience between numbers. He joked, he cajoled, he did everything but juggle. It became clear that Once Again's set was the work of good musicians who were inspired by others and not trailblazers on their own. But they were entertainers and they understood the concept of pleasing an audience.

It worked, to some extent. The noise level among the audience dropped and attention was paid. Applause, albeit not incredibly wild applause, followed each song. And after seven of them, Bill leaned into the mic again and said, "We're Once Again. Thank you." And the band left the stage.

Josh nodded at me as I stood and the message was implied. He'd stay here, but he'd be watching. If he was needed, he'd be available. Even the nod was superfluous; I knew that already.

But as I made my way toward the band, who were heading toward the back of the room where presumably was whatever passed for a dressing room, I felt a presence over my left shoulder and turned to look.

Liz Seger was following me.

That was bizarre. "I have to work now, Liz," I said even as I kept walking toward my quarry. I was just close enough now, so I said, fairly loudly, "Bill," and watched as he stopped and looked at me.

Bill Mastrovy looked puzzled. "Do I know you?" he asked.

"No, we've never met. I wanted to ask you about Vanessa McTiernan."

His eyes widened a little and the right side of his mouth twitched. "Why?" He looked behind me, where I knew Liz was still standing, inexplicably.

"I'm a private investigator and I'm trying to find out what

happened to Vanessa. Is there somewhere we can talk?" I could practically feel Liz's breath on my shoulder. She seemed absolutely enthralled.

"You're a private investigator?" Bill sounded astonished. Can you blame him?

I get that a lot, so I already had the license in my hand and showed it to him. He looked at it for about ten seconds, which is a long time. Then he looked at me.

Then he looked at Liz. "Who's she?" he asked.

Well, *she's a friend of my boyfriend* didn't sound especially professional, so I was stuck with, "She's my assistant." Liz blinked a couple of times but didn't say anything. "Now is there somewhere we can talk?"

Bill's expression suggested he'd prefer not to, but he nodded. "There's a dressing room, sort of. Follow me."

He led us out of the main room and down a staircase to the basement, where players from tonight's bands were milling around in various stages of dress, or un-. A few doors down a fairly depressing corridor was one marked *Storage*, and he opened that door for us to enter.

There were already three people in the overcrowded room: the other members of Once Again, and a woman who clearly (and I mean *clearly*) was with the lead guitarist they called T.B. or "Teeb," and now Bill, Liz and me. When we walked in, absolutely no one looked up. The drummer, introduced onstage as Sammi Fine, sat at a mirror taking off her stage makeup, which meant dabbing at her eyes with a cotton ball.

"This is as private as it gets around here. So what do you want to know?" Bill leaned on the table Sammi was using and folded his arms, which I took to be a gesture of defiance. Why he needed to defy me was Bill's business.

"You were Vanessa McTiernan's boyfriend, weren't you?" I started. I tried to hold up the tote bag I was carrying, which held my voice recorder.

"For a while, yeah." Bill's voice, now that I could hear him in a slightly less noisy environment, was pure Jersey Shore. That's half I'll-bust-you-up and half why-are-you-pickin'-on-me. I noticed Sammi look up in the mirror without turning to face us, and she was looking right at me. She didn't care for the topic of conversation, it seemed.

"So were you there when she died?" I asked. I looked at Liz, who was transfixed by the guitarist and his girlfriend, who had obviously been told to get a room and had chosen this one. Our luck.

"Hell no," Bill said. "Anybody who told you I was is a liar."

"Nobody told me you were," I countered. "I'm trying to figure out what happened, and part of that is reconstructing the scene. Do you know who was there?"

"I have no idea. So I can't help you. Sorry." Bill turned to look at Sammi, now angry enough at him—apparently for having a dead girlfriend—that she wasn't returning the glance.

"Hang on," I told him. "Liz?"

I looked at her; she was still gaping at the amorous couple in the back of the room. "Huh?"

"Are you taking notes on this?" I asked her. She was, after all, supposed to be my assistant. If she wanted to bulldoze her way into this situation she could at least act the part.

"Huh?" Liz repeated. "Oh. Yeah." She started rummaging through her purse, presumably for a pad and pen. What were the odds she had those?

I shook my head theatrically for Bill's benefit. "Assistants. Can you ever get one to be efficient?" I pulled the voice recorder out of my tote bag. "Do you mind?"

Bill Mastrovy stared at the little battery-operated device like it was a phaser set to kill. "What do you need that for?" he asked.

"So I can transcribe it for my report later," I said. He hadn't asked me who my client was, which simplified my process enormously. No need to make up someone who might care how Vanessa McTiernan had died. "Now, how was Vanessa's relationship with her father?"

Bill puffed out his lips in a sneer of contempt. "Ooh, the famous Vance McTiernan? Front man for a band that had exactly two hits?" I could think of six, but that was me. "She never heard from the old bastard."

"Never?" Liz sounded scandalized.

"Not from what Vanessa told me. The guy was dead before I met her. She said oh, maybe once every couple of years he'd get in touch to see if she still remembered he existed, but let's be real—he considered himself a great big deal in the music business, yet he never once lifted a finger for his own daughter." Bill rolled his eyes. "She believed in that man until she died—literally. And he let her down every time."

"You know he's been dead for eight years," I pointed out.

"Yeah, and what did she get in his will? Nothing, that's what. If he cared so much about her, you'd think that would be the one time he'd show it since he'd have nothing to lose. Nothing."

"What was she like?" I asked. "I really don't have a strong sense of Vanessa."

Bill smiled wistfully. "Oh, she was fun," he said. "She could get a little spacey sometimes, just stare straight ahead and mumble to herself like she was in a trance. But that was how she was—she was completely in herself, but would let you look in to see her once in a while. She was a good soul." Sweet, but I didn't see how that was going to help Paul solve her murder. He'd asked me to pose the question and I had, eager to show him we were back in our normal roles.

Paul also wanted me to ask about Vanessa's supposed record contract. "I understand she was about to release a solo album with Vinyl Records?"

Bill's eyes bulged a bit and Sammi's almost closed. Opposite reactions to the same information. "Yeah," Bill said. "She had just signed the deal."

"And that didn't have anything to do with her father's reputation?" After all, no matter how he drove me crazy, he *was* Vance McTiernan.

Bill puffed out his lips and made a rude sound. "No. It was all due to Vanessa's voice. And her material, some of which was mine."

"You wrote the songs?" I asked.

"Depends on who you talk to."

"What does that mean?"

Sammi chose this moment to interrupt my interview. She turned away from the mirror and looked me in the eye. "Look. What does the music have to do with anything? Vanessa and I were never all that close but apparently she did something stupid and it killed her. What's the big deal?"

"The 'big deal' is that she was *murdered*," Liz piped up. I had only met Liz two hours before, but she was climbing up my list of people to be annoyed at for the next few years. Wait. She was a friend of Josh's and he cared if I liked her. Okay. Liz was trying to help. That was it.

Sammi curled her lip and made a noise usually associated with other areas of the body. "Sure she was," she said, unwrapping a piece of gum and popping it in her mouth.

But Bill, whom I'd been watching for a reaction, certainly had one. He pulled his lips in and his eyes got wild. It wasn't anger or shock—it was fear.

"Murdered?" he said quietly. I'm not sure if he was talking to me or to himself.

"There's a very strong possibility she didn't die accidentally," I told him. "What can you tell me about the day she died?"

Bill looked stunned. He was staring blankly, half at the floor and half at the air in front of the floor. He probably wasn't seeing anything really. "What?" he muttered.

"The day Vanessa died, Bill. Tell me what happened."

He seemed confused. "Nothing happened," he said. "She died. I heard about it the next day."

"Yeah, I get that. What was happening *before* she died? Focus, Bill. What do you remember?"

Sammi cracked her gum. Perhaps she was looking for a way to be more clichéd, and she'd found it. "For chrissakes, Bill. You weren't there when she died, right? That's what you told me."

Bill's head was bobbing around. I was getting dizzy looking at him. I crouched down because he was still looking at the floor. Liz looked like she might sit down, considered the rug and decided against it.

The two people making out on the couch were unaffected. I couldn't really catch Bill's gaze but at least some of me was in his line of sight. "Bill," I said. "Is that right? You weren't there when Vanessa died?"

"Tomorrow," he said. "I'll talk to you tomorrow. I need to figure it out. Tomorrow night."

That didn't make tons of sense but I was about to agree when Liz once again decided to be helpful. "She can't," she told Bill. "She's showing *Ghost* at her guesthouse tomorrow night." In an earlier moment of delusion, I'd invited Liz and A.J. to the showing. It had seemed like a good idea at the time.

"*Ghost*?" Bill didn't seem to be hearing everything that was being said; it was like he was listening in on a long-distance call from 1932.

"It's a movie," I said. "But that doesn't matter. Tell me now. Were you there when Vanessa McTiernan died?"

"No. Yeah. Well, earlier. Not when she died."

Sammi stood up. "*What?*" she bleated. "You were there? You told me you'd broke up with her weeks before! We were *together* already!"

"I gotta go," Bill said. He pushed his arm out like a running back in a 1950s football movie. "I gotta go now."

For reasons I couldn't begin to explain, we all backed off and cleared a path for him. He moved, still watching his own feet, all the way to the door and then out, and nobody said a word.

After a long moment, Sammi spit her gum out on the floor and stormed out, but she didn't call after Bill and she didn't seem to be following him. She just left.

Liz looked at me. "Was that a good interrogation?" she asked.

"What did you think of A.J. and Liz?" Josh asked later.

Liz and I had maneuvered our way back to the table while the new band was playing, and looks all around had concluded that staying to hear the show would be a poor idea. We didn't even sit down. Josh and A.J. stood up and we left to the comfort of the outside, where it was cooler and, thankfully, much, much, quieter.

It was a relatively late night for someone who got up around dawn every day to prepare for guests and someone else who got up around the same time to open a paint store, so we said our goodnights to Liz and A.J. in the parking lot and now I was driving Josh home.

"What did you say?" I asked. I was stalling for time because I was driving at night and because I'd actually been thinking about Bill Mastrovy and Sammi Fine, not about how I was going to sugarcoat the fact that Liz was something of a pain and that I'd barely talked to A.J.

If Bill Mastrovy really had been present around the time Vanessa McTiernan died, it opened up vast new possibilities that I was sure Paul would explain to me. But even a detective like me—not that there are any detectives like me, which I mean in an anything but arrogant fashion—could muddle over some of the implications of what he'd said.

Vanessa had died from a reaction to soy sauce, but there was no other food in her digestive tract when she suffocated.

She knew she was severely allergic to soy products and would never have willingly eaten any on her own. Would she?

Now I could put Bill Mastrovy, the man with whom Vanessa had just ended a relationship, in the room the day she died. But he'd looked genuinely freaked out at the prospect that Vanessa had been murdered, like it had never occurred to him before. If he was the killer, he was an awfully good actor as well. The point is, I believed him.

And that was a problem.

"I said, what did you think of A.J. and Liz?" Josh repeated. *Oh, yeah.*

"Well, I really didn't get a chance to talk to them that much," I said. "The music was so loud."

"Uh-oh."

"What, uh-oh?"

"You don't like them," Josh said. He sat back in the passenger seat and closed his eyes for a moment. "I was afraid of that."

"You're rushing to judgment." I was hoping to traverse the remaining three miles in about six seconds, but that would probably mean points on my driver's license. "All I'm saying is that this wasn't the best environment for me to get to know them. I'll see them tomorrow at the guesthouse."

"You'll be in a room with your whole family, only some of whom I can see, and all your guests," Josh pointed out. "*And* you'll be showing a movie. Somehow I don't think you're going to have tons of time for my friends tomorrow, either."

This was a little touchy. Josh hadn't introduced me to many of his friends. He's in the store for twelve hours a day, six days a week. I live at my work and have to be available to my guests at any hour of the day or night, literally. It hasn't left a lot of time for us to collect a posse.

"I'm sorry," I said. "I was preoccupied with talking to Bill Mastrovy tonight. I probably should have said it was a bad night but we never seem to have a good night and I wasn't even sure until we got there whether or not they were just part of our cover story. Look. I have one night free next week and I suggested to Liz that they come for dinner." The thought of subjecting myself to Liz's barrage of questions wasn't a terribly appetizing prospect, but the thought of disappointing Josh was worse.

He looked at me without turning his head, like he wanted me to see him looking amused. "You sure?" he said.

The look on his face was enough. "I'm sure," I said. But between you and me, I wasn't the least bit sure.

Still, the rest of the drive—which lasted six minutes—was not at all tense. We talked about the music mostly from this afternoon at my house, which Josh agreed was awesome (and that was even without the benefit of hearing the vocals) and had some not-awkward silences. I'd worry about dealing with Liz tomorrow. I dropped Josh off, then headed home.

I hadn't expected the guesthouse to be entirely quiet when I got back—it was a Saturday night and I'd left instructions with Mom to either bring out the karaoke machine The Swine had foisted upon me a while back or to have a ghost Q&A if Paul and Maxie were willing to float still for it.

But I was surprised to find every light in the house on, and every guest in the den. It looked like the place had been buzzing while we were out. I wasn't all that concerned that Melissa was still awake, since it wasn't a school night, but I was a little peeved that the Levines were teaching her to play poker. At least she was winning. Too bad they weren't playing for money.

Berthe and Jesse were watching the poker game, Tessa was playing, and Maureen, bless her, was sitting by herself with her e-reader. A whole library full of books and she was never away from her e-reader.

Mom was standing behind Liss eyeing the cards, and

Dad, floating near the ceiling, was looking at everybody else's hand. If they were cheating for their granddaughter, they'd get a serious talking to from her mother. That's me.

None of that would have seemed terribly out of place, but Paul and Maxie were both at the door the second I walked in.

"Something's got to be done," Paul was babbling as I took in the scene. "This investigation is being jeopardized."

"Since when do you care?" Maxie countered. "Until tonight you didn't even want to hear about who killed Vanessa."

"What are you two talking about?" I was trying to keep my tone light so the guests would be in on the idea that the ghosts were there but not concerned about their presence. Even people who come willingly to a haunted guesthouse are skittish around spooks who seem upset.

I hadn't even been able to fully brief Paul before Berthe chose that moment to walk into the den and must have assessed our faces. "Is something wrong?" she asked. I handed Paul the voice recorder, which he stashed in his pocket to make it vanish. He sunk into the basement.

"I'll be back," he said. He didn't even have the good taste to do an Arnold Schwarzenegger impression.

I stood up, back in hostess mode. "No, not at all, Berthe," I said. "Is there something I can help you with?"

"Alison, I don't want to complain, truly. I've loved all the little shows and everything that goes on here at the hotel." You can tell them a million times it's a guesthouse; they'll call it what they want and you'll agree because the customer is always paying. "And the musical performances have been lovely."

"But?" I said.

"*But* when it gets a little later in the evening, even nice music is something that can be, well, too much. Do you know what I mean?"

"Music?" I asked Berthe. "What music is that?"

Vance was out somewhere and I was pretty sure John Lennon hadn't come back already.

"Well, it sounds like it's coming from the library to me."

There was nothing to do but go and look. Maxie came along as I followed Berthe to the library. Berthe led the way, in case I'd forgotten where the rooms were in my own house.

Sure enough, when we got there, a ukulele was (to Berthe's eyes) playing itself in one of the armchairs. And making quite a lovely sound, although I couldn't really recognize the tune.

Sitting in the armchair, playing the uke, was a ghost who looked to be in his seventies, though quite fit for a person who had passed away. His longish gray hair was pulled back in the requisite aging hippie ponytail, and his eyes sparkled as much as a ghost's can when he saw us walk in. He stopped playing.

"I swear I heard it a second ago," Berthe said. She shook her head and walked out, mumbling something about a hearing test.

"Ah, good!" the ghost shouted. He had a fairly thick Cockney accent, so understanding him was going to be a challenge, I could see. Hear. You know. "The music brought ya in! Glad to see it. Which one of you is the innkeeper?"

He didn't seem especially dangerous, but that didn't mean anything. Still, I *was* the proprietor of the place, and with all the musicians passing through here lately, it didn't seem too risky to admit to it, so I did. "Alison Kerby," I said. "And you?" I asked, though I was pretty sure that even with the wrinkles, I knew the face.

"I'm Morrie Chrichton."

"The bass player for the Jingles?" I asked. I was a little jaded after meeting Vance McTiernan and John Lennon, but hey, not bad.

"The same. I heard through the grapevine that Vance

McTiernan's been through here lately. I was hoping you might direct me toward where old Vance might be keeping himself."

"He's not here now," I told him truthfully. "Why do you ask?"

"Because I'd like to strangle the old swine with me bare hands," Morrie said, still smiling.

"You're too late," Maxie said.

# Thirteen

Morrie Chrichton had made it to the age of sixty-six before he'd died a mere eight months previously, he'd told us, from "extremely natural causes"—a heart attack sustained while playing electric bass in a recording session for a trio called Squirrel Meat.

"So I'd like to find the swine who forced me into playing these cheap boring gigs for the last twenty years of my life and probably contributed to me keeling over with a Fender in my hands, playing the dreariest repeat riff in the history of rock 'n' roll," Morrie told us, demanding to know where Vance was and if anyone could find a way to make a ghost feel a great deal of pain. Cost, he'd mentioned, would be an object.

Although he hadn't reverted to a younger self, I still recognized Morrie from old Jingles album covers, though he said he'd stopped getting royalties after Vance McTiernan had sued him and thrown him out of the band—not necessarily in that order—when the Jingles were already on their way down in popularity. (Many believed *Jell-o*, the only Jingles album without Chrichton's input, was the band's weakest.) I couldn't expect to be paid handsomely for my information "because McTiernan, that louse, took all my money and reduced me to living in New Jersey."

Morrie Chrichton wasn't making a great number of friends in my house.

I'd assured him that I had no idea where Vance McTiernan might be, which was technically true because Vance hadn't told me where he was going and I hadn't asked.

That was my story, and I was . . . well, you've got it by now.

Melissa had quit the poker game to see what was going on and suggested to Morrie that, with all eternity awaiting both him and Vance, maybe it was time to bury the hatchet.

"That's a good idea," Morrie said to my eleven-year-old. "Maybe I can bury it between a couple of his ribs."

At that point, I asked Morrie to vacate my premises, ostensibly because I didn't like the way he had talked to Melissa, though she seemed completely unperturbed by what he'd said. The fact was, I didn't want Morrie around the house when Vance returned and I had no idea when that might happen.

Morrie, calm as the surf at low tide, nodded, made the ukulele disappear into his coat and rose up through the ceiling to exit. "I'll be back," he intoned as his head broke through into the rooms above (I estimated that was Tessa's room).

Once he'd vanished into the rafters, Liss looked at me with a wisdom that belied her tender years. "What a jerk," she said.

"Got that right."

Paul chose that moment to rise through the floor. "The recording of your interview with William Mastrovy is interesting," he said. "But I didn't hear anything from any of the other band members except the woman, and that was only an occasional comment. What did the others say?"

*Um* . . . "I didn't get to talk to them," I admitted. Total honesty with Paul was my latest resolution; we'd see if it lasted longer than that whole thing about exercising every day. "The one guy was really, really occupied with the woman on the couch, and I think he's new anyway. The other guitarist wasn't in the band when Vanessa died."

Paul did his best not to look impatient. We were healing our relationship, and we both knew it. "What about the woman?" he asked, tone flat and consciously nonjudgmental.

"Sammi didn't want to talk," I told him, and that was true. She'd simply stared blankly at me and then walked out.

Paul, clearly having decided he would do what it took to make this arrangement work, nodded. "Very well. You'll get to them next. Our priority now should be to find Vanessa's mother and half brother."

Given the chance, I told him about our encounter with Morrie. Paul is an excellent listener and waited until the end of my tale to put his hand to his goatee and say, "I'm not sure if this simplifies matters or complicates them. This might be a side issue unrelated to Vanessa's death."

I considered Morrie. I'd never had the same blind admiration for him as I'd developed for Vance when I was a teen. In interviews, he'd seemed almost contemptuous of the fans, as if we were somehow a necessary inconvenience that went with his true goal, living the rock star life. It could be somewhat off-putting.

"If I didn't know better, I'd swear he was drunk," Maxie chimed in.

There was no sign of Vance or Morrie in the den. Quietly (as if I didn't want to disturb the poker players' concentration) I asked, "Where *is* Vance?"

"I have no idea," Paul said. "I haven't seen him since before you left."

"Well, Morrie's not here now," I said. And perfectly on cue, I was proven wrong.

Morrie Chrichton sank down through the ceiling, which meant he'd passed through at least one of the guest rooms. I wasn't crazy about that. And as soon as he saw me, he pointed a somewhat shaky finger—it really *was* like he was drunk!—and said, "You're hiding him! Where is that dirty Vance McTiernan?"

"I have no idea," I said. "I'm just the innkeeper."

"We know, dear," Tessa sighed. She must have wandered in from the card game. "I'll be going up to my room now." And she turned and left.

This conversation with Morrie would just be easier elsewhere, I realized. "I'm going into the kitchen," I said.

Liss, Paul and Maxie followed me, and after a second, Morrie did, too. We walked through the den on our way, and my mother, sensing something was up, came in behind us without asking questions.

Once we were all in the kitchen, I turned to Morrie. "When my guests are present, you're going to be civil and you're going to let me tend to them," I said. He looked confused. "Is that clear?"

"What, can they hear me?" Morrie tried to focus.

"No, but I can. And are you drunk? How can you be drunk? You can't drink anything!"

He smiled wryly. At least, that's what *he* thought. "It's all sense memory, my pet. I spent so much of my life like this I can pretty much summon it whenever I want. It's a kick, isn't it?"

I looked at Paul, who shrugged. "I never drank much," he said.

"Oh, you should try it," Morrie suggested. "Do you a world of good."

"Well, I need to talk to you seriously right now," I told him. "Can your senses remember how to be sober?"

"Yeah, but it's not half as much fun." Suddenly his eyes focused, his expression sharpened and his voice lost a percentage of rasp. "Now tell me where Vance McTiernan is and I won't trouble you again."

"I have no idea where Vance is right now, and given the way you've been talking, I don't think I'd tell you if I did. I don't know what went on between the two of you but I'm not going to leave him open to whatever warped idea of revenge you have in your mind. So stop haunting the place, pal. You're not going to find what you want here."

Paul looked proud, and Maxie looked astonished, which wasn't very flattering. I can be very authoritative when I put my mind to it. Ask my daughter.

Okay, maybe *don't* ask my daughter. But it's true.

Morrie stared at me. It wasn't a pleasant gaze. "Why would you protect that swine?" he asked, using an unfortunately familiar word. "What has he got on you?"

*What did that mean?* "He hasn't got *anything* on me," I said. "He's a guy who made music that matters to me, and he's asked me to help him with something that's weighing down his whole being. His daughter is dead and he's distraught. Why should I turn him away?"

"Because he's a lying snake! *I* wrote most of that music you're so nostalgic about," Morrie answered, completely sober. "He's a fraud and that daughter of his never meant anything to him until she was dead."

My eyes must have narrowed unconsciously because the amount I could see decreased. "How would you know that?" I asked.

"I was his bandmate and supposedly his friend all those years until he died," Morrie said. "For the first twenty years of her life, I never heard one word about his daughter in all that time except when Vance complained about some bird in the States trying to squeeze him for money."

Paul took over the questioning, which was something of a relief, given that I had no idea what to say. This was not the Vance I'd seen. Of course, the Vance I'd seen had changed moods and intentions so many times I wasn't sure I knew anything about him at all.

"Why would Vance suddenly develop an interest in his daughter after she died?" Paul asked Morrie. "What is the advantage for him?" Paul was lightly stroking his goatee, a sign he was in Sherlock Holmes mode.

"It must be almost impossible for a parent to survive the death of a child," Mom chimed in, looking concerned.

"He didn't survive it," Paul corrected. "He died years before Vanessa." Forgive him; he can't help it.

"Vance has always been a drama queen," Morrie answered. "It's always about him. *He* wrote the words; *he* wrote the music. Or so *he* said. He had to have it that way in every press release, every interview. His daughter was trying to make a name for herself in music and he didn't lift a finger, did he? Then she passes away and the next thing you know *he's* the grief-stricken dad out for revenge. He makes the story about him, again. If Vance can get his name back in the papers and on TV, he'll be a happy man."

"But the press won't know he's trying to get revenge," I said. "They'll have no idea Vance is around driving the investigation. That doesn't play into this publicity push you say he's trying to generate."

Morrie shrugged. "Doesn't matter if the punters know he's behind it. What matters is that people will be talking about him and playing the records again. He'll be able to float around and hear his voice coming from people's houses. What could be better than that?"

"Why did you just arrive?" Paul asked. "You've been harboring this resentment since you passed away."

"I died in New Jersey," Morrie reminded us. "McTiernan was in England."

"You could have gone there," Mom pointed out.

"And give him the satisfaction?"

It was all starting to make too much sense to me. Vance

clearly had a pretty healthy ego, which wasn't the least bit surprising for someone in his line of work. Vance might very well have simply seen Vanessa's death as a way to attract publicity, even from beyond the grave. Given what Bill Mastrovy had said about Vance's relationship with Vanessa, I felt the trap springing around me.

Suddenly everyone seemed to be looking toward me, waiting for some defense of Vance, but I didn't have one. The only thing I could muster was, "It doesn't matter. If what the autopsy report says is right, somebody probably killed Vanessa McTiernan. What difference does it make if Vance wants to be seen as a hero as long as we find out who did it?"

"Who wants to be seen as a hero?" The voice behind me was familiar, mostly from hours of listening to his recordings. I turned.

Vance was floating just inside the kitchen door, looking at me with a perplexed expression. Then he looked up.

"Chrichton," he said.

"That's right, you old villain," Morrie said. "I'm here to settle with you."

Vance pointed to himself. "Settle with *me*? About what? About you wanting credit for work you never did? Will you never get off that one?"

"You don't get to take that tone this time, McTiernan," his ex-bandmate said. He swept his hand majestically around the room. "They're not taken in by you anymore."

Mom held up a hand. "Now, boys," she said. "This is no time to bicker about who did what all those years ago. Isn't it time to forgive and forget?"

My mother, spreading reason and just-getting-along from birth to the afterlife.

But the two Jingles weren't hearing it. They drew closer to each other, which necessitated Vance actually moving through me. This time his sensation was hot, fueled by anger.

"You claimed every idea, every guitar lick, every drum-beat as your own," Morrie Chrichton said. "Nobody could *ever* have an idea, especially not a good one, when Vance McTiernan was in the room!" His fingers curled into talons as Vance approached.

"And you thought every little note from your bass was genius," Vance countered. "If it wasn't for you hitting that D sharp, the whole band would have collapsed, right?" Vance's sneer, his go-to expression when not trying to charm, took on some seriously scary undertones.

"The whole band *did* collapse! Under the weight of your gigantic ego!"

"Liar!"

"Thief!"

"Plagiarist!"

"Fraud!"

Vance howled in anger and lunged at Morrie. The two men grappled for a moment, grunting with effort, until Maxie slammed two frying pans from the hooks over my center island together. It made a dreadful noise, and they stopped their wrestling match and stared at her, as did everyone else.

"Knock it off," she snarled. "You're both dead."

Mom nodded her approval up to Maxie, who put the frying pans back on their hooks. I marveled at the fact that she could do that, and also considered that the pans probably hadn't been used at all for a while, since Mom insists on bringing her own cookware when she's making dinner at my house. It doesn't make any sense, but that's Mom.

Paul was stroking his goatee fervently, watching Vance very closely.

"This isn't over, McTiernan," Morrie Chrichton said. He let go of Vance's triceps and flew out the side wall into the night.

"You're damn right it isn't," Vance said. Then he looked

down at me. "Now, then. What lies has that louse been telling you?"

My head felt overcrowded. I'd begun this enterprise because I believed in Vance, defended him to Paul; then Morrie had made me question my loyalty, and now Vance was asking me what lies Morrie had told me about him. I looked up, auditioning responses rapidly in my head, and finally said, "I have to get Melissa to bed. She's been up late playing poker."

And I turned and walked out of the kitchen. I'm pretty sure I got a glimpse of Mom beaming proudly at me as I left.

# Fourteen

There was no more discussion that night. I did indeed break up the poker game, as it was after midnight and my daughter was in fact eleven. The rest of the guests went to bed almost immediately, as none of them was close to eleven and all were considerably more tired than Melissa. This is the logic of parenting.

Mom, realizing that I wanted no more talk about murder, music or old wounds, packed up her backpack, beckoned to my father and hit the road in her Dodge Viper. At the rate of speed she drives at night, the fifteen-minute trip to her house wouldn't take much longer than a half hour.

I went upstairs when Melissa did and holed up in my bedroom. Vance was hopefully aware by now that barging in uninvited would be a serious problem for me, and Paul and Maxie certainly knew better.

Nobody dropped in on me and after some initial tossing and turning, fatigue won out, so I slept fairly well, except for the itching in the back of my throat. In the morning I'd definitely pick up that allergy medicine.

The next morning, I woke, got myself presentable, did some tidying for the guests and was ready for an assault-by-ghost just as Paul arrived in the kitchen; early, even for him. Maxie was a late sleeper and Vance, having been a rock star when he was alive, I figured could be counted on to stay out of circulation until noon at least.

"We should consider our position in this investigation," Paul began.

I was getting urns of coffee and hot water for tea ready for the guests (I don't serve meals, but I consider providing caffeine in the morning a basic nutrient), and looked up to see him tilting slightly to the left—Paul lists a little when he's thinking hard—while floating half inside the fridge. Luckily, there was nothing in the fridge but some batteries, milk, a little cheese and assorted vegetables I'd have to assess for freshness (or the lack thereof) shortly.

"You're not backing out on me again, are you?" I said as I braced myself to carry the coffee urn into the den and place it on the side table, the one where Paul does *not* attempt the tablecloth trick.

The urn was heavy, but I do this every morning and I'm used to it. I lugged it into the den, hovered it over the table and dropped it from an altitude of about an inch. It landed with a rather unsettling sound. Maybe "used to it" was overstating things.

"No, of course not. I'm saying that we need to evaluate where we are and what we should be doing." The goatee wasn't being stroked yet, but you knew it was only because he was holding himself back for later. One had to time one's goatee stroking for maximum effect.

"So, where are we and what should we be doing?" There was something very soothing about letting Paul take the reins in the investigation. It would have been soothing, frankly, to let *anyone* other than me take the reins. Sherlock Holmes, Jessica Fletcher, Gilbert Gottfried. It didn't matter. But Paul was an especially comfortable caretaker.

He also likes nothing more than to recap. "We have a victim of about forty who might or might not have known she was ingesting something that could be lethal to her, so one of our priorities should be to discover if she was alone when she died. We know she was alone when the police found her body, but that proves nothing."

He was just getting warmed up. "We have Vanessa's ex-boyfriend William Mastrovy, who apparently told his current lover that he'd had no further contact with Vanessa but suddenly admits to being present on the day she died, a claim which might or might not be true. However, you said that he seemed legitimately surprised by the possibility she might have been killed. That would seem to place some question on his viability as a suspect, but as a witness, he is invaluable. He should be interviewed again as soon as possible."

"I don't know where he lives," I told him. "That's why I had to go find him at the bar."

"That is something Lieutenant McElone might be able to clear up for us," Paul said. His right hand moved toward his chin, but—no.

Talking to McElone again wasn't my favorite plan but it was far from a deal breaker. "What else?" I asked. I can prompt with the best of them.

"Ah. There's Vanessa's mother, Claudia Rabinowitz, and her half brother, Jeremy Bensinger. We have almost no information about either of them, so we can't include or exclude them from a list of possible suspects. We should contact them very soon, as well. Your plan to go to Marlboro today is a good one. Find Jeremy and ask about his mother, among other things."

No goatee stroking yet. I went back into the kitchen to get

the urn of hot water, which is lighter because it's empty when I bring it into the den, then fill it with water from a pitcher.

I hardly grunted at all carrying this urn. Why didn't I put coffee in the pitcher and then fill that urn the same way? Sometimes I scared myself with my own inability to see the obvious. To cover, I chided Paul. "I love how whenever you say, 'We should contact them,' or 'We need to interview him,' you mean that *I* should do it."

Paul has perfected his dry look and sent it now in my direction. "I have certain drawbacks which prevent me from doing the legwork," he said. "I don't think you'd like to change places with me."

"No, but going out to talk to murder suspects might just increase the possibility that I could be joining you sooner, and that's not something I'm crazy about."

"Neither am I. So let's make sure *we* take precautions." That usually meant bringing someone with me to serve as security/backup, and since Maxie is the ghost who can move around outside my property line, she is the one who usually fills that role. Spending a day with Maxie might also increase my chances of dying sooner but I'm not prone to suicidal thoughts. "Meet him outdoors where there are people around. You won't need backup on a first meeting."

"Yes, chief. What else is on the agenda?"

Paul stopped, meaning his drifting slowed to an almost imperceptible rate and he appeared to be "standing" still. "You might want to talk to this Sammi woman about Bill Mastrovy. Angry lovers make excellent sources of information."

"You're not giving me any assignments I actually want to do," I said.

"Do I ever?" The wry sense of humor surfaced again. How endearing it would be if only it were funny.

I went into the kitchen for the large pitcher of water for the tea urn. I started to fill it in the sink. "That's a riot, truly, but is it possible Maxie might chip in here with some

Internet research? Something that can fill in the holes while I'm out asking a bunch of strangers whether they killed Vance McTiernan's daughter?"

"That is one thing you need to do," Paul said. "You have to train yourself to stop thinking of Vanessa as Vance McTiernan's daughter."

"Um . . . she *was* Vance McTiernan's daughter."

"No, she was Vanessa McTiernan. She was an adult who had a life that might have been taken from her. You are her advocate. You can't think about her only in relation to him. Are you only Jack Kerby's daughter?"

Now, that was hitting below the belt. "No, but Vanessa had a famous father, and it's inevitable that people would think of her that way, especially since she used his name."

"And how do you think she felt about that?"

"What am I, her therapist?" I picked up the full pitcher to take into the den and remembered why I didn't do this with the coffee urn, too—it wasn't *that* much easier. A cart. That's what I needed. "How do I know how she felt about it?'

"That's exactly my point," Paul said with his annoyingly calm tone. "You *don't* know how she felt about it, so limiting your thinking to one segment of her life, one that might have been relatively unimportant, inhibits your ability to see the whole picture. That can be a hindrance to this investigation."

"So what am I missing?" I asked Paul. "Don't the facts remain facts, no matter if Vanessa was Vance's daughter or Bill's girlfriend or Jeremy Bensinger's half sister?" Paul was big on facts, so this was my way of showing him I had indeed paid attention when we'd talked in the past.

"Yes, but you might be missing a connection when you limit your perspective."

"This thing's heavy," I said, grunting as I lifted the last pitcher to fill the urn. That's when it hit me: It wasn't a cart I needed. It was a way to get Paul to carry the pitchers from now on.

Nothing. Not even a goatee stroke.

"The point I'm making—"

"I understand the point you're making," I told Paul. "You don't seem to understand the point *I'm* making—these pitchers and the urns are heavy. I could use some help in the mornings."

"Why not get a cart?" Melissa, awake uncharacteristically early for a Sunday, had appeared while I was dealing with the water. "You could just roll it out in the morning after the urns were ready and then roll it back when we're done with the coffee and tea in the morning."

She started pouring herself what we've decided to call a latte—about two-thirds milk to one-third coffee. I decided to look for an inexpensive cart in town after I visited Jeremy Bensinger today.

Sometimes you just can't fight the tide.

"Nessa was my sister," Jeremy Bensinger said. "There wasn't anything 'half' about it."

We were standing in one of the parking lots in Jeremy's apartment complex, which had seven "villages" (the names were so cute, too; he lived in "Londontown," which looked exactly like "Villa Paris," "Chalet Moritz" and "Piazza Tuscanne"), each of which was simply a quad of garden apartment buildings. Finding Jeremy had been a stroke of luck—I hadn't been able to find his number before I came but had located the unit with his name on the door, which he'd been coincidentally walking out of when I'd arrived. I'd asked if he knew Jeremy Bensinger (since I had no idea what the man looked like) and he'd confessed to being one and the same.

Since I wasn't going to walk into his apartment, discovering him outside was even better, and there were, as Paul had anticipated, people around.

I'd told Jeremy that I was investigating his sister's death

on behalf of an insurance company representing the apartment complex where she died. It didn't make any sense, but people tend not to question that much when you show them a license.

Jeremy wasn't averse to talking about Vanessa McTiernan, but he was going out for the day—I didn't ask to where because it felt like prying (yes, we've established that I'm a bad detective)—and had only a little time. We talked by his car, a current model Hyundai Sonata.

"You had different fathers," I pointed out. "And different last names." I don't know what significance that last fact was supposed to have, but it was important, Paul always said, to have areas of conversation and see where the subject went with them.

In this case, Jeremy went with a light scowl. He wasn't an unpleasant guy, in his mid-thirties and in shape although not ostentatiously so, but he clearly didn't like the suggestion that his connection to Vanessa was anything less than a full sibling relationship. Which was fine with me, as it kept him talking.

"We had different fathers," he said. "So do lots of brothers and sisters. There isn't just one definition of a family anymore, you know."

I knew. My ex-husband lives in Southern California. Somewhere. It's hard to keep track.

"As for our last names," Jeremy went on, "Mine is from my father. Nessa had Mom's, but then changed it for professional reasons. I guess 'Vanessa Rabinowitz' didn't sound like a rock star to her."

"She was serious about her music," I said. It was a question in statement form. I wouldn't be a great contestant on *Jeopardy!*

"Music was her whole life," he said, breaking eye contact with me. He seemed to be staring off into space so he could look especially contemplative, and it was working fairly well. "She thought it was in her genes or something. Maybe she felt it was a way to connect to her father, but as far as I know she only heard from him every couple of years or so."

That statement, at least, was becoming consistent. Vance had not been a fabulous, hands-on type of dad. Yes, he'd usually been thousands of miles away and yes, his daughter would have preferred more contact with her father, but . . . were we talking about Vance's daughter or my own?

"Was she any good?" I asked Jeremy. Lots of people can play a little and many try to make it a career, but quite often they persist because no one has the heart to point out that they're not especially talented.

"Of course," Jeremy said. "I had just made her a deal with Vinyl Records to release her first album and it was gathering steam. The album's still coming out in about six months, so people will hear what a great talent was lost."

"You made the deal?" I said, as if I hadn't heard this before. "You acted as her agent?"

Jeremy nodded. "I cowrote seven of the songs and produced the album, too. I can't play an instrument or sing, but I do know music. The people at Vinyl were going to give it a big push. Vanessa would've been on her way."

"They must have really heard something in those tracks," I said.

"Hang on." He opened his car door, sat down and started the engine. This was a very unusual way to flee an interrogation. I did notice, though, that the interior of the car was immaculate. There were even little squares of carpet on the floor, green shag. Hideous, but they didn't have any mud on them at all.

Instead of peeling away in his getaway car, Jeremy pulled a CD out of a door pocket and slid it into his dashboard player. Music began playing almost immediately. "This is Vanessa."

It was lovely, hypnotic and dreamy. Not the sort of music I would have expected from Vance McTiernan's daughter, so maybe Paul was right about not pigeonholing her. Her voice was smoky and calm, engaged with expressing, not manufacturing, the emotions her music conveyed. The melody was unexpected, nontraditional. The arrangement was understated but definitely in sync with the songwriter's intentions. It was like sitting in on a late-night session at a blues club after the civilians have all left and the players are just amusing themselves and each other. It was almost too intimate, but never uncomfortable.

"Wow," I heard myself say.

"That's right." Jeremy stood up out of the driver's seat and met my eyes. "'Wow' is right. Now you tell me if you think she was any good."

"She was amazing," I said honestly. "You wrote the music with her?"

He tilted his head. "Not all the time. She also worked with her boyfriend, Bill, on a couple of things, but he basically just added a hook or a suggestion."

Bill Mastrovy? The plot thickens. I listened to more of the music, and Jeremy watched for my reaction. I'm sure the one he got was the one he'd hoped for. "That was terrific," I said when the song ended.

"Thank you. Nessa wanted to just release it herself, you know. Bypass the record companies. She didn't think she was good enough for wide release. But I convinced her."

"What do you know about the day she died?" I asked Jeremy.

He looked at his shoes and brushed flecks of the carpet off them. "I wasn't there," he said. "They told me she might have done it intentionally. I don't believe it."

"Why not?" The music continued to play, a new song that was more upbeat and pop-ish. I liked it, but it wasn't connecting the same way the first one did.

"Because Nessa wasn't depressed. She was about to sign a great record contract, what she'd wanted all her life. She wasn't crazy about her love life at the moment, over forty and thinking about kids, maybe, but she wasn't terribly down about it. I think it was just an awful accident. She ate the wrong thing and didn't know it."

I didn't think not to say it; it just came out of me. "She accidentally drank straight soy sauce?"

Jeremy looked at me, confused. "Soy sauce? That's what did it? She would have known better than that. Where did you hear that?"

"The medical examiner's report. You didn't see it?"

Jeremy's mouth twitched. "I didn't want to talk to the police anytime I didn't have to; I don't like the police. When it first happened, the word from the detective . . . what was her name?"

"McElone."

He snapped his fingers. "Yes! You're very good. Detective McElone said it was an allergic reaction. I didn't ask anything more than that." He stared off again.

After a moment, I had to press on. "Can you tell me how to get in touch with your mother?" I asked. Jeremy just shook his head negatively. I pushed on. "Could anyone have wanted to hurt your sister?"

Jeremy looked surprised. "I can't imagine anybody being that mad at Nessa. I've been trying to make sense of it for months. But the thing is, it *doesn't* make sense. There was no reason to want her dead. It doesn't benefit anybody. She didn't leave a will; she had no money. She wasn't cheating on Bill, so he had no reason to be jealous."

Except maybe I knew something he didn't. "She was still dating Bill Mastrovy when she died?" I asked.

"Yeah. Why?"

"Because his current girlfriend didn't know that."

Jeremy looked at me again, his head turning at a faster rate of speed than thirty-three and a third revolutions per minute, to be sure. "Bill has a new girlfriend?"

"That's right. And when I saw her yesterday, she was

surprised that he'd been in touch with Vanessa at all." Paul would hear this interview from my voice recorder, but he'd want me to describe Jeremy's facial expression when he heard that news.

It was one of astonishment.

"Who is she?" he rasped.

"I don't think I should tell you that," I said. "I don't want to create suspicions until I'm certain of my facts." But perhaps it was a little too late for that. This whole selected-information-for-selected-people thing was complicated.

Jeremy seemed to think that over, his eyes unfocused as he muddled. Finally, he nodded, once. "That's fair," he said, "but when you do have your facts straight, I'd like you to tell me what you know."

"I promise I will." Time to try again, with a new tack. "Maybe your mother can shed a little light on some of this. Sure you can't give me an address or phone number where I can find her?"

It was becoming a pattern; Jeremy stopped looking me in the face again. "I haven't been in touch with my mother for years," he said. "She and I argued about my line of work. I wanted to be involved in music and she hated it because of Nessa's dad. She didn't want Nessa in music, either, but knew it was a lost cause. I ended up working at Ace Equipment Rentals and I hate it to this day but I need the money. We had words five years ago. Both of us said things we can't take back. She quit the business two years ago and ended up in the Midwest somewhere without saying a word to us for six months. She didn't even show up for Nessa's funeral. So I don't talk to her anymore."

"Does she try to get in touch?" I asked. The third song on Vanessa's CD was playing, and it was more in line with the first, but up-tempo. It could have been a swing song from the 1940s, complete with brass section.

"Once in a while. She got my cell number somehow, and

she'll call when she needs something. Last time was probably a year ago, complaining about some tax problems, expecting me to bail her out. I didn't, she screamed at me, and I don't even keep her number in my phone anymore. She calls when she calls, but I don't answer."

"Well, if she calls you again, just write down her number and give it to me," I said, handing him one of the investigator cards I had made because I like business cards. "You don't have to talk to her to do that."

Jeremy took the card. "I'll do that," he said. "But I wouldn't count on it happening anytime soon."

"When the album comes out, are you planning on leaving Ace Equipment Rentals?" It would go a ways toward clearing Jeremy—his success hinging on his sister's would mean he'd have no reason to want her dead.

"That was the plan," he admitted. "Don't know if it'll be possible with no follow-up album, though."

"I understand," I said. "Thanks. One last thing."

"You want a copy of Nessa's songs?" He grinned.

"How did you know?"

"Everybody who hears it wants them. She was going to be a big star."

# Fifteen

I listened to the CD of Vanessa McTiernan that Jeremy Bensinger gave me all the way home, which admittedly wasn't that long. Vanessa didn't have a great voice, but she had a supremely interesting one, a voice that should have been allowed to flourish and grow. Yes, she was forty when she died, but she still should have had a lot of creative years ahead of her. Someone had taken those away and now I wanted to find that person and see them punished.

The detective thing gets to you after a while.

I reported back to Paul after dealing with a couple of guest issues (Tessa wanted a good bakery, and that was easy; Roberta Levine needed a replacement contact lens, which was a little more complicated, but doable) and talking my mother, who had been staying with Liss, into letting me order dinner in that night before the movie. It had taken some doing, given that Mom is virtually a walking food truck, but I wanted her to be fresh for the debut of the movie room and I thought pizza was a better food for the cinema, anyway. In a burst of magnanimity (and okay, maybe bribery), I'd told all the guests that the guesthouse would provide free pizza to tonight's movie viewers.

I was proud of the way that room had turned out and was anxious to see it in full bloom. Dad was in there now, checking over every finishing nail and every hidden wire in the electronic connections. The man was a perfectionist when he was alive and now he literally had all the time he'd ever need to make sure things were just so.

With only a couple of hours before the movie showing, I went back out for some extra ice and found the ghost with the wagon standing directly outside my house. "Have you found Lester?" she asked. It was like her mantra or something.

"Not yet, but I haven't given up," I said. The guy across the street walking to his car waved, perhaps thinking I was talking to him.

"Don't," the ghost said, and started pulling the wagon away. I don't know why she'd reached me so deeply, given her sullen attitude, but every time she showed up I really wanted to find Lester. Instead, I went and found six more bags of ice at the Rite Aid.

When I got back, Paul was anxious to discuss the case.

"He hasn't been in touch with his mother in two years?" Paul said after listening to Jeremy Bensinger say precisely that on my voice recorder. The goatee stroking had made a comeback. "That seems odd. And it was because they had a disagreement over his career?"

"You heard it. Why are you asking me what he said?"

"Alison," my mother said. She has an odd concept of when I'm being rude.

Paul was pacing, something he likes to do when he's thinking. It doesn't even rate a notice anymore that he's generally doing so in midair. I'm so jaded.

Melissa, whose room we were using for this impromptu meeting, was lying on her bed above the blanket. "He's mulling," she told me.

"I am reviewing the information to better organize it," Paul said, not looking at either of us. Maxie, who was suspended from the rafters like a bat (strictly for her own amusement), sniffed a little.

"It's a way to stall because he doesn't have any ideas," she said.

"Maxine," my mother said. She has an equal opportunity stance on rudeness.

"Where's Everett?" I asked Maxie. "You're so much more pleasant when he's around." Mom didn't say anything but I knew what she was thinking.

"He's guarding the Fuel Pit. He'll be here for the movie tonight." Everett is very protective of the local gas station and his military training is perhaps a bit more effective than even the Army might have desired it to be. He's a lovely man, but a little gung ho.

"The interesting thing is the album of music," Paul mused. "If Vanessa really was gaining interest in the industry, there could be a motive there."

"Look," I said. "There isn't much to plan for the showing tonight, but I want it to be special, so I'm going to be taking a break from any more investigating today. You guys figure out all you need to figure out but I'll be downstairs obsessing over details with Dad, okay?"

"What's the guest list for tonight?" Everyone turned to look toward the door, where floating there was Vance McTiernan. I wasn't looking at Paul but I was willing to bet he was scowling.

"What are you doing up?" I asked Vance. "It's isn't even one in the afternoon yet."

"I wanted to be sure to talk to you before Morrie Chrichton

returned to sully my name some more," Vance responded. "That man filled you with lies about me and I could see the whole room start to doubt my good intentions."

"Your good intentions?" Paul asked. Vance was *definitely* scowling when Paul spoke. "Your intentions seem to change from minute to minute. What are your intentions today?"

Vance gave a smile I recognized from all the publicity photos for the Jingles. It was warm, trustworthy, understanding . . . and, I could now tell, completely insincere. He didn't like Paul and he wasn't especially good at hiding it.

"My intentions are the same as they've always been," he answered. "I want to find the person who did in my little girl and see to it that justice is done. Is that so hard to understand?"

This was becoming very investigation-y, and that was the very thing I'd just announced I would not be doing today. "Yesterday you said you didn't want me to look into Vanessa's death anymore," I reminded Vance, for different reasons than I might have had the day before. Now I wanted him to tell me to stop, just so I could do so for today. By tomorrow, he'd have changed his mind and I'd do what I planned to do anyway.

"That was a mistake," Vance said, and I could see my relaxing day of worrying about the movie room vanish before my eyes, which was more than I could say for Vance. "I need to see this thing through for my little girl." There was a slight catch in his voice as he said that last part, which I completely would have bought only two days ago. Now it was an irritant. Like the pollen making my eyes water, even with the antihistamine I'd finally bought on the way home. It was worse up here than it had been downstairs.

"I talked to Vanessa's brother, Jeremy," I told him. "He said you were almost never in touch with Vanessa at all."

Vance's face changed expression three times in less than a second. Surprise to anger and then concern. The last one seemed the least believable.

"I wouldn't put much stock in what that little git says," Vance told me. "He's trouble, that one. Poisoned my relationship with my little Vanessa. Told her I wasn't a loving dad, but it wasn't true, love, none of it. He had an agenda and that was making my daughter see him as her whole family."

Paul coughed, which was clearly an attention-getting device, since he had stopped using his bronchial system a few years earlier. "What possible reason could Jeremy Bensinger have to alienate you from your daughter?" he asked Vance.

Vance's hands went to his hips in a gesture of exasperation. "Why, because he wasn't my son! Couldn't let Vanessa be different from him, so he tried to erase me, that's what it was. The less there was of me, the more he had to bond with her. It was a little unnatural, if you're asking me."

Before I could answer that I was not, in fact, asking him, Mom stepped in, no doubt aware that I was thinking of saying something she would consider rude. "Mr. McTiernan," she said, "this isn't about whether you were a good father. I'm sure you would have liked to have been closer to your daughter when you were alive. This is about your behavior for the past couple of days. You've been telling my daughter that you wanted her to find out what happened to Vanessa, and then you said you were over it and didn't want the investigation to go on. Now you're back here saying it's important she do some more asking around. Can you tell us why you've changed your mind so many times?"

That's Mom. She'll find a way to make everything positive even when she knows for a fact that it's not. And she'll do it in a way that you won't see coming, so you feel good about answering her.

And it worked again; Vance smiled warmly at Mom, this time genuinely, from what I could tell. "I've been conflicted," he said to Mom. "At first I was just angry. I knew that this someone killed my girl, and I wanted to do them harm, I'll admit it. But then I thought Vanessa wouldn't want that. She wouldn't want someone to suffer for her. So I told Alison here to stop. But Morrie Chrichton being here reminds me of the responsibility to my daughter I never accepted, and I'm ashamed. I know I should have explained better, but I'm not used to trusting people."

"You should trust Alison," Mom said. "She'll always tell you the truth."

Maxie stifled a laugh. Maxie is not the person you want when tact is called for. In case you were wondering.

"I don't understand," Melissa piped up. She had her smart girl face on and was no doubt about to bring up a point none of us had yet considered. "What does Mr. Chrichton have to do with your daughter dying? I thought he was angry at you about who wrote the songs and things."

It was a good question. That had gone by a little too fast for me to notice.

This time Vance's expression only changed once. His face hardened and his eyes showed an old, deep anger. But he didn't address Melissa; he looked at me.

"I don't know if I should get into this right now," he said, his eyes darting back and forth toward Melissa and then to me.

"He means it's something that's too adult for me," my daughter said with no particular inflection. Just statement of fact, as if she were translating from another language. But she just wanted him to know he wasn't fooling anybody.

"*How* adult?" I asked Vance. I noticed Maxie leaning down a little more, anxious not to miss anything especially juicy. "Melissa's input is usually pretty valuable if it's not something especially outrageous."

Vance laughed lightly. "Well, I'm clearly up against someone much smarter than I am," he said, nodding to Liss. "Very well, then, let me see if I can say this delicately. The real reason the Jingles broke up was that Morrie Chrichton and I got into a pretty serious row."

"About the authorship of your songs?" Paul asked.

Vance didn't look at him; he held my gaze. "No. Over Vanessa." He glanced at Melissa. "See?"

According to Vance's somewhat carefully worded explanation, he and Morrie Chrichton had been bandmates and friends for years without the least bit of friction (which, having met both men, I found a little hard to believe). Then one summer Vance convinced Claudia Rabinowitz to allow Vanessa to go on tour with the band so he could better get to know his daughter, who was in college at the time and showing an interest in music. It had taken a good deal of cajoling, but Claudia had finally given her consent, and Vanessa joined the Jingles in London after school had let out for a four-week sojourn through Europe with her dad, the rock star.

And his band. And that was the problem.

Vance said Morrie had shown "an unhealthy interest" in Vanessa from the start and that he and Morrie had started to argue about it even before the tour had left England. Vanessa, whom Vance described as "star struck and young, a disease cured by time but not soon enough," had shown some attraction to Morrie, who was twenty-five years her senior and was, after all, "as old as her dad, yeah?"

Vance had shown what he considered to be reasonable concern and Morrie had laughed in his face, he said. He'd continued flirting with Vance's daughter until they reached Hamburg, where Morrie suddenly told Vanessa that he was no longer interested.

At that point, Vance said, the two men had confronted each other in a hotel room because "that's where rock bands go to bust stuff up." Vance, relieved that his daughter was no longer involved with his bandmate, was nonetheless incensed with the way Morrie had broken it off with Vanessa, who had immediately flown home. Claudia, Vance said, had then reported to him that their daughter had not left her bedroom for four days.

"We came to blows in Hamburg," Vance said. "Actually

beating on each other. That's when Morrie started taking credit for everything the band had ever done. Every shake of the maracas had been his idea all of a sudden. And he wanted money for it. There. On the spot. After he'd booted my daughter and broken her heart. I went for him and he didn't run away. We both ended up in the hospital. I don't know who ended up paying for the hotel room. The band was over for all intents and purposes then, and I never saw Morrie alive again. My luck he finds me here in New Jersey when we're both dead."

I looked over at Paul, hoping for some guidance in how to respond. I got nothing. He was in mid goatee stroke and frozen in that position (albeit tilted a little to the left). Maxie seemed less struck by the moment, doing a few slow somersaults through the air.

My mother instinctively tried to pat Vance on the arm, and her hand went straight through.

Melissa looked thoughtful.

"I'm sorry, Vance," I said.

He looked up from his thoughts, seemingly startled, but gave me a smile. "Water under the bridge, love. We're all gone now. But now you know why I'm especially keen on finding out what happened to my Vanessa if Morrie's around, eh?"

It was Liss who caught on first. "You think Mr. Chrichton killed Vanessa?" she asked.

"No," Vance said. "He's crazy, but he's not that crazy. He's the one who started her on a path all those years ago. Maybe she really did end up doing herself in, and it started with Morrie."

Paul started stroking his goatee again.

# Sixteen

"It's perfect," Dad told me.

I had a little trouble hearing him, but once he repeated it, I smiled broadly. Dad gestured around the movie room, which was filled close to capacity. And its capacity was not small.

Running the length of the house of the north side, the movie room was now the center of activity in the guesthouse, with our screening of *Ghost* only a few minutes away. It was a warm night, and the bodies gathered in the room were making it warmer.

Those were just the living ones, too.

Besides me, my mother and Melissa (the alliteration trio), my best friends, Jeannie and Tony, had shown up early for pizza with their son Oliver, who was now a full-fledged toddler based on his newfound ability to walk around and cause trouble. Ollie was a little overwhelmed with all the faces to look at right now.

Jeannie, who is just a tad overprotective of her son, had

considered leaving Oliver with his babysitter for the evening because she thought the movie "might be too violent for his sensibility." I'd be amazed if he even understood that there were people on the screen, but Jeannie had finally relented when her babysitter had mentioned tickets to see a Broadway show on Sunday with her boyfriend and had politely declined.

Tony had also given the seal of approval to the movie room. He's a professional contractor, and next to Dad, my most trusted home-improvement guru, so that meant quite a bit to me.

Oliver had not commented on the room, but was probably distracted by Melissa playing with his toes for a good long while, which he found hilarious.

Josh had come by himself a couple hours before showtime, and A.J. and Liz arrived a while later. I was warming to A.J., and as for Liz . . . I was warming to A.J.

All six of my current guests were in attendance, and I'd given them the best seats in the house, right up front and center, something Liz had commented on. She'd tried to pretend she was kidding, but . . . I was warming to A.J.

Actually, only five of my guests had seats front and center. Maureen Beckman had insisted on taking a back-row chair because she had to leave her walker in the aisle and didn't want to be a bother to anyone. I'd told her I would be happy to store it for her while the movie was showing, but Maureen planted herself in the back row as soon as she entered the room and refused the help.

Among the less-living crowd, of course Paul and Maxie were in attendance, Maxie wearing her best "I'll Bet You Do" T-shirt, Paul in his traditional jeans and dark shirt, this time paired with a somewhat worn sports jacket. Everett had shown up in fatigues because Maxie had told him it was a "casual premiere." Which it was, particularly if few of the guests could see what you were wearing anyway.

Vance was not in the room, yet, and I wasn't sure if he'd be coming. I had told him he was welcome but he wouldn't be asked to perform or make his presence known at all if he didn't want to.

He'd been philosophical this afternoon after telling us the story of his and Morrie's falling out. The ways of two old rockers, he'd said. Yeah, it was possible his bandmate had done him some damage and possibly ruined his daughter's life decades before, but what could be done about it at this late date, with all three of them dead? He'd hit all the right notes and said all the right words.

I hadn't believed a word of it.

Paul had agreed that we needed to redouble our efforts to find Claudia Rabinowitz, and I agreed but had no immediate suggestions other than asking McElone for help. I'd sighed and said I'd do so tomorrow.

"I'm not so sure about perfect," I told Dad now, "but I am pretty proud of the way it turned out."

"Don't sell yourself short," he said. "I've looked at every inch of the room and I didn't see anything wrong."

He was right that it looked impressive. The overhead lighting was not too bright, never in your face, but warm and inviting. The re-stained paneling looked like real wood with a light grain, not at all artificial. The chairs were covered in nappy blue fabric, which didn't match but complemented the area rug. (I'd added some folding chairs for the overflow crowd tonight.) And the big-screen TV at the far end was about to make everyone's eyes pop.

Although not as much as they would if *Lawrence of Arabia* were showing. Just sayin'.

"I love you," I said to Dad. Josh looked over, saw I was talking to no one from his perspective and smiled. Then he went back to talking to A.J. and Liz.

Jeannie walked over smiling, for once without her son, whose diaper was being changed by his father in the downstairs bathroom at the moment. "You sure know how to draw a crowd," she said.

"Are you kidding? I practically had to bribe a couple of the guests to stay in tonight, but the free pizza helped."

"You sell yourself short," Jeannie said. Her happy face was hiding something.

"Are you having another baby?" I asked.

"What? Where'd that come from?" But Jeannie would not look me in the eye (this was becoming endemic), and she *had* gone on a romantic cruise with her husband recently. I know, because I took care of Oliver while they were away.

"You are," I said accusingly.

Her voice dropped an octave. "Nobody knows yet. Our parents don't know yet. *Tony* doesn't even know yet." My best friend and my contractor mentor have an interesting marriage. It's based on the kind of trust where you can trust one isn't telling the other something at any given moment.

"Why not?" I asked.

"There was some . . . question about whether we wanted to have another baby this soon," Jeannie explained, looking at her fingernails and pretending she cared whether they were perfectly polished or not.

"This wasn't a planned baby?" I said.

She avoided eye contact. "Depends on who you ask. You have to keep it quiet."

"Who am I going to tell? Phyllis Coates doesn't run guess-who's-pregnant notices in the *Chronicle*." I had invited Phyllis too, but she'd declined on the grounds that "it's not really much of a story for the paper now, is it?" She had a point, but giving her a scoop hadn't really been why I was inviting her. Sometimes Phyllis can be a little single-minded about the paper. Like, all the time. "You've got to tell your husband, Jean," I admonished. After eleven years of being a mother, admonishing is among my most well-honed skills. And Melissa requires less than a very large percentage of her peers.

"I will. I am," Jeannie said, waving her hand as if to ward

off the harsh words coming her way. "I just don't know how he'll react."

"He's Tony. He'll react first by rolling his eyes at you and then he'll get excited and tell everybody he meets that he's going to be a dad again." I'd introduced Jeannie and Tony, so I knew both of them before they knew each other. It makes a huge difference.

"Well, I didn't think he'd divorce me or anything." But she looked relieved, huffed for a moment, then went back to grinning like a monkey. Tony joined her and they found seats for themselves and Ollie, who was eating a cookie and taking in the room as only small children can: with genuine wonder.

Josh waved me over to where he was standing with A.J. and Liz. I gritted my teeth mentally and smiled as I walked over. Dad floated a little above and to my left and said, "Which one don't you like?" He's known me all my life.

"This is lovely," Liz said as I approached. Of course *lovely* is a word people use when they've decided to use the word, which requires forethought. In other words, it was not an honest reaction, but a planned one. I might have been overthinking this just a tad but I doubted it. All of that had all gone through my mind in a split second. "I love the room, and the whole house, really."

"It looks really cool," A.J. said. His tactic seemed to be that he'd be as casual as possible to balance his girlfriend's formality and maybe reach a middle ground. He was in there trying. "Thanks for inviting us."

"Ah," Dad said. "The girl. I get that." He floated off to Mom, presumably to share his insight.

"We're about to start," I told them. "Thanks for coming. I hope we have a chance to talk later." Smooth, right? A quick expression passing through Josh's eyes indicated maybe not smooth enough.

There was no time for that now. I walked to the front of the room, stood just in front of the mammoth screen and held up my hands. "Okay, everybody," I said. The clamor died down and people who had not taken seats began filling some. Melissa stood at the back because she knew I'd reserved a seat for her but she wanted to get a good look at the crowd in case something was needed at the start of the showing. Melissa is an excellent assistant. "We're just about to start. I want to thank everybody for coming tonight to our premiere."

Vance McTiernan showed up just next to the big TV, surveyed the crowd (no doubt to size up his ability to enthrall it, despite having no performance planned—it was a reflex) and floated down to what approximated standing among the mortals.

"I don't get it," Jesse said from the first row, just to my left. A different younger guy might have been able to sit farther back and let some of the elders get a better view, but Jesse was not that kind of guy. "What's the big deal about seeing an old movie on DVD?" Jesse was clearly a deep thinker.

"We're inaugurating the new movie room with our state-of-the-art screen and sound system," I said, talking to the crowd and not just Jesse. "We're very proud of the work that's gone into creating this environment and we hope it'll enhance the experience of seeing this very special film"—I didn't stumble over that part at all—"here in a house with *real* ghosts."

A few rows back, Jeannie snickered. Jeannie, despite every nutty thing she's seen happen at my house, refuses to believe in ghosts. She thinks the whole thing is a scam I'm running to give my business some novelty. So she thinks it's a riot.

On cue, Paul billowed the drapes and Maxie shook the chandelier, which in my opinion she did just a little too enthusiastically. I'd worked hard on smoothing out that ceiling. If so much as one speck of wallboard dust fell from it, I was going to hold Maxie personally responsible. Vance did not participate in the production; after all, if he wasn't going to play music, what was the point? He was just here as a spectator.

A few of the guests looked up in wonder, despite having already seen a number of spook shows at the guesthouse. Because I can see the ghosts, sometimes I forget the effect they can have by simply manipulating objects when they are invisible to the viewer.

"But we're not here for an encounter with real spirits tonight," I said. "We're here for a fun time with a very appropriate movie. Please enjoy *Ghost*."

Just at that moment Morrie Chrichton leaked in through the outside wall, looked around the room, fixed his gaze on Vance and headed in his direction.

I didn't get to see what happened when Morrie reached Vance because at that moment Liss hit the light switch at the back of the room as Mom sat in a last-row seat. It was pitch-dark in the room, more so than I had anticipated. I hit the button on the remote control to start the movie, and that illuminated the room—or at least the front half of it—enough that I could find my way to an empty seat while the FBI warned us not to reproduce this film, something I had no intention of doing.

I will say this: For the first twenty minutes or so, the movie worked like a charm and I was rethinking my resistance to showing it. It wasn't that I didn't like *Ghost*, it was that it hadn't seemed "important" enough for the occasion. Maybe that was something else I'd been overthinking.

The entertainment system was working beautifully. The flat screen provided a picture so sharp and clear it seemed even better than a movie theater, and the speakers spaced out around the room provided ambient sound without drawing attention to themselves. The research and work I'd put in designing and constructing the room was paying off.

A few minutes later, I heard some movement behind me and felt a light breeze. It had been getting a bit warm in the room, so I figured Mom or Liss had gotten up and opened a window. They were always one step ahead. It got more comfortable almost immediately.

But that didn't last long. Perhaps ten seconds later, I heard a muffled wail of pain from somewhere behind me, a man's voice grunting. There were footsteps but I couldn't tell how many people were up. I stood to try to navigate my way back, but it was still very dark, and turning away from the screen made everything seem just a little darker.

Then I heard Mom cry, "Alison!" Her voice was urgent and it was alarmed. I stopped being dainty about my steps and ran toward her voice as my pupils adjusted to the darkness. I reached for the cell phone in my pocket and used it as a flashlight.

As soon as I followed Mom's voice to the hallway outside the movie room (where the lights were also off) and saw from the glow of my flashlight app what was on the floor in front of me, I said loudly to Mom, "Get Melissa out of here." Mom didn't respond but I heard Liss say, "Grandma . . ." and heard footsteps walking away.

Once I figured they were out of the room, I said, "Paul," in a conversational tone and didn't so much see as feel him by my side.

"Oh my," he said.

"Tell my mother to get Josh and keep Liss out of here," I told him.

"I should observe . . ."

*"Now."* Paul was gone in an instant. I knew he'd be back quickly, but I couldn't wait for him.

There was no choice—I had to turn on the lights. Patrick Swayze had his own problems but they weren't a concern of mine anymore. I had much more to deal with right at the moment.

Of course everyone looked back to see what had happened when the lights switched on but most people stayed in their seats, except Josh who reached my side, a look of intense concern on his face. Behind him I could hear Liz saying to A.J., "In the middle of the movie?"

Josh's eyes were now the size of quarters (yeah, they're bigger than you think) and he started breathing through his mouth. "Call the police," I said. "Ask for Lieutenant McElone." He nodded and pulled out his phone.

"Are you all right?" he asked as he dialed.

"Better than him," I said.

There were mumbles and confused looks from the crowd. Maxie, floating overhead, let Everett take the lead. He swooped to the hallway, then back, and when he returned his eyes were dark. "It's not good," he said. Like I didn't already know that.

"What's going on?" Jesse wanted to know.

What was "going on" was that lying facedown and bleeding all over my pristine hardwood floor, which I'd sanded, stained and urethaned within the past year, was a man with a very large knife in his back, just below his neck. I looked to the side where his face was turned and said to Paul, who had materialized at my side, "It's Bill Mastrovy."

I had to tell the crowd something, mostly because I was afraid someone would use the wrong exit from the movie room. "Please stay in this room," I told them. "Something very bad has happened, and we're waiting for the police to arrive."

"What happened?" Berthe asked.

"I'm afraid a man has been badly hurt in the hallway. So please stay here. The police will be here very soon."

Jeannie was standing, looking at me, trying to determine if this was some hilarious prank I'd devised. But she saw my face. "Watch Oliver," she told Tony, and rushed to my side.

Maureen, leaning on her walker a few feet away, strained to see past Josh, who was doing his best to block the doorway. "If this is part of the show, it's in very bad taste," she said.

Jesse, of all people, had the good sense to reach for the

remote and pause the frame on the screen. "I can't hear the movie," he complained without looking to the back of the room.

"The ambulance is on its way," Josh said as he put his phone away.

I nodded, grateful for the news, but I knew it wasn't going to do any good. There wasn't even any reason to feel like I should be doing something for Bill Mastrovy.

He was dead.

"This wouldn't have happened with *Lawrence of Arabia*," I said to no one in particular.

# Seventeen

"This is not going to sound good," said Lieutenant Anita McElone. "How do I report that the chief suspects are ghosts?"

True to her word, McElone had sent an ambulance, which had arrived within minutes of our discovering Bill Mastrovy's body in my hallway. In that time, A.J. had seen the stab wound and fallen back on his chair, the Senior Plus guests (especially the Levines) had freaked out just a little—except Berthe, who said very calmly that we should wait for the police, and Jesse, who had suggested we put the movie back on until the cops came. Tony had thrown a blanket over Oliver's head, presumably to block his view (despite the fact that he was fast asleep and stayed that way), and I had attempted to keep everyone calm—a losing proposition—while Paul had observed everything there was to observe in the hallway, Everett had taken on a security mission, blocking the door with a drill rifle he just happened to have with him (not that he could have stopped anyone and the rifle wasn't loaded), Maxie had changed into a trench coat and a green visor, which she thinks makes her look like a detective, and Dad had suggested three different ways to get the blood stains out of the floor.

Vance and Morrie were not visible once the lights had come back up. I asked the other ghosts and nobody had seen them leave.

Melissa was now standing in the front of movie room, telling the uniformed officer that she certainly had almost seen the body and might be needed to help with the investigation later on, despite her grandmother, steadfastly by her side, determined not to let her within ten feet of the hallway until the paramedics had done what very little they could do for Bill Mastrovy.

"What was the deceased doing here tonight?" McElone asked me. "Was he invited for the movie?" There wasn't the usual tone of sarcasm in her voice; this was her business and she was a professional.

"No," I told her. "I have no idea what he was doing here, and I don't even know when he came in. It must have been when the movie was on and the lights were out. It got pretty dark in here."

McElone was taking notes on a small yellow pad she carried with her. "That's stupid enough to be true."

So we were back to our old routine again. There was something comforting in that. I was grateful for it.

"I met him last night at a club in Asbury Park," I told the lieutenant. "He was playing in his band. Josh and I went to see him and I talked to him after the set, but I have no idea even how he knew where I lived, let alone what he was doing here."

"What were you talking to him about yesterday?" McElone asked. "His name came up with that allergy victim you were asking me about, didn't it?" Nothing gets by the lieutenant; she remembers everything. Why she was taking notes at all was beyond me, but maybe the Harbor Haven PD required it.

"That's right," I said. Tony had lain Oliver down across two chairs where Tessa and Jesse had been sitting, and he (Ollie) was as asleep as someone can be in a room with four cops, twelve living people (plus four ghosts) and all the lights on. I wished I could sleep like that. Instead, I was noticing my eyes itching and my throat closing up again. And I'd actually taken an allergy pill before dinner. "He was Vanessa McTiernan's boyfriend at the time she died and he told me last night that he'd been with her the day it happened."

An eyebrow went up. "Really," she said, her tone not betraying anything. Although the eyebrow was practically a scream of surprise itself. "What did he say happened?"

"That's the problem. He didn't. He just said he'd been there, then pushed his way out of the room, saying he'd talk to me today." I told McElone the whole story, including Sammi the girlfriend's reaction, which the lieutenant seemed to find interesting.

"I'm going to ask you something I wouldn't ask anybody else on this planet." The lieutenant's voice dropped to something that would have been a whisper if it had more oomph to it. "Was Vanessa's daddy the vengeful ghost here when our pal Bill bit the dust?"

I didn't want to rat out Vance, but there was no chance I would lie to McElone on something like this. Or anything else, for that matter. "He was here," I said. "He's not here now, but he was here then. But I don't think he did it."

"Why not?"

"I'm pretty sure he was busy talking with one of his old bandmates at the time. He was when the lights went down, anyway." I hadn't actually *seen* Vance and Morrie arguing; in fact, they'd seemed to have been getting along all right just when Morrie had come in. But once the movie started, I couldn't even vouch for their location or say they were still in the room, and I said that to McElone.

She looked around the room, paying more attention to

the ceiling than she would in most other crime scenes, I guessed. "I'm never getting used to this place," she said.

The interrogations took some hours and we never did get to see the rest of *Ghost*, although I don't think anyone was much in the mood to do so by then. Roberta and Stan Levine, despite my best efforts, packed up their stuff and called Senior Plus to send a van, heeding McElone's warning that they not leave the state; they lived in Maplewood after all. The other guests opted to stay in the house, particularly Berthe and Jesse, who had not seen much of anything. Tessa said she didn't think it was my fault and since she'd been saving for this vacation all year, she'd just spend most of her time outside for the next couple of days.

Maureen, who had been closest to the hallway entrance and might have caught a glimpse of the body, just looked grumpy. She didn't say it, but she certainly looked like she felt this was an inconvenience aimed directly at her and she wanted to find the killer just to give him a piece of her mind. The four of them went to bed after the police dismissed them.

All of us had our turn with McElone or the other officer, and I got the impression which cop you got hinged on how seriously McElone saw you as a witness or a suspect. Mom, Liss, Maureen, Tessa, Jeannie, Tony and the Levines got the officer. Josh, Jesse, Berthe, A.J., Liz and I got the lieutenant.

Nobody questioned Oliver.

Meanwhile, I continued to look for signs of Vance or Morrie. I found none. I didn't see Lester, either, but I probably wouldn't have known if I had.

But finally we were all completely debriefed, the lieutenant and her crew—who had long before removed Bill from my previously pristine floor—left, and I sat, exhausted, on one of the folding chairs. Josh sat next to me, arm casually draped over my shoulder, while Jeannie and Tony let Oliver sleep for another few minutes and sat in the row in front of me.

A.J. and Liz appeared to be uncomfortable but for some

reason didn't make a move to leave, yet didn't come close enough to be in the group. Maybe I was supposed to invite them?

Despite Mom's best efforts, Melissa forced her way into the hallway as soon as the last flashing light disappeared from my windows. She saw a lot of police crime scene tape, a stain on the floor that I'd asked McElone to cover and was denied ("in case we need more samples") and a number of depleted adults, dead and alive, sitting around wondering what had happened here tonight.

"Who was closest to him when it happened?" Liss asked as soon as she took in the scene.

"You were there," I said. "It was dark. There was no way to know."

Mom appeared behind my daughter and shook her head. "You shouldn't have been in there, Melissa," she tried, but I waved a hand.

"It's okay, Mom," I told her, knowing it was a useless battle. "Liss is a big girl."

"*I'm* a big girl, and I wish I hadn't seen what I saw," Jeannie contributed.

"I can't figure it," Josh said. "What was Bill even doing here?"

"He did say that he wanted to talk to me today, but Liz told him I'd be too busy," I said, loudly enough that Liz, who must truly have been the embodiment of the adage that the sound people most respond to is someone saying their name, looked up and tentatively walked over, trying not to look in the direction of the hallway. "Maybe he came here because he needed to tell me something about Vanessa."

"This is a weird place," Liz said, apropos of nothing. I'm not saying it isn't true but there really wasn't a context at the moment.

"If Mastrovy had a message, he could have gotten in touch another way," Paul said, floating where he could best see into the crime scene, as if the position of Bill's fall would break the case wide open. "He knew your name. Did you give him a business card?"

"I think so."

"You think so what?" Liz asked. She looked in the direction I was looking, except I saw Paul and she didn't.

"She just does that," Jeannie told Liz. "You have to go with it."

"If you gave him a card, he could have just called you," Paul went on. He's gotten used to these conversations, too. "He didn't have to come here. There has to be another reason."

"Someone killed Mr. Mastrovy here," Melissa said. "We don't know who it was. Maybe whoever killed him also sent a message telling him to come."

I put an arm around her shoulders. "You're a smart girl, you know that?"

Liss rolled her eyes. "Mom." And I saw my own mother giving me a familiar look.

Oliver made a waking noise that indicated he was awake, and the next thing I knew, Jeannie (giving me a look that indicated I should stay silent about her news) and Tony had picked him up and whisked him out to their car. Death, murder, ghosts, whatever: You don't mess with a sleepy one-year-old.

Liz told A.J. it might be time for them to follow suit. He hadn't said much since what I was now processing as the Incident. I had not provided a great evening for Josh's friends to get to know me. Not that I could have anticipated what was going to happen, but that didn't seem to matter much at the moment.

Once all the civilians (Josh does not fall into that category) had left, which felt like it had taken a very long time, Paul floated down a little and was stroking that goatee like he's never noticed it on his chin before.

"The problem has multiplied," he said. He says stuff like

that and nobody blinks. If I ever tried to say, "The problem has multiplied," I'd get laughed out of the room.

"Before we were investigating a four-month-old death," Paul went on, oblivious to my resentment of his ability to project authority, "one that we weren't even sure was a murder. What happened tonight definitely is one."

My concerns were elsewhere. Now that everyone except her grandmother and the ghosts had left, I could ask Melissa, "Are you okay?"

She thought about it. "Yes. I didn't really see anything, even though I tried. I'm glad you didn't let me. Sort of."

Paul went on as if I had not spoken, which is his habit. "We don't know why Mr. Mastrovy was here tonight, and we can't be sure who knew he would be here. But it seems logical that whoever killed him certainly had prepared for it and had probably been in touch with him, arranging for him to come to this house."

"How does that help?" I asked. "The only people in the room were my guests, who couldn't have known Mastrovy, Jeannie and Tony, who certainly didn't kill him, A.J. and Liz . . ."

Josh, who had been understandably quiet since the lights had come back on, looked at me. "Please. They didn't kill him."

"Right, and us. And I'm pretty sure none of us decided to stick a knife into Bill Mastrovy's back. I, for one, had no idea he was even in the house until he was dead."

"You're overlooking someone," Paul said.

"Yes," Mom said. "Vance McTiernan was here, and so was his friend Morrie Chrichton."

"Seriously?" I asked. "Vance and Morrie? They had barely shown up when the movie started. Besides, they were all the way at the front of the room and Mastrovy got killed out in the hallway, all the way in the back."

Maxie gave me a look that had some pity in it. "Right," she said. "They couldn't have done this." She swooshed back and forth from the movie room to the hallway through the walls three times before I could so much as raise a finger.

Not that I wanted to raise a finger. Well, maybe one finger.

"You've made your point," I said when she finally stayed in one place long enough to make eye contact. Her smug grin was not a welcome touch.

Everett moved over from the entrance and put an arm around Maxie. "Stand down," he said to her. "Ghost Lady is trying to work it out." (Everett is the only person I allow to call me that.)

"Party pooper," Maxie answered, but she snuggled into his shoulder.

"What we're missing," Paul said, trying to regain control of the meeting, "is that we have no physical clues; it's all conjecture. We can guess motives for Vance or for Morrie, but we don't know about anyone else."

"Who else?" I said.

"Perhaps someone who slipped in to do the killing and out after," Paul answered. "None of us saw the murder happen."

"Thank goodness," Mom said. She looked up at Dad, who floated down specifically to put his hand over hers.

"Agreed," Paul said. "But there might have been someone who had a grudge against Mastrovy and wasn't on the guest list for the showing tonight."

"But that person would have to know that Mastrovy was going to be here," I argued. "Who could have wanted to kill him that bad and known he'd show up uninvited?"

Josh looked thoughtful. "Sammi," he said.

It wasn't much, but it provided, as Paul put it, "a path." Tomorrow we—or rather, McElone, which was the plan I was advocating—could look into finding Sammi. Paul didn't seem to have any serious objections.

It was a couple of months past Melissa's bedtime and a school night to boot, so I made sure she went straight to her room. She protested, but not wholeheartedly.

Mom and Dad left soon after. It wasn't only because the murder had put a serious damper on the evening; it was late, and the absence of their granddaughter just took a little of the allure out of staying.

I got Josh to come into the kitchen with me, ostensibly to help clean up, although the only thing that had to happen was for some pizza boxes to get recycled. Once there, I interlaced my fingers behind his back and gave him a very therapeutic hug.

"I didn't do great with A.J. and Liz tonight," I said. "I'm sorry."

Josh smiled at me with that what-a-nut-my-girlfriend-is look I get more often than I suspect most girlfriends do. "Did you kill Bill Mastrovy?" he asked.

"What? No!"

"Then I don't see how this is your fault." He held me a little closer, to which I did not object. "Don't worry—I'm not going to dump you if you're not best friends with Liz and A.J."

That was, sadly, something of a relief. "You sure?"

"I'm sure. Hey, she annoys me sometimes, too. And besides, you offer things I can't get from my friends." He kissed me quite adequately.

And that was when I heard the voice from behind me. And a little above.

"Isn't that sweet?" Vance McTiernan said. "I do wish I had a camera."

I must have broken off the kiss and turned at the speed of sound, because I think I still heard the smack of our lips when I was already facing Vance. "You have some nerve," I said.

"Not really. I do that all the time," Josh said. But he was looking up where I was looking, so he knew someone was there, even if he didn't know who.

"Me?" Vance said. "I have nerve? What'd I do?"

"You keep showing up in my house, in my rooms, at times when I'd prefer to be left alone," I said. "But the real point is, you vanished out of the movie room before the lights came back up."

"I didn't like the movie," Vance said. "If I don't like the movie, I leave the cinema."

Josh leaned against the center island and watched me. I was, after all, the only other person in the room actually refracting light. I guessed. I'd have to ask Paul how that worked.

"When you can look me in the eye and say that, I probably still won't believe you," I told Vance. "Were you there for the main event? You know, when Bill Mastrovy ended up with a knife in his back?"

Vance seemed unfazed. "Yeah, I heard when it happened but I didn't do it."

"Of course not. You expressed a specific desire to do precisely that to that exact man, but you had nothing to do with it actually happening. Convenient. Did it occur to you that he might *not* have killed your daughter?"

Vance McTiernan lost the grin he'd been wearing when he thought he was being witty. Now, his face looked pained. I almost felt bad that I'd brought up Vanessa's death. But the bloom was definitely off this rose. Yeah, he was the hero of my adolescence, but I wasn't buying any of Vance's acts anymore.

"Yes, it did," he said with the requisite touch of sadness in his voice. "That's why I *didn't* kill him. Because from what you told me, I can't be sure what really happened to Nessa. I wouldn't have really done it, anyway. I'm a passionate man, not a violent one."

"What about Morrie Chrichton?" I pointed out. "He was there with you before the movie started and nobody's seen him since."

"I can vouch for Morrie," Vance said, raising his hands as if to hold me back. "I was with him the whole time."

"I understand Morrie vanishing," I told him. "Of course he did. There's no reason to come back here now; the business is finished, isn't it? What I don't understand is why you came back at all, Vance."

He looked me straight in the eye as if I were in the front row of a concert and he was putting over the most tender ballad you've ever heard. Like "Violet" on the Jingles album *Enemy of the Mind*, the one that had been playing on eternal rotation in Vanessa's apartment when she died.

"I came back because I know who killed William Mastrovy," he said.

# Eighteen

"Speak very slowly and carefully," Paul said. "I don't want anything to be misheard or misconstrued."

When Vance's bombshell dropped in the kitchen, I immediately insisted he accompany me to the movie room, despite not having wanted to go back in there until a crime scene cleaning crew had done its magic. I'd have to find an affordable one on the Internet in the morning.

I wanted Paul to hear Vance's claims and explanations directly. Maxie and Everett had left, heading to the Dunkin' Donuts sign on Route 35, one of Maxie's favorite vantage points. She used to enjoy moving the donuts in the shop around, to the consternation of the late-night crew, but Everett has mellowed her. A little.

Josh came with me into the movie room and made sure we were seated at the front of the room near the screen, facing away from the tape outline in the hallway. Josh looks out for me without my asking. I try to do that for him, too, but he doesn't need very much. I'd have to grit my teeth and invite A.J. and Liz to dinner. He deserved it.

"I know who killed William Mastrovy," Vance repeated, slowly and clearly. "It was Claudia."

*Claudia?* "Claudia Rabinowitz?" I blurted. "Vanessa's mom?"

"The same."

"That doesn't make any sense," I said. "We don't even know where Claudia is, and she certainly wasn't in the room with us tonight. We would have seen her." Vance was clearly just rambling or trying to divert our attention from something.

Before he could ask, I relayed the conversation to poor Josh, who was sitting there watching my face get more and more concerned and not understanding why. "Is this recent or before Vance came here?" he asked.

"Her presence drew me to this house," Vance answered, though only Paul and I could hear him. "And then when I was in the room, I could tell she was near. The same thing tonight."

Too much information was coming at me at one time. "You think Claudia was here all along? Like her spirit lives here? Impossible; she's alive. Isn't she?" I said.

"No, I don't think she's a ghost. I think she came here as a guest."

There was silence for quite some time after that one. "You think one of my guests is actually Claudia Rabinowitz, and that she came here specifically to kill Bill Mastrovy? That's crazy."

"Stranger things have happened," Vance suggested. I couldn't actually think of one, and I live in a haunted house.

Paul, stroking away at a breakneck pace, considered Vance, and to my horror, seemed to be taking him seriously. "Do you think Claudia is here now or was here as a past guest?" he asked.

Vance shook his head. "Can't be sure," he said. "You know how you sense a presence sometimes? I get that pretty strong for Claudia. It's what drew me here. But you have to remember I only . . . met her . . . the one time, and that was more than forty years ago. I have the feeling, but I can't say I'm perfectly certain on it."

He'd flown right past it, but that caught me. "Wait. You only met Claudia *once*? The night Vanessa was conceived?"

Vance's face registered surprise, like that point should have been obvious. "Yeah. What did you think?"

"You fathered a *child* with this woman, she grew up here in Jersey and you never once came to see her? Not even when you were on tour, playing in New York?"

Vance must have seen the trap closing on him, but it was so outside his life—or death—experience that he didn't know how to react. "Well, no. I sent money."

"How does that help your daughter have a father?" I demanded.

"Alison," Paul suggested, "this might not be the time."

"No, really! What kind of a dad never sees his child?"

Vance held up his hands. "Now, I didn't say that, love. Didn't say that. I said I hadn't seen *Claudia* again, because that was the way she wanted it. I saw Nessa. She came over to see us once in a while and I always visited when we played the States. Always."

"And what about your will? You didn't leave her a dime!" I'd had such admiration for Vance McTiernan. Before I knew him.

"The sad truth is, there wasn't much of anything left, love."

"How is this about the murder?" Josh asked. And he hadn't even heard the other half of the conversation.

They were right; I was off topic. "Okay. So you believe you sensed Claudia's presence in my house, both tonight and once before, when you were playing that song— "Claudia"—in my library. How did you know it was her?"

Vance looked at Paul for some kind of affirmation. "You

know how it is," he said to the other ghost. "You can't really say how you know something, but you know it?"

Paul nodded. "It's true," he told me. "It's similar to what you call the Ghosternet. I don't hear the messages from other spirits as much as I feel them. It's difficult to describe."

"But it's reliable?" I asked.

"I have found it to be, yes."

Okay, if we were going to treat it that way, I could dive in. I turned and looked at Vance. "You said the 'presence' you felt drew you here to the house. When did you first sense it? Were you still walking the ocean at the time?"

"No. It was when I had arrived here in New Jersey. I had come this way because of what I'd seen about Nessa, because she had been here."

"Why should I believe you?" I asked. "You haven't said one thing that held still long enough to be true since I met you." I was playing it a little over the top, but it felt right. A showman like Vance would respond to that. But I had a clincher. "You even got some female ghost you know get in touch with Paul and say she was Vanessa, didn't you?"

Vance looked away and tilted his head. "I did. This bird I knew in Leicester. A *very* long time ago. I thought it would give you a little more push. At the time I wanted you to stop digging, stop doing what you were doing. I pushed too hard. I do that."

"You lied to me and you lied to Paul," I told him. "That's not the way you get people to do the things you want them to do. That's how you make us feel we can't trust you."

"I deserve that," he said, his voice slightly wounded and ashamed. He was a much better actor than I would ever be. "I don't have any reason to give you. I can't say you should believe me because I mean it this time. I would have said that all the other times, too. But the fact is, I *know* Claudia was here tonight."

"Even so," Paul interjected. I think he was trying to defuse the situation. "Let's work on the assumption that you are correct and the woman with whom you had a daughter was in the room. What proof do you have that she killed Mr. Mastrovy?"

Vance's head was hanging like a schoolboy caught trying to grab a cupcake without paying at the bake sale. "I have none."

"All that from intuition?" Paul asked. He shook his head. "It's more than I could do."

"I can't explain it. If it was a lie, I'd be able to make it sound more plausible." Of course, his saying that made it sound more plausible. It was a difficult conundrum.

I leaned back in my chair and Josh's arm found its way around my shoulders. "It's incredibly late and I passed 'tired' about an hour-and-a-half ago," I said. "I need to go to sleep."

Josh, clearly thinking I was talking to him, nodded. "Me too. I have to open the store in about four hours."

"I wasn't trying to get you to leave," I said. "I still have more apologizing to do."

"Tomorrow. If you tried now it might kill me." He stood up and so did I. He kissed me quite pleasantly, right there with the ghosts looking on, and left, promising to call the next day.

Dad was right. Josh was a keeper.

Once I was the only living person in the room, I looked over at the two ghosts. Paul was standing, hand on his chin but not stroking. Maybe he was tired, too. Ghosts don't sleep, but that doesn't mean they don't get at least mentally worn out.

He was watching Vance, who looked the exact opposite—he seemed like he was on amphetamines. He was moving around the room, not exactly floating but propelling himself in unpredictable patterns around the room, just navigating the space without a conscious effort. Or maybe this was what he was like when he was tired.

Except Vance was a former rock star. This was the shank of the evening to him.

"Fellas," I said, "if you two want to rehash the whole subject some more, feel free, but I have to get at least twenty minutes of sleep a night or I'm completely useless the next day."

"Is that it?" Vance said, staccato delivery and with an expression that cried out for sweat. "You're just going to sleep when I told you a murderer is here under your roof?"

It wouldn't be the first time, but I didn't feel like telling him that. "I'll deal with it in the morning." I turned to head for the hallway, the first move to the staircase. My bed was getting closer.

"I think Claudia killed Vanessa, too," he called out.

"Good night, Vance," I said back.

I don't remember if I even brushed my teeth; I was in bed within seconds. And then at about two in the morning, I was awakened by what I would swear was the sound of a dog howling, briefly, somewhere nearby. Just the sound of it made me sneeze.

I began to form a theory.

The next morning, I got up to a house with two fewer guests than the night before, one hallway completely off-limits until such time as I could get professional cleaners into it and a somewhat pessimistic view of life.

Ignoring the more complicated concerns, I spent the first twenty minutes looking online for an urn cart. I found one after some doing but decided first to see if the independent furniture store in town, Sit On It, might have something I could use. The itch in my throat and my eyes was a reminder that antihistamines were also in order. I'd given up wondering what I could possibly be reacting to at this time of year and simply decided I must've developed an allergy because I was older than I used to be.

Berthe Englund was already up when I got downstairs, which was something of a surprise. I apologized to her for sleeping in—it was six a.m., after all—but Berthe waved a hand and said I shouldn't feel guilty.

"After last night, I couldn't sleep very well," she said. "I figured I'd go out and try to catch some waves early, work out the cobwebs a little."

"I feel awful that the special night I'd planned for all of you turned out to be such a terrible experience," I said.

She smiled a little crookedly. "It's okay," she said. "I've already seen *Ghost*."

"Anything I can do for you today?"

Berthe thought a moment. "Treat yourself well," she said. Without another word or look, she turned and walked to the glass doors, no doubt about to pick up her rented surfboard from the shed in back, where I'd told her she could store it.

That was it. She was too nice to be Claudia Rabinowitz and a murderer. That left me with Tessa, Jesse, Maureen and the Levines (because let's face it, they had hightailed it out of here awfully fast last night) as candidates. Assuming Vance was correct and not lying.

Two very large assumptions.

It would be another four hours before the morning spook show, if we decided to go ahead with one. I hadn't gotten a strong read on the remaining guests the night before. If they were too upset after what had happened—and who could blame them?—I might curtail some of the more ghost-oriented events for the next two days.

The only thing to do was ask the guests when they came down for the morning. If the consensus was that they wanted a hiatus, we'd stop, but if they preferred to keep the spook shows going, we'd do that.

Paul rose up through the floor as I was moving the coffee urn, sans cart, and grunting like an Olympic weightlifter during the clean and jerk. "Why don't you just let the guests into the kitchen for coffee in the morning?" he asked.

"Shut up."

I finished with my Andre the Giant impression and saw Paul, tea urn in his arms, moving into the den and setting it on the side table next to the coffee. "Well, thank you," I said. "Where have you been all my life?"

He looked stymied. "I believe you know where I've been," he said.

Go teach Jersey sarcasm to a British Canadian ghost.

"So what do you think?" I asked Paul when my breath was coming in regular intervals again. "Should we believe Vance this time?"

Paul tilted his head. "It's a difficult question. He's been inconsistent with his story for the few days we've known him, but he did seem particularly sincere after Bill was killed. I have been thinking about this all night, and there is one issue I have been unable to reconcile."

We were back in the kitchen, where I was making myself a toasted bagel, having defrosted one in the microwave and cut it in half. It pays to plan ahead. "Just one?" I asked.

Paul chose to be focused. "What possible motivation would Vance have to claim his ex-lover Claudia Rabinowitz was here in the house, posing as one of your guests?"

The bagel had not yet popped—I like them nicely toasted if they're not fresh that day—so all I had to do for the moment was sit and think about what Paul had said. "You make a good point," I said. "But I can throw one back at you."

He cocked an eyebrow. "Really."

"Yeah." The toaster popped, so I got up and picked a plate off a shelf in the cabinet above the toaster. "Why would Claudia be here at the guesthouse? She would have had to book the trip well in advance, and I had never even heard of Bill Mastrovy before Friday night, so there was no reason to think she could find Bill here if her goal was to knife him."

Paul grinned, which I did not expect. "You know, you really are progressing at this," he said. "You wouldn't have thought of that a year ago."

"Don't butter me up. You're only saying that because I was mad at you a couple of days ago."

"No, I mean it. I think you're doing quite well. I hadn't considered that position. Claudia, assuming she was the one who killed Bill, would had to have presumably lured him here somehow for the showing of *Ghost* last night. If she'd booked her trip three months ago, how would she have known such an event would take place? Why would she choose to murder him here? Why not go to where he was living and do him in at home?"

"Great. So we have tons of questions. How do we answer them?"

Paul pursed his lips. "The first thing to do would be to try and reconnect with Jeremy Bensinger," he said. "He might have some idea about his mother's whereabouts."

"He said he didn't. He said that once they had their fight, she pretty much disowned him." Having now spread the bagel with cream cheese (something not especially easy to do with a very hot bagel), I sat down to eat.

"Well, that might also mean he has no strong reason to protect her. Tell him you have some reason to believe she might have been involved with the murder here last night. See if that changes his position."

"After I finish this," I said, chewing vigorously.

"There are times I don't mind not being able to eat anymore," he said.

"What do I do if Jeremy doesn't immediately cave in and hand over a print out of his mother's address, phone number and Social Security information?" I used a napkin to wipe a little cream cheese off the corner of my mouth. Daintily, of course.

"I'd say get in touch with Sammi Fine," Paul said. "According to the voice recording you gave me of your interview with Bill Mastrovy, Sammi didn't know he was still involved with Vanessa McTiernan at the time Vanessa died.

But if she found out, she might have been angry enough to do something about it."

The second half of the bagel was calling to me, and I was responding. "How come I always get the good jobs?" I asked.

"Because you're the one who's still breathing," Paul reminded me so drily I think some dust might have escaped from his mouth.

"For the time being."

"I'm so sorry. Is there something I can be doing for *you*?" He thought he was kidding.

"Yeah," I said. "Get Maxie and her dancing keyboard fingers on the case of Claudia Rabinowitz, and while we're at it, find out who else was in the room when Vanessa died. And you can do one other thing for me."

"What's that?" Paul asked.

"Get on the Ghosternet and see if you can find a short blond guy named Lester from Topeka, Kansas."

# Nineteen

Finding Sammi Fine was not hard, but strange nonetheless. The only Samantha T. Fine I'd seen listed in the tristate area was at an investment firm called Plantiere and Associates in Red Bank, which seemed unlikely (*incredibly* unlikely, to be honest), but it was all I had to go on. So I went on it.

If you're wondering why I didn't start with a follow-up interview of Jeremy Bensinger instead of searching for Sammi, it was because Jeremy hadn't responded to my text messages or voice mail, and wasn't home at his apartment when I'd dropped by this morning. Jeremy, after having met me once, was apparently ducking any further contact. Imagine such a thing. I decided I'd have to drop by his place of business later.

There'd been a general consensus from the guests that we could continue the spook shows in the afternoon—"especially if there'll be that wonderful music," as Tessa had suggested— but this morning had fallen into the too-soon category. I'd agreed with that sentiment, took Melissa to school (despite her protests that having a murder in the house exempted her for the day) and headed out to invade Samantha T. Fine's professional venue.

I drove to Red Bank and sat in my Volvo across the street from the investment firm's offices, pondering possible courses of action. Stomping into the investment firm and asking for Sammi Fine seemed somehow unwise, like I'd be doing damage to this poor woman's reputation just by showing up. The PI license in my wallet probably wouldn't do her a ton of good, either.

The idea of this Samantha Fine and the one I'd seen drumming for Once Again two nights before being the same person was laughable. Plantiere's website had not offered a photograph of Ms. Fine, so I couldn't be sure she *wasn't* Once Again's drummer, but I just had a hard time imagining that people would actually hand over their savings for investment to a woman who had dated Bill Mastrovy and played at a club called the Last Resort. Or if they did, I wanted to call each one and warn them personally. The woman behind the drum kit had three nose rings, tattoos on both upper arms, a very healthy streak of orange in her hair and a very serious chewing gum habit. I worried about gum being a gateway drug to, I don't know, Twizzlers or something. Stay in school, kids.

It was only nine thirty in the morning, so waiting out here in the hopes that Samantha would wander out for her lunch break was a bad plan. Not to mention that if she wasn't the Sammi Fine I'd seen, I'd be sitting out there all day waiting and never actually know whether I'd come to the right place or not.

So, following Paul's sage investigator's advice, I was about to be sneaky. Paul called it "creative," but we both knew what that meant.

I'd forgone my usual sort of outfit—fine for an innkeeper, especially one often working on home repairs—and worn something more businesslike, with a skirt and everything.

I figured having dressed up, I might as well show myself off, so I got out of the car, smoothed myself out, pretended my hair looked the way I wanted it to and crossed the street to the three-story office building.

It wasn't quite as fancy or off-putting as I'd expected. Not every place is a Wall Street firm, and the sad fact was that I'd never had enough money to consider investing except for the time I was foolish enough to sink every last dime I had into a charming but somewhat rickety Victorian on Seafront Avenue. So perhaps I wasn't the savvy investor this sort of place usually attracted.

A very pleasant-looking receptionist inquired if she could help me, which was something I was wondering myself. I asked if I could see Ms. Fine and she asked if I had an appointment.

Of course, I did not. And I couldn't rely on the old movie trick of looking at the handwritten list of appointments in front of her and claiming to be one of those people because this was the twenty-first century and computers had been invented in the interim. The one on the receptionist's desk had a screen that faced away from me.

"I'm afraid I don't have an appointment," I said. "But I have one quick question that will only take a minute of her time."

The difference between, say, a lawyer's office and an investment firm, I knew (from being married to The Swine, who was in that business), was that the investment firm doesn't gain anything from turning a potential client away. The law firm might not want to deal with your kind of case and probably deals with a lot of people who are, how shall I put this delicately, crazy. Walk-ins are not encouraged.

An investment firm, on the other hand, is happy when someone they don't actually seek out comes to talk business. Since so much of the business is generated by word-of-mouth, getting a "free" client is a boon. So I was betting that Samantha T. Fine, whoever she was, would be glad to talk to a wayward investor for a few minutes.

"I'm afraid she doesn't have anything available today," the receptionist said.

Another in a long list of ways my ex-husband has failed me. I should have known.

"Not even for a minute?" I pleaded.

"I'm sorry."

It was time to play hardball. "Could you please just mention the name William Mastrovy?"

The pleasant-looking receptionist looked up from her screen. Her face didn't read worried or astonished, just confused. "I'm sorry?" It was her favorite phrase because it was so versatile.

"William Mastrovy."

Her eyes narrowed. "Is that you?"

"No. Please just call her extension and say someone is here about William Mastrovy. If she doesn't want to see me, I'll leave. How's that?"

Probably more out of curiosity than anything, the receptionist punched a button on the console in front of her. She spoke into the earpiece she was wearing in a professional, unobtrusive tone. "Ms. Fine? There's a woman here to see you. No, I have your schedule. She said to mention the name William Mastrovy." Impressive that she didn't have to ask me for the name again. This girl was earning her money.

She listened for a moment, betraying nothing with her expression. Then she said, "I will. Thank you." And she punched the button on her console again. She immediately pulled a pad out from under her desk. "Name, please?" she asked.

Ms. Fine's office, I was told, was one floor up and three doors down on the left. So I followed the directions and ended up in front of a plain wooden door, not especially fancy (in keeping with the rest of the décor in the office), but bearing the nameplate "Samantha T. Fine." I knocked.

"Come in."

Sure enough, seated behind the standard-issue desk was the drummer from Once Again. It took me a moment to recognize her because she was wearing a very sensible power suit (I thought those had gone out of style, but maybe they were making a comeback), her hair up in a bun. The tattoos were covered with a white blouse and a gray jacket was draped over the back of her chair. The nose rings were nowhere to be seen.

"You," she said.

"I could say the same." I didn't wait to be asked; I just sat down in front of her desk. Luckily, there was a chair there for just that purpose. "I figured I had the wrong Samantha T. Fine."

"Hey. It's the day job. I have to make a living until the music starts to pay off."

"I guess so." Every bar-band member has a dream. One in a half million realizes it.

"How did you find me?"

I produced the PI license from my tote bag and said, "I'm looking into Bill's murder." Technically that didn't answer her question, but I didn't see how that was a big deal at this point.

But Samantha's (she just didn't look like Sammi now) eyes widened to maximum density and she gasped. "Bill was murdered?"

"Oh, come on. The cops must have called you by now. I gave them your name when they questioned me."

She shook her head. "I swear. This is the first I'm hearing about it. I was so mad at him, I haven't spoken to him since that night at the Last Resort." Her eyes were tearing up, and unless she was a graduate of the Actor's Studio, the tears were real. "What happened?"

I told her about the previous night at the guesthouse and how it had ended, permanently, for Bill. Samantha sat back deeper and deeper into her leather chair until her head seemed almost encased, but she kept shaking it back and forth.

"Why?" she finally said. "Why?"

"Once we find out who, we'll know why," I answered. If I could focus her on the task at hand, it might be possible to delay the emotional scene I'd prefer to avoid at the moment. "What can you tell me? Why was he at my house last night?"

Sammi dabbed at her eyes, but not in a theatrical way. Her eye makeup was running a little, so she dabbed at it with a tissue from a box on her desk. Investment counselors were like doctors, The Swine used to say. If the news was bad, you wanted to have some Kleenex at the ready. "I don't know. He was acting all weird even before we met you. Said he'd run into an old friend but he wouldn't tell me who, and then he canceled rehearsal last night. Said he had to be somewhere."

"So it seems like he planned to be at my house."

"No, this was before you showed up," Sammi pointed out. "He said there was something big going on and he wasn't going to tell me until it was all done. Bill was like that—he liked the big gesture." She started to well up again. "He's really dead?"

Sammi looked so distraught my heart went out to her, but I had to see if there was some information that might help. I told myself finding Bill's murderer would give her closure. "Who do you think the old friend was?" I asked.

"Oh, man, I don't know. I mean, it sounded like a music thing the way he was talking. And he could piss people off, you know. But killing him? Who'd want to do *that*?" Sammi seemed legitimately upset and sniffed back tears a few more times.

"That's what I'm asking you. What did he tell you about the day Vanessa McTiernan died?" I watched her face for a reaction the way Paul always says I should, and I got one: her lips pursed and curled a little at one side. Sammi was back, and she didn't like the mention of Bill's old girlfriend, even if now they were both dead.

"You think this is about Vanessa?"

"She used to be in your band. She used to date Bill. And she died a few months ago. It's at least possible there's a connection." *And her dead father the rock star asked me to find out. That's not weird, right?*

"I mean, don't get me wrong: I'm sorry she's dead, you know? But I never liked her. Maybe that's bad to say, but she was weird. She used to stare off into space and talk to people who weren't there. It freaked out everybody in the band except Bill. Then her brother started coming around and saying he was her manager, and she needed to sing her original songs in the set. We're a cover band; you can't do that. So she quit Once Again and went off to record or something. That's when Bill and her broke up."

"Did you steal him away from her?" I asked. When Sammi found out that Bill was still seeing Vanessa when she died, she had not looked pleased. I wanted to see if I could get the same reaction now.

"Nobody stole anybody from anybody," Sammi said, her mouth twitching a little, maybe another attempt to keep from crying. "Vanessa and Bill were a thing. They broke up before she left the band. He and I started up later. Then she died."

The look on her face had changed and I wasn't really convinced about this last part, so I pressed the issue. "When he said he'd seen Vanessa the day she died, you looked surprised. Then you got so mad you didn't talk to him again."

Sammi let out an involuntary sob. "Yeah. Now I can't ever talk to him again." *Would it comfort her to know that I might be able to, if he showed up in the right form?* She started to

cry, not steadily, but not just choking it back, either. I wasn't
sure whether to leave her to herself or if it would be cruel to
abandon her when she felt so awful. But Sammi gathered herself and went on. "I was mad at him because he was stupid for
going to see her. I don't remember that day exactly, but I know
he wanted her back in the band so we could do some Fleet-
wood Mac. Vanessa sounded a little like Stevie Nicks."

"You think he was going there to ask her to come back?
What did he tell you about that day?"

"He *said* he never went," Sammi's voice froze over and
she put down the tissue, which wasn't going to be needed now.
"Said Vanessa canceled because her mom was in town."

"Why? Did Vanessa not see her mother often?"

"No, her mom had moved to, like, Ohio or something,"
Sammi said. "But she was in town now and wanted to see
Vanessa. They'd had some fight about her brother or something; I don't remember. So her asking to get together was
a big deal. But I guess it was all a lie because then Bill told
you he was there the day Vanessa died."

Claudia being around on the day of Vanessa's death did
seem to jibe with Vance's claim that she had something to
do with Bill's murder . . . I made a mental note to have
Maxie look for Claudia Rabinowizes in Ohio.

"Vanessa had a severe allergic reaction to peanuts," I
said, being intentionally misleading. "Can you think of a
reason she'd eat peanuts if she knew they could kill her?"

"I hadn't talked to her in weeks when she died," Sammi
said with a shrug. "So I don't know what she was upset
about. But it wasn't peanuts; it was soy sauce. She was allergic to soy sauce. She was a big pain about it," Sammi went
on. "Whenever we'd go out for Chinese, she'd make a big
deal out of it: 'Oh, don't put any soy sauce on it,' like she
was so special. You just wanted . . ."

"To kill her?" I asked.

Sammi didn't answer. I didn't want to cause her more grief if she wasn't the killer or be nice to her if she was, so I got up to leave.

On the way out I passed Lieutenant McElone on her way in. She looked surprised.

"She's all yours," I said.

# Twenty

"You think Sammi might have been that angry?" Paul Harrison was more transparent than usual, standing in the sun outside my back door. Okay, *standing* might be an overstatement, but Paul was there, and given the angle of the light, he was sort of hard to see.

"Can you float over to the shade by the deck?" I asked. I was shielding my eyes with my hand to begin with, so Paul's habit of pacing as he thought was making the whole process more difficult and, frankly, a little painful. Light, dark, light, dark, light . . .

Paul moved to the designated area so I could face the house rather than the ocean and put down my hand. "I think you're missing the larger point," Paul said. "Concentrate less on Vanessa's love life and more on her suddenly promising musical career. Did Bill Mastrovy see her as an ex-girlfriend or an ex-bandmate about to hit it big?"

"Unless you've heard from Bill, there's no way for us to

know," I said. Paul shook his head. "Well then, I think we have to see both love and money as possible motives here."

"You really have learned," he marveled. Maybe a little too vehemently. "Very well. I imagine you would argue that if it was the romantic angle that was in play, Sammi is the more logical suspect."

"I would," I said. "Nobody else seems to have been involved. The guitarist I saw the night Josh and I went to the Last Resort wasn't in the band when Vanessa was, Sammi told me. The guy who used to play with them moved to Los Angeles right after Vanessa left."

"Very well," Paul said, enjoying his role as proud professor just a little too much. "So if the motive was the money Jeremy said was likely coming Vanessa's way, who is the beneficiary of her dying? And why kill Bill Mastrovy?"

"That's a good question," I said, looking down. "In fact, it's two good questions. Here's a third: What's this about Claudia being in town on the day Vanessa died?"

"An excellent question. If she's still in the area . . ."

"She could be here in the guesthouse."

Paul nodded. We were alone in the backyard for the moment. Liss was still at school, Mom and Dad were not coming over today as far as I knew and Josh was at work at Madison Paints. The remaining guests were out enjoying the Jersey Shore in early fall on this lovely September day, and Vance was off doing whatever it is he did during daylight hours. I'd rarely seen him except at night. Morrie had been scarce since the murder; when I asked Vance where his old pal was he shrugged and said something about "Morrie being Morrie."

"Where's Maxie?" I asked, realizing it had been a while since our resident poltergeist had made an appearance. "We have a spook show in a couple of hours."

"She's in the attic or on the roof, working on some

research," Paul said. "I asked her to find out whatever she could about Claudia Rabinowitz even before you came home with this allegation. She hadn't gotten much when I saw her, but she was just starting out. You know Maxie."

"I know Maxie," I agreed. Maxie is many things, not all of them wonderful, but she is a whiz at Internet research. For someone whose job was creative when she was alive, she had developed into a very accomplished techie.

"Well, how confident were you with what Sammi told you?" Paul asked. "Did she seem credible?"

It was weird, but in a way seeing Sammi in her business guise had somehow made her less credible in my eyes, and I said so to Paul. "I mean, I realize she can't look like Drummer Sammi when she's at work, but knowing that she's able to put on a whole new persona sort of made me trust her less."

Paul doesn't have a lot of patience for intuition rather than fact, but he trusts my judgment, which might be a flaw of his. "Did you believe her when she told you that?" he asked again.

"Actually, yeah," I said. "It's not even that she wouldn't have a reason to lie. Maybe *she* killed Vanessa and Bill; I don't know. But the look on her face when she heard he was dead . . . I just thought she was telling the truth."

"Don't let your emotions cloud your judgment," he reminded me.

I looked at Paul, which could now be done without squinting, even while wearing sunglasses. "What's our next move, chief?"

"I think a consultation with Lieutenant McElone is in order," he said. "I'd be surprised if she doesn't show up here to follow up on last night's mayhem anyway."

That was right, I'd forgotten. After I wowed McElone at Sammi's office, she'd said she'd be back this afternoon with any further questions for me and the guests. She might wait until after Melissa was due home in case she thought my daughter might have seen something else or been too sleepy to fully report the night before. She didn't know Melissa that well; my little Nancy Drew had given every detail she could possibly have mustered and offered a few theories on the possible culprits without being asked.

"Until then?" I asked.

He shrugged a little. "Try to find Jeremy Bensinger," he said.

With the guests gone, my business was mostly to make sure the house was in order. "First I'm going to find a cleaning service for the hallway," I told him. "Then we can find Maxie for the show, assuming the guests straggle back in. Once that's over, I can go to Ace Equipment and talk to Jeremy."

"I'll do my best raising William Mastrovy, but you know that's probably a losing proposition at least for a few days," Paul admitted. "It was so dark in the room, and he was attacked from behind. Even if I could talk to him, it's possible he wouldn't know who had killed him."

"Well, the one person who might be able to confirm this thing with Claudia might be Vance," I thought out loud. "If you see him, ask him about that." I started up the steps of the deck to the back doors, then turned back to look at Paul, who was in the sun again. I saw a little blue denim floating toward the basement doors. "Oh, hey. Any luck on Lester?"

"Not yet," he said. "I found two ghosts named Lester from Topeka, but both dark-haired. One was a Civil War veteran." He vanished through the basement doors to his favorite hideaway.

I went to my bedroom and accessed my absurdly old laptop to find a cleaning service. It only took about twenty minutes, eighteen of which were engrossed in getting the computer to warm up and find the Wi-Fi signal that any other device in the house could access in seconds. Once I could get to the Internet, I found a service called Master Clean that promised to take care of any problem in one visit. They got the job and said they would send a crew out that evening.

One problem at a time. And by that I mean Maxie was dropping through the ceiling wearing her trench coat, which meant her laptop couldn't be far behind.

"I've got something for you," she said. It struck me that I was pretty sure nobody had said hello to me at all today. She pulled out her laptop, which was much better than mine despite the fact that Maxie had been dead for three years. "It's a picture of Claudia Rabinowitz."

Sure enough, the screen on her computer showed a woman in a short skirt and tight top, hair piled up on top of her head. She was also wearing a wide-brimmed hat, which obscured part of her face. She was not smiling in the picture, which appeared to be from a newspaper article. I could only see part of the headline, but it was about the woman taking Vance McTiernan to court over his "love child."

"This picture is from 1978," I told Maxie.

"Do you think I have access to her family vacation pictures? Claudia isn't on Facebook or Instagram." Maxie, expecting to be lauded as usual for her incredible ingenuity in finding anything on the Internet, frowned at me. "How much do you think *you* would have been able to dig up?"

I looked at the woman to see if she bore a resemblance to anyone I could remember being a guest in the house recently. Oddly, she did seem vaguely familiar but I couldn't place her.

"Do you think she looks like anybody?" I asked Maxie.

She swooped down to where I was holding the laptop and angled herself to get a clean view. Unfortunately that involved sort of pushing herself through me, but you get used to these things after a while. I'm told.

"With different hair, she would look like Taylor Swift," Maxie said.

Sometimes Maxie causes slow, deep intakes of breath. I finally looked at her and said, "Do you think she looks like anyone who's been here recently?"

She squinted, I think just to make it look like she was

thinking hard about the question. "It's an old picture. Do you think she looks a little like your mom?"

"Get Paul," I said. Maxie made a face but she dove down through the floor without saying anything else.

I studied the photograph for a long moment. I can't say I saw a really strong facial resemblance to anyone I'd seen recently—or to Taylor Swift or Mom—but the picture was almost forty years old and in black and white. These were not the best conditions to evaluate such a thing.

My phone rang while I was waiting for Paul and Maxie to emerge. I checked to make sure the caller wasn't Jeremy calling back, but it was Phyllis, so I answered.

"I don't have the ME's report yet," she began.

"Thanks for calling. I haven't actually found a cure for cancer."

"Woo, cranky! What's going on, sweetie?" Phyllis has known me since before I started dating. And I started early.

"I lost a couple of guests because of the dead body on my floor last night."

"Yeah, how about that?" Phyllis sounded offended. "A fresh murder in Harbor Haven, right there in your house, and I'm not your first phone call?"

"No, crazy me, I thought I'd call the cops first. Why are you calling, Phyllis?"

She made an irritated sound that bore some resemblance to a steam engine pulling into a station. "I'm hearing stuff about the guy who turned up dead on your floor last night," she said.

"Stuff? What kind of stuff?"

"This William Mastrovy, right?" She didn't wait for an answer. "Worked fronting a band around the Shore, but he also had a day job, if you catch my drift."

"I didn't even see you throw a drift. What do you mean, a day job?"

Phyllis's "coy" voice wasn't terribly attractive. "The kind you don't get from Monster.com," she said.

"Bill Mastrovy was a United States Senator?"

She sighed; I was spoiling all her fun. "Drugs, baby. He was dealing, just a little weed, nothing serious, but the cops knew about him. He wasn't up for major time, but his name was around."

It would be inconvenient to walk around all day with my eyes closed, but it felt kind of nice, like I was taking a nap while sitting up on my bed. Maybe I could just stay in this one place all day. But then I heard Paul say, "Who's on the phone?" I opened my eyes. He and Maxie had obviously materialized during my brief respite and were now hovering about three feet above me, looking concerned as if my simple desire to sit quietly was a sign of some deep psychological disorder, like fatigue.

I knew Paul wanted me to put the call on speaker so he could hear it, but I resisted the urge. For one thing, I'd have to come up with a phony excuse that Phyllis wouldn't believe for my doing so and for another, I was in a contrary mood and felt like keeping the call, or at least her end of it, to myself.

"See? That's the kind of thing a *real* reporter would find out," I said.

Paul turned toward Maxie and said, "It's Phyllis Coates." Maxie looked blankly at him. "The newspaper editor." Maxie nodded oh, yeah.

"I have sources who say Vanessa's brother, Jeremy, and Bill were at odds over her." Phyllis likes nothing better than knowing stuff before other people. It's what drove her into journalism. "One wanted her to be a big music star and the other wanted her to be his girlfriend and play on weekends. So tell me, what do you know about Vanessa McTiernan's career?"

"I know she had an album ready and there was a contract

from a record company," I said. "I know it was good, at least to my ears."

"But do you know Bill was going to Vanessa's apartment to try to talk her back into his band on the day she OD'd on soy sauce?"

"You know, I often wonder why you call to ask me stuff you already know," I said.

"It's called confirmation, sweetie, and you didn't know, so you can't provide it. I'll call you later." And just like that, she was gone.

I put the phone away and tried, wearily, to shake my mood. I could be cranky with Maxie—she's used to it—but if I start being rude to Paul, well, I'd seen what getting him upset was like and I preferred having him on my side. I looked up at them.

I held out the laptop and refreshed the screen. "Does this woman resemble anyone we know?" I asked.

Paul's brow furrowed. "Wait. What was the phone call with Phyllis about?"

"Picture first. Phyllis later."

Paul gave me a puzzled look but floated down to examine the newspaper photograph on the screen. He scrutinized it carefully from three different angles and looked over at me. "No."

"No?"

"No. I don't recognize her. It's a grainy picture scanned from a newspaper's archives of four decades ago. That could be a picture of my own mother and I wouldn't necessarily recognize it. Now, tell me what Phyllis said."

I gave him the edited recap and the goatee stroking started right up on cue. "Interesting," he said. "You said that Mastrovy made a quick exit from the dressing room as soon as you said that someone might have killed Vanessa. And he admitted to being in the room the day Vanessa died."

Maxie lay on her back, pretending to sleep. "We know this already," she said in a dreamy voice.

"But we didn't know then that Mastrovy was selling drugs and might have been worried about police entanglements. This information makes it more likely that he at least knew something about her death."

"We're going in circles," I complained. "We keep coming back to the same facts, but we don't have a reason anybody would want Vanessa or Bill dead."

Paul frowned as Maxie, still frustrated that she wasn't being showered with praise for finding an unidentifiable picture of Claudia, grabbed the laptop out of my hands and started tapping away at it furiously. Sometimes a lack of attention is all it takes to motivate Maxie.

"I think you're right," Paul said. "Motive is the key to this case."

"And?"

"And we're ignoring the notion that Vance sensed Claudia Rabinowitz in this house. How does she fit in?"

"Maybe she came to town to buy her daughter some lo mein and things didn't go well," I said. The whole eyes-closed thing was feeling attractive again.

"The medical examiner's report didn't show any definitive signs of defensive wounds on Vanessa, so it's unlikely the person who gave her the soy sauce had to force it down her throat," Paul said. "How do you get someone to drink straight soy sauce?"

"By putting it in something else?" I suggested.

Paul shook his head. "Diluting it wouldn't have the same concentration as the autopsy found. She drank it as soy sauce. It leads to the conclusion that the cause of Vanessa's death was taken intentionally."

"What about the knife sticking out of Mastrovy's neck?" I said. "*That* wasn't suicide."

There was a knock at the door, and I started. Guests very rarely come looking for me in my room, although they're certainly welcome to do so if they need me. I walked to the door and opened it to find Tessa and Jesse standing there.

"I hope we're not interrupting," Tessa said. "It sounded like you were talking to someone in here."

"It's that kind of house," I told her. "How can I help?"

"We're wondering," Jesse said, "if after the whole hoo-hah yesterday, is there going to be a ghost show this afternoon?"

I'd asked Tessa this morning what her preference might be in this area, but that seemed to have been forgotten. "That's up to you guys. If nobody is too upset, we'll do the show. And of course, anybody who *is* too upset certainly has the right to avoid it if they choose."

"Cool," Jesse said. "I really like the tunes." Berthe was the only bona fide surfer I'd ever had stay at the guesthouse, yet Jesse's speech patterns fit the stereotype so much better.

Um . . . I had no idea if Vance was going to be present or not; Vance was not "under contract" to perform, at least not the way Paul and Maxie were. He showed up when it suited him, and only for the past couple of days. "Well, that was a special event we've been lucky enough to have this past weekend," I said. "It's only going to happen if our resident musician is here at the time. I don't really have control over that." Better to warn the guests than to disappoint them.

Jesse's face sort of froze. He wasn't exactly the sharpest scissor in the drawer, so it was possible he wasn't following me. "Bummer," he said.

"Well, he might be there. I just don't know yet. So stick around to find out."

Tessa, who had not looked as enthusiastic as Jesse to begin with, nodded. "We'll see," she said. "I might want to pick up some souvenirs on the boardwalk." She waved a hand as if she were going far away. "See you later."

She led Jesse away by the hand like one does a small

child. I hadn't had to do that with Liss for at least four years. Probably five, but I hadn't been taking any chances.

"They make such a cute couple," Maxie said. "The proud mother and her son."

"Oh, cut it out," I said after I closed the door again. "They're entitled to whatever it is they want."

"The case," Paul reminded us. "We have to make some plans."

"Don't tell me; let me guess," I said. "Jeremy Bensinger?"

Paul didn't even grin a little. "You read my mind," he said.

# Twenty-one

Before I could go see Jeremy, we had to get through the spook show. It would have been better if we hadn't.

Vance McTiernan did not materialize, so there was no special musical performance to cap off the festivities. But that was only the icing on a very unappetizing cake.

Maureen, Berthe and Jesse all came to the show. Jesse said that Tessa was off shopping for mementos on the boardwalk, which might even have been true. But without the Levines or Tessa, the den—the largest room in the house, so a bad choice for this event—seemed especially empty. And because Paul and Maxie were sensitive to the possibility of frightening the guests (yes, even Maxie), the performance was . . . let's call it lackluster.

Boring is such a strong word.

Paul moved some random objects around the room. Maxie just juggled a little fruit, mussed Jesse's hair (he complained about the assault on his "do" and asked whether we'd hear any "hot tunes") and sort of called it a day.

Then Lieutenant McElone walked in, reminding everyone of the crime scene the night before, and the group just generally dispersed without a smile on anyone's face. I couldn't blame them.

"I have a few follow-up questions," McElone said.

"And here I thought this was a social visit," I said. An awkward moment passed between the two of us as McElone just looked at me. "What with the murder last night and everything."

It was as if she'd been reanimated—she just stopped being still and nodded her understanding. Being closer had actually made McElone and me more uncomfortable around each other.

"We've run as many checks on Roberta and Stanley Levine as were possible, because they cut out of here pretty fast after the crime. The Maplewood police did some interviewing on our behalf this morning," McElone said. "They came up without any connections to William Mastrovy or Vanessa McTiernan."

Swell. I couldn't wait to hear from Senior Tours after the Levines got through telling them how humiliated they were being questioned by the cops just because they'd decided to see some ghosts on their vacation down the shore.

"So you're assuming the two deaths are connected," I said, not a question.

"That's right. It's way too big a coincidence, even though McTiernan's death has not been ruled a homicide. It was an allergic reaction. But the Levines didn't seem to have ever heard of either one of the dead people before last night."

"How can I help, Lieutenant?" I wanted to be through with this by the time Melissa got home from school and I still had questions of my own to ask.

"Do you have any paperwork on the guests that you got

from the service that books them for you?" McElone asked. "It would be helpful to see what their backgrounds are, so I know if there are questions I should be asking."

This led to an ethical question for me. I assumed McElone did not have a warrant for such information or she'd just have handed it to me. So I had to decide if my guests' privacy was more important than finding out whether one of them was a cold-blooded killer, living (albeit temporarily) under the same roof as my eleven-year-old daughter.

On second thought, it wasn't that much of an ethical question. "I keep the records in my bedroom," I told McElone.

"Would you please get them?"

On my way up the stairs, McElone directly behind me (presumably so I couldn't destroy any evidence, although possibly out of fear of being left alone with the ghosts), I noticed that the higher up I walked, the more I felt the urge to sneeze and the more my throat itched. And this was with allergy medicine in my bloodstream.

Something in the house was irritating me, and for once it wasn't just Maxie.

We got to my bedroom and I unlocked the door. With strangers constantly in the house, I keep it locked all the time. I tried to say, "Come on in, Lieutenant," but with my throat reddening and tightening by the second, the best I could manage was, "In."

Just my luck, Vance McTiernan—having learned absolutely no rules of etiquette since arriving—was hovering in my bedroom, directly over the dresser. My first thought was to check and make sure all the drawers were closed; they were. My second thought was: *Where the heck were you when we needed you at the spook show?*

"Oh, there you are, love," Vance said when I walked in, McElone just behind me. "I have an idea about identifying Claudia that might work."

I suppose I *could* have responded to Vance even with the

lieutenant in the room, but she was still freaked out enough about ghosts and frankly, I didn't feel like having a conversation with him at the moment. So instead I looked at McElone and said, "Did you find out anything more about Claudia Rabinowitz, Lieutenant?"

"Ooh, gossip," Vance said, and assumed a sitting position in midair.

"What do you know about her?" McElone answered. It was a classic police trick, answering a question with a question, but I didn't mind sharing information. If she caught the murderer, I could concentrate on my upcoming lawsuit and subsequent bankruptcy.

"From what I hear, she was in her early twenties when she met Vance McTiernan. They spent one night together when the Jingles were playing the Arts Center in Holmdel. What do you know, nine months later Vanessa is born, there are court proceedings verifying Vance's paternity, and not much contact afterward."

"Now, that's just not true," Vance protested, but under the circumstances, I got to control what McElone got to hear. "I saw Nessa whenever I could."

"There appeared to be no love lost between Claudia and Vance," I concluded.

I went to the little table I use as a desk and opened the top drawer, where the guest information I printed out each week is kept. I riffled through it and remembered that Maureen Beckman's paperwork was not there. "There's one missing because Maureen was a last-minute addition," I told McElone. "I have the information in a file on my laptop, but it'll take until your next birthday for that to boot up. Do you need it?"

"Yes, but not now. What else do you know about Claudia?" McElone seemed to be scrutinizing me closely, and I believed it was a test—had I found out about Claudia's extracurricular activities? Would this be an opportunity for me to shine in the lieutenant's eyes?

Wait. "What do *you* know?" I asked. "I asked you first."

McElone sighed a little; it was the cost of doing business with someone like me. "She married Neil Rabinowitz when Vanessa was born, then he died and she married a Randolph Bensinger and had a son, Jeremy, three years after Vanessa. Divorced Bensinger and tried to make a living in the music business as a publicist for local bands on the boardwalk when Asbury Park was the place to be. Didn't do too well, so she got a job for a company that rents construction equipment. Did very well at that, to the point that she ended up president of the business ten years ago and employed her son, Jeremy, as its general manager five years ago. Almost immediately after that she retired to Davenport, Iowa, of all places. And then about two years ago she vanished. All traces vanish. No credit card bills, no rent, no nothing. Nobody ever found any evidence of foul play, or evidence of anything else. I'm asking the Davenport police for all records they have of her and that should come through any minute."

"She spent all that time looking for a replacement for me," Vance said dreamily. "It's kind of touching."

I jumped in to answer both of them. "I hear that Claudia was in town around the time Vanessa died and had made contact with her," I said.

McElone looked like she wanted to say something, then stopped herself.

Vance stood up, which would have hurt a normal man since the top of his head went through the ceiling. "What?" he croaked.

I couldn't help but look up at him, and that was when I realized McElone hadn't been studying me so much as trying to see where I might be looking. "Who's there?" she asked me quietly (but not so quietly that Vance couldn't hear).

"It's Vanessa's father," I said. "Vance McTiernan."

"How did he react?"

"How did I react?" Vance echoed. "How does she *think* I reacted?"

"He's surprised," I told the lieutenant. I am nothing if not a master of the understatement.

She looked serious and continued to stare in Vance's direction, which I knew was doing her no good at all.

"I knew Claud could be cold because Nessa would tell me that," Vance went on, talking mostly to me, which was logical. "Claud always sort of blamed her for being my daughter. But she raised that girl mostly alone. I wasn't there." Vance looked seriously shaken.

I relayed most of that to McElone, who made eye contact with me when I was talking. She didn't bother to look up at an empty space in the air again and told me to ask Vance whether Vanessa had, to his knowledge, had a history of depression. I didn't say anything to Vance, since he was perfectly capable of hearing McElone, who seemed embarrassed to be pursuing the line of questioning with someone she would have bet money wasn't there.

"I didn't know anything about that," Vance said. "She wasn't happy with all that went down when she joined us on the tour, but depressed? I'd say no."

I didn't point out that he'd barely kept in touch with his daughter and had never actually filed for custody, according to what Maxie had unearthed. What was the point of getting the man upset eight years after he died? Besides, I needed him to be in a cooperative state of mind for McElone, and reminding him of his parental failings wouldn't have been the best prescription for that.

"The half brother, Jeremy Bensinger," McElone said after I'd relayed Vance's message. "Do you know whether he had anything to do with the deal that was supposedly coming between Vanessa and Vinyl Records?"

I'd met Jeremy and told McElone so. "He said he was the

one acting more or less as Vanessa's agent with the label."
I looked at Vance but he just shrugged; he'd been dead for
years and on another continent when all this happened.

"That doesn't mean it's true," McElone responded, again
searching the air for Vance and getting fairly close to his actual
location. There was something she wasn't saying that she might
have said if she didn't know Vance was there. "People tend to
exaggerate their importance after someone else is gone and
can't argue."

"I don't know the boy well," Vance said. "His dad was some
artist relations guy or something at a music label and she
divorced him about fifteen minutes after the boy was born,
Nessa told me later. Claud wanted to be a music publicist and
then the husband didn't want her to work. She left."

If McElone had been using a notebook, she would have
flipped it shut at that moment. Instead, relying on her memory, she nodded in Vance's general direction and thanked
him. "Are there any other dead people in the house that
might know something?" she asked me.

"Just the regulars."

"If they tell you anything I can use let me know. But
nothing I hear from you that you didn't see yourself isn't
evidence anyway, because no sane judge on the planet would
allow it. So we'll keep this quiet, okay?"

I'd been doing that for years, so it wasn't difficult to agree
to keep doing it. "Sure."

"There is one thing," said Vance, holding up a finger as
McElone and I were turning to leave the room.

I twisted back to face him. McElone, noticing only my
movement, stopped. "What?" I asked Vance.

"Like I said, I think I can find Claudia so your copper friend
there can question her," he said.

I chose to wait for Vance's brilliant plan before informing
McElone of his claim. "Let's hear it," I said.

"Hear what?" the lieutenant asked.

"Maybe 'let's' wasn't the right word," I told her. "Vance?"

"I told you, I can feel her presence," he said, looking smug. "All I have to do is fly through everyone in the house and then tell you which one she is."

"What did he say?" McElone asked. I realized I'd been standing there looking blankly at him for too long a moment.

"Nothing," I told her. "Nothing at all."

"What do you mean, nothing?" Vance demanded. "I can solve the whole thing right now."

I looked at the lieutenant. "He's suggesting we use an arbitrary method to find Claudia that would involve something you definitely couldn't use in court and I absolutely couldn't confirm for you."

"Of course you could confirm it, love," Vance insisted. "I'd tell you the very first. You could just pass the information along."

"You don't think this . . . guy is a reliable source of information?" McElone asked me, perhaps forgetting that Vance was present.

Now, you have to understand. I've said that Vance McTiernan and the Jingles had gotten me through some rough times when I was an adolescent, and I mean *rough* times. I'd had some problems with rebellion then, my parents were at their wits' end and I had not handled it well. I sat in my room and listened to the Jingles instead of doing something really, really stupid. So it hurt—badly—when I had to look at Vance, then turn to McElone.

"No," I said. "He's not reliable."

Vance's look was absolutely devastated, and devastating. "Okay," he said softly. He evaporated quickly into the air.

McElone must have read my face. "What's wrong?" she asked.

"He didn't care to be seen as unreliable," I said. "He left."

"Oh." She walked out of the room and I followed. "Why isn't that one reliable?"

"His story's been changing every hour on the hour," I said as we walked down the stairs. "I think his heart's in the right place, so to speak, but 'reliable' would be a stretch."

McElone's eyes were still scanning the ceiling. "This place is so weird."

"Tell me about it." I hadn't even told her that Morrie Chrichton had made his first appearance since the murder just over her head when we reached the landing. McElone spotted Maureen sitting, walker to one side, at the entrance to the den, and headed that way. I went to the front door and out to the porch to wait for the cleaning crew, ostensibly. Morrie followed me, which I had expected him to do.

"Where have you been?" I said casually as I stepped onto the porch. It was still a nice warm September day, the incredible heat having abated (for the time being) and the chill that announced winter not yet arrived.

"Trying to make sense of what happened in your house last night," Morrie answered. "I mean, I've seen some freaky stuff in my time. I'm dead, after all. But that took it."

"There's talk Bill Mastrovy was killed over an album Vanessa had recorded. You were alive around here until six months ago. Had you heard anything about that?" I asked him.

"After what went on during the Jingles tour, I stayed away from Vanessa," Morrie said. "But I did catch the odd bit of information. Her brother was definitely talking it up, and from what I hear, Vanessa was just as big a goniff as her old man."

I looked sideways at Morrie, whose big cheesy grin indicated he thought he knew something juicy. "What would that mean if it were in English?" I asked him.

"It means Vanessa was stealing copyrights just like Vance did to me. Other people wrote her songs and she took the credit."

# Twenty-two

Paul was not convinced. "Just because Morrie says so doesn't make it factual," he said, sounding just like Mc-Elone. He floated above the railing on my front porch while I pretended to watch a couple of tourists go by and not acknowledge anything at all incredibly confusing going on. Paul looked at Morrie. "No offense meant."

"Oh, none taken, guv. I love it when people tell me I'm a liar and say I shouldn't be offended." Morrie, enjoying the spotlight—this was the closest he'd ever come to being a front man—was stretched out on his side in the same pose Maxie likes to take.

She, nonplused by Morrie's copping her attitude, folded her arms across the part of her T-shirt that read, "Hulk Smash," and "stood" to one side, frowning at Morrie like he was a bad piece of whitefish.

"I didn't mean that you are a liar," Paul explained. "I was

only saying that your information might not be accurate. I have no doubt that you believe it."

"So I'm either a liar or a moron." Morrie actually smiled. He seemed to enjoy making people uncomfortable, and he was having that effect on Paul.

"Neither. But that's not the issue right now," Paul hurried on. "If Vanessa didn't write the music on an album that was never released, does it really matter?" Paul was watching Morrie's face intently, which was a trial for me because he was sort of blending in with the tree behind him, whose leaves were beginning to think about changing. I've never asked whether ghosts can see each other better than we can see them. It hadn't occurred to me before now.

"As I *understood* it," Morrie said, "Bill Mastrovy wrote some of the songs and her brother wrote the others. But the buzz was big. Vinyl Records was buying it, and even if they weren't the biggest in the business, they could make a splash. You don't make money on records anymore, anyway, because the kids all steal the music. It's touring that makes you a pile."

The tourists were out of sight, so it was easier for me to talk now. "So then why would anybody care about the credit on the songs?" I asked Morrie.

Morrie gave me a look that indicated I was one of the things he'd felt accused of being, and it wasn't a liar. "Credit always matters, dear," he said. "If that song gets played on the radio, that's money. If someone downloads it, that's money. If they use it in a movie, money. I heard the record was hot enough that a decent amount could be had. And besides, it's your work." His gaze bore a hole into my forehead. "A person should be given proper recognition."

"But Vanessa wasn't a household name," Maxie said, trying hard to point out a flaw in Morrie's tale. "Why would her music be worth that much?"

"I'm just guessing," Morrie said, looking like someone

should peel him a grape and feed it to him from above. "But think about it. The music was getting buzz. Even in this terrible business climate, a recording company was going to pay cash money for it."

That was the first shoe, so I waited for the second to drop. "And?"

Morrie did an innocent face that was the opposite of innocent. "Think. What happens to a painting's value when the artist dies?"

"It goes up," Maxie answered. She probably didn't consider that Morrie's question might have been rhetorical.

Paul, stunned enough to forget his goatee for once, gave Morrie a look from head to toe, which in his horizontal state was more like end-to-end. "You think someone killed Van essa to make the value of the recording go up?"

"I wouldn't know, guv. I'm just a washed-up old bass player." Morrie wanted our pity and our respect. He was really just getting me annoyed.

"We can't be sure," Paul said quickly. "Mastrovy told you he was in Vanessa's apartment the day she died. That could mean he killed her or it could be motive for Sammi to have killed him."

:"Then why would Sammi have killed Vanessa?" I asked.

Paul tilted an eyebrow. "Maybe she didn't. Maybe there are two killers."

I sneezed.

"You people seem to have a problem to work out," Morrie said with a nasty grin. "I wouldn't want to hold you up." He vanished before we could question him further.

"So do I tell the lieutenant?" I said.

"Tell the lieutenant what?" McElone was standing in my front entrance, straight as a pine tree and while not nearly as tall, bearing herself as if she were a giant redwood.

Well, the cat was out of the bag anyway (not that we had

a cat, or I'd *really* be sneezing!). "Apparently there are rumors Vanessa was cheating other people out of song-writing credit on her album," I told McElone.

"Uh-huh. And you got this information from one of the people I can't see?" It was clearly a feat of incredible self-control for McElone to keep from rolling her eyes, but the lieutenant was a professional and a good one. Her gaze held steady.

"That's about the size of it," I said.

"Okay. I'll keep it under advisement." She said nothing else as she walked out to the curb, got into her car and drove away without so much as a furtive glance back toward me and my deceased posse.

"What do we do now?" I asked Paul.

"Some of this seems to center on Vanessa's coming album," he answered. "The person who knows the most about that is Jeremy Bensinger. I think we need to talk to him again."

That actually turned out to be a little bit more compli-cated than I would have expected. First, Melissa walked in about ten minutes after our spectral conference, gave me a cursory hello, didn't stop to hear the news about our case and headed up to her room as if it gave her the life force she needed to survive. I began to worry that she might really be turning into an adolescent right before my eyes.

But I had to go see Jeremy and I made Melissa come with me because there was no responsible (i.e., living) adult in the house, but she wasn't happy about it, nor was she pleased when I sniffled and coughed my way out of Harbor Haven. The open window in the car seemed to help. I couldn't say the same at the moment about the allergy pills.

On the way out of town I saw the ghost with the wagon. I almost stopped, but I doubted that she'd be able to tell me anything more about Lester and I didn't have time to talk to her and Jeremy and get back in time to keep my guests—who were already a little shaky—entertained for the evening.

Once away from her room, Liss was pretty much her usual self and listened as she always did with interest and consideration. She asked a couple of good questions and gave a nod when the answers confirmed what she'd already thought.

I had to get that girl to law school before she decided to become a detective. I had only ten years before she'd be out of college.

"Did you believe Morrie?" Liss asked finally. "He's not really the nicest ghost I've ever met."

"Nice and reliable don't always go together," I said. "Sometimes even if a person is not very nice, they still tell you the truth. Sometimes they do it because they want to be mean and the truth isn't very easy to hear."

"You think Morrie wants us not to like Vance, right?"

"I do think he holds a grudge, and yes, he wants us to stop liking Vance. But to answer your question, I don't know if I believed Morrie. He was enjoying it just a little too much, but that doesn't mean he was lying."

"Do you think Vance stole Morrie's songs?" Liss asked. She was clearly trying to determine whose side we were on.

"I think it was a really confusing time and things were happening fast and maybe which idea was whose got mixed up a little," I said. I'd come to realize that all the interviews I'd read when I was a little older than Liss was now were probably stage-managed and sanitized; the truth was in between what was said and when it was said.

We pulled up to Ace Equipment Rentals just after four in the afternoon. I expected that they'd be getting ready to quit for the day, but it appeared to be bustling. Men in hard hats (which were probably mandated by state law) were walking in and out. It took a minute to find a parking space.

The building wasn't much, but the lot behind it was enormous, with tractors, cranes and other construction equipment parked in neat rows, ready for rental. Melissa and I walked up to the entrance and let ourselves in to find what

I guess you'd call a reception area, with a window behind a makeshift counter. I got the impression this wasn't a place that got a lot of walk-in business.

There was no one in the window (really a cutout through a false wall, paneled over in about 1978) but there was a bell on the counter, so I rang it. A young man in a nicely tailored suit appeared from the office area behind, which was visible, and smiled as he approached.

"May I help you?"

I didn't dare steal a glance at Melissa or we both would have broken out in laughter. The man hadn't done one thing to make us react that way, but his elegant appearance was the exact opposite of what I'm sure both of us were expecting, and surprises tend to make us both guffaw. It's a family thing.

"Yes, please," I said. "We're looking for Jeremy Bensinger."

The young man immediately looked concerned. "Yes," he said. "So are we."

"I beg your pardon?"

"He didn't come in to work today and didn't call," the man said. "We're all very worried about him."

Melissa's eyebrows dropped about three inches, which indicated she was fairly concerned as well. She'd already seen one man die during this case (well, she'd been there; I don't think she really saw anything) and now another was not where he was supposed to be.

"Is that unusual?" I asked.

The young man nodded. He still hadn't asked me who we were or why we were asking after Jeremy. "He's never called in sick before, let alone simply not shown up."

That wasn't good.

"You've tried his cell phone?" I asked the young man. I had, but I figured he was just ducking me.

"Oh, sure. A number of times. That's the scary part." He shook his head, banishing the evil thoughts. "I hope everything is all right."

"So do we," I said, and turned away to leave. There was nothing else he could tell me.

"Are you his sister?" the young man asked.

That was odd; if Jeremy was the big cheese around here, wouldn't Vanessa have dropped by occasionally? Wouldn't everyone have heard when she died? Maybe the young man hadn't been working here very long.

"No. I'm a private investigator, but Jeremy isn't in any trouble. Does he talk about his sister a lot?"

"Just about her record. She's supposed to be some kind of great singer."

*Jeremy never told his coworkers Vanessa had died?* "I just want to ask him something."

"You're a detective? What's going on?"

"Sorry," I said. "I'm not authorized to talk about it."

Melissa suppressed a laugh. I didn't have the opportunity to scowl at her.

"I understand," the man said.

Now I felt bad—here this guy was trying to help us, and seemed genuinely concerned about Jeremy, and I was treating him like a functionary. "I'm sorry," I said. "What is your name?"

He didn't so much as blink. "I'm not authorized to talk about it," he said.

# Twenty-three

I called Paul from the car. He could hear but not respond, so I did all the talking (ghosts can't be heard on the phone, seen in photographs or reflected in mirrors; I'm pretty sure they can e-mail). Then he texted to Melissa (it saved time to talk to him and then have him text), since I was driving, and told her Vance was back in the house and we should come home.

Which was just as well, since I hadn't planned on going anywhere else.

When we got there we found Mom and Dad had arrived unexpectedly. Mom said they'd just been in the neighborhood but I knew she wanted to see how Melissa and I were reacting to the events of the night before. We were fine—or at least Melissa was—and that satisfied her enough to stay for the Chinese food I was ordering in for dinner. After greeting her grandparents, Liss of course hightailed it for her room and would no doubt hibernate there until called for feeding.

Vance was indeed back, looking sad and disappointed. He hovered over my currently unused stove like a depressed basset hound, sighing and not saying much. Mom was poring over the menu like she'd never seen one before. Paul floated up from the floorboards and noted Vance, who was doing his forlorn vulture impression and not speaking. Paul stopped rising for a second, considered and shook his head slightly.

"Now can we talk about the case?" he asked. Once he'd been back on the job, he'd become just as zealous and overbearing as before. Why had I missed this?

"Jeremy," I reminded myself.

"Exactly." Paul hovered, not really moving around the room, which was an indication he was thinking hard. If he started tilting to the left I'd know the problem was a real stumper.

"What about Jeremy?" Vance asked.

We all started at the sound of his voice; he hadn't spoken a word since materializing in the room. I wanted to repair our relationship, so I made my voice very tender when I answered, "Jeremy is missing. You heard me tell Paul that before."

Paul shook his head. "You told me on the phone. Vance wasn't here then."

"Missing?" Vance said. He seemed to be in a fog. Not literally, although I'd seen that before.

"Yes. Alison tried to find him on his cell phone and at his job, and he wasn't there." Mom was talking to Vance like she talked to me when I was six and wanted to know why there were no GO signs.

"Who cares where Jeremy is?" Vance wanted to know. "Why aren't you looking for Claudia?"

"You heard the lieutenant," I reminded him. "Claudia disappeared in Iowa after she left the construction house."

"And then she turned up in Vanessa's apartment the day she died," Vance shot back. "That can't be a coincidence."

"It's true," Paul said, although his face looked like it hurt to agree with Vance. "Claudia's disappearance is ominous and her presence so close to Vanessa's death . . ."

"We don't know about that part for sure," I argued. "We know that Sammi said she heard from Bill that Claudia was in town and wanted to see Vanessa. That's like fourth-hand information. I agree we should be looking for her." I looked at Maxie, who rolled her eyes but went upstairs for the laptop. "But we shouldn't forget about Jeremy, or Sammi, for that matter. She was pretty mad at Bill and resented Vanessa."

"You're correct," Paul said. "We shouldn't eliminate any possibility until we have facts that support a theory."

Maxie floated down with the laptop already open (once she cleared the ceiling) and clacking keys madly. "I don't have anything on Claudia Rabinowitz yet," she said. "So don't ask. I'm working on it."

"We're going to have to hire on some operatives," I told Paul. "I can't look for all these people myself." I looked up at Vance. "How'd you like to follow Sammi around and report back on her movements?"

I thought I'd get a lascivious comment but Vance's eyes were cold. "I don't know if you can trust me. You told that copper I wasn't *reliable*." Vance looked down into my eyes with a wry-ness unconnected to any smile. He was making his point.

And I didn't like it. The adolescent worship had worn out—you should never meet your heroes. "How do I know what you're telling me now is *reliable*?" I challenged.

He crossed his arms. "You don't."

My father, who had been quietly observing from a point above the stove (no danger even to a living person of any-thing happening there when Mom and Liss weren't cook-ing), crossed his arms. "Bickering isn't going to help you solve your problem," he said. "Alison, this man was your idol for decades; he deserves some respect."

I'm not used to hearing my father call me out, so I stopped and stared. "Daddy?" I said.

Dad turned toward Vance. "And Mr. McTiernan, you shouldn't *ever* raise your voice to my daughter in my presence, is that clear? It's people like her, never forget, who gave you the life you wanted."

"Understood," Vance said. "My apologies, Alison." Damn! I believed him!

That's when the doorbell rang and the van from Master Clean was at the curb outside my house. A woman in what appeared to be a somewhat stylish sort of hazmat suit was standing at the door and identified herself as Maggie Reznick. She showed me a piece of identification she could have gotten online, but I nevertheless let her and two men into the house. I led them to the hallway, which I had admittedly been avoiding all day.

I stopped at the entrance to the movie room. "If you have any questions, I'll be in the kitchen." Then I told them where the kitchen was, because in a house this big, that can be a question. You don't really need a map but a Sherpa guide isn't an awful idea.

Maggie looked inside briefly. "If it makes you feel any better, I've seen worse," she said.

"That doesn't make me feel at all better. But thanks."

I went back into the kitchen, where apparently Vance was once again trying to sell his plan to somehow intuit Claudia's presence. This time he was peddling it to Paul.

"You understand," he said. "You know what I'm talking about. If I just fly into each one of them, I'm sure I can figure out which one she is."

I didn't have a chance to argue the point before Paul, shaking his head slightly, said, "I don't know. Based on your remembrance of a woman from more than four decades ago? A woman you really only knew for one night? I don't like to deal in feelings, Vance. I need facts."

"I'm telling you, I can do it." Vance's face was impassive, stubborn.

"Well then, why do you need our permission?" I asked. "You keep acting like you're asking for our approval. If you think you have this special power to find Claudia Rabinowitz, why is it necessary for me and Paul to okay it for you?"

Vance's head turned quickly, as if he hadn't realized I'd reentered the room. "I asked you to help me with this," he said after a moment. His voice was quieter now. He seemed almost embarrassed. "It would be wrong for me to take off on my own after I asked for your work."

I had no idea whether to believe him or not. Vance could sell a story, but that one seemed weirdly genuine. It was flimsy but it was the kind of logic that might come from the same guy who wrote an acoustic album and called it *Electric Spur*.

But I didn't get to respond to him (which might have been a blessing, since I had no idea what that reaction would be) because Maggie, the cleaner, appeared at the kitchen door. "Excuse me, ma'am," she said.

I know it's a cliché, but for a split second I actually thought she was talking to my mother. I'm not used to "ma'am." I recovered quickly enough and asked, "What's up, Maggie?"

"Your room is not in bad shape," she reported. "It isn't a very hard job. But we found something in there that you might want to take a look at, if you have a minute."

Paul's eyes lit up, at least as much as they can, and he was out of the kitchen through the wall before I could tell Maggie that I'd be right there and follow her out, trailed by Mom. Dad and Maxie were no doubt following Paul's route.

We got to the hallway and I assessed the job Maggie and her crew had done. "You really did well, and so quickly," I said. I sounded like a TV commercial but you want people like this on your side.

She walked to one of the men in the plastic suits, which in the scope of things were probably an example of overkill. "Where is it, Tom?" she asked.

"The small bin." Tom pointed to what was actually something the size of an ashtray.

Maggie nodded. She was just a step away from where Tom, who was applying some sealing compound to the hardwood floor, was standing. She reached over and picked up the dish.

"These fibers were about where the outline would indicate the person's left thigh would have been on the floor," Maggie said. She showed me the contents of the dish, and at first I thought it was empty. "I'll have to report it to the investigating officer, of course, but I wanted to show you first before I handed it in for them to analyze. I'm surprised the crime scene team didn't catch these."

I leaned over a little closer. Melissa, who had not said a word since entering the room (against her grandmother's wishes and best attempts to keep her outside) was staring at the floor, no doubt trying to determine where the outline must have been. Maggie said she'd called the Harbor Haven police and gotten permission to remove the tape and all signs that something *unusual* had occurred here.

Now at close range, I could see a few strands inside the black dish. "What is it?" I asked.

Maggie flattened her mouth and gave a "can't be sure" gesture. "Some kind of fiber. I'm thinking maybe from a mohair sweater or something like that, but they're very small so it's hard to tell. The cops can do a better analysis."

"They're green."

She nodded. "Yeah. From what I know of the incident, I'm thinking that the victim fell on the fibers heavily, and that kept them from getting covered in . . . anything."

"Do you think it's a clue?" My mother likes to clarify things to the point of obviousness. It's actually a useful tactic. Meanwhile, Paul had studied the strands in the dish and was now assessing the area of the floor Tom was finishing, which to the naked eye was pretty much in the same condition it had been before Bill Mastrovy had made the unfortunate choice of crashing our premiere.

Dad was hovering next to Mom, his permanent place for all eternity, no doubt. But he was watching Tom work and paying special attention to my floorboards.

"I wouldn't have any idea," Maggie answered. "I do the cleaning. The cops decide what's relevant. I just wanted to give you a look." She produced a plastic bag from a box on the floor and put the dish and its contents inside. "This will go to the police as soon as we leave here, and I imagine you'll hear from them if there's anything helpful in the sample."

Within minutes she and the crew had packed up and headed for the door, making sure to warn us not to walk on that section of the floor for at least an hour. Since nobody wanted to come in and finish our viewing of *Ghost*, that didn't seem to be a problem.

The second they were out the door, Dad (who no one in the crew could have heard anyway) said, "Green fibers. Was anybody in the crowd wearing something that color green?"

"I don't think so," Maxie answered. "It's pretty bright. I'd remember."

"It looks like something but I can't remember what," I said.

"Welcome to my life," my mother told her. "About thirty years early."

Paul leaned back as if he were going to rest on the window sill and stopped short of sticking his head into my driveway. "It looks like we have a lot of work to do," he said.

# Twenty-four

Questioning one's guests in a murder investigation is sort of a tricky proposition. Add to the equation the fact that the people being interviewed were *paying* guests, and it gets more complicated by a geometrical factor.

I got a D in geometry. Suffice it to say, I was prepared to tread very lightly today.

The previous evening's huddle had narrowed our list of suspects, but not by much. Paul noted that Tessa and Jesse had been sitting in the front row of the movie room so they could have the cushiest chairs, and that they were still in those chairs when the lights came back on. "While it's not impossible that Tessa could have snuck to the hallway, stabbed Bill Mastrovy and then made it back to her chair before you turned on the light, Alison, I find it very difficult to picture."

Jesse, of course, was not a suspect as a possible new identity for Claudia Rabinowitz any more than Stan Levine, Josh or A.J. Didn't mean he hadn't killed Bill Mastrovy, though.

My boyfriend and his friend were disqualified not just due to gender, but also age: They weren't born when Claudia gave birth to Vanessa.

So just playing the which-one-is-Claudia game, that left Maureen, Tessa, Berthe and Liz. It seemed unlikely that Liz would want to kill Bill Mastrovy, but she had after all insisted on being present when I'd questioned him after Once Again's set at the Last Resort. Was that level of interest a sign of hostility?

No, because there was that whole too-young-to-be-Claudia thing again. But Claudia was not the only suspect.

Let's face it—all I knew for sure at this point was that I definitely hadn't killed Bill Mastrovy. And I was sure I could vouch for my parents and Melissa. I was willing to stand up for Josh. Everybody else was going to have to fend for themselves.

Any one of the other people in the room—dead or alive—might have done it out of revenge, fear of exposure or the desire to really test out a great sharp kitchen knife.

Hey. Wait a minute.

I walked into the kitchen and did something I should have done immediately after the *Ghost* fiasco: I checked my block of knives on the kitchen counter.

The block was full. No knives were missing.

"Well, that's weird," I said aloud, to no one in particular.

I thought. Paul, having slipped into the room at a point when I wasn't looking, asked, "What's weird?" I started a little from the surprise of his voice, but I hoped he didn't notice.

"All the knives are still in the block," I explained.

I didn't have to elaborate. "So where did the knife come from that ended up in Bill Mastrovy?" Paul said, clearly not expecting an answer. "Very good work, Alison. I'm amazed we didn't think of it sooner."

"McElone said it was a kitchen knife," I told him. "She must have already checked in here because she didn't ask me if it was one of mine. So she at least has the same information. But whoever was planning to kill Bill at the movie screening must have brought their own knife. Where would that have come from?"

"Is there a store in town that would sell such items?" Paul said. Since he doesn't get out of the house and didn't live in Harbor Haven at all (his apartment had been on Long Beach Island in Surf City), he doesn't know the town or its merchants nearly as well as I do.

"There are a few," I said. "Assuming they didn't come here packing their own weapon, I can ask around and see who might have sold it. They might remember which of my guests made that kind of purchase. I just wish I remembered exactly what kind of knife it was, and I'll bet you McElone won't share that information."

Paul smiled. "I had Maxie take some crime scene photos with her laptop," he said. "For exactly this purpose, so we could review any evidence. I'll get them from her and see if she can use them to identify the knife." Before I could agree, he was through the ceiling. I thought about his "waking" Maxie at this hour and did not envy him the task.

Of course, the one I had before me was to make my treasured guests feel like I thought each one of them might be a murderer (which technically was the case), so I wasn't exactly thrilled with the morning's potential, either.

Berthe Englund came into the den first, after Melissa had made herself the coffee/milk hybrid and then taken it upstairs to fortify herself through the dressing-for-school process. Berthe, having spent a decent amount of time on her vacation in the surf of the Harbor Haven shoreline, had taken on something of a glow, which I mentioned to her.

"Thank you," she said. "This has been a very interesting

week for me, reconnecting with the sport after some years. I didn't realize how much I'd missed it."

"I'm glad that what happened the other night hasn't ruined your vacation for you." *See how slyly I could bring the gruesome murder into the conversation without being accusatory? Maybe Paul was right; I was getting the hang of this after all.*

"Well, it's not the kind of thing you expect when you go for a relaxing holiday," she admitted. "But I know you didn't plan it. Have the police found out any more about who that poor man was and why someone would want to do something like that to him?"

How to bring this up delicately . . . "The theory is that he was involved in the death of a woman a few months ago and that someone the woman knew did it for revenge." *That wasn't bad. It didn't actually say that McElone or the cops had this theory, but that the theory existed. You'd be amazed how fine a line you can walk once you decide to do some snooping for dead people.*

Speaking of which—Morrie and Vance passed through the wall from the kitchen at that moment, pointing fingers at each other and raising a racket only I could hear.

"You didn't write lyrics!" Vance was insisting. "You listened to what I wrote and you made suggestions!"

"Right, and then you changed the lyrics to what I said they should be!" Morrie countered. "So that's me writing lyrics, isn't it?"

I must have flinched at the sheer volume of it because Berthe looked at me funny and asked, "Is something wrong?"

"No." *Recover quickly, Alison! Some of the guests are still queasy after the murder!* "It was just that I was thinking about the poor man and why someone would hurt him like that." Now I had to shift the focus back onto Berthe. "I guess you didn't actually see what happened, did you?"

"That's like saying that the guy who transcribed *Hamlet* deserves credit," Vance persisted.

"No," Berthe said. "Thank goodness. I was watching the movie and didn't know there was anything wrong until there was all that commotion and the lights came on."

"So now you're Shakespeare, are you?" Morrie and Vance exited as they had come, through the opposite wall. I could be sure that if I asked them later, they wouldn't remember being in the room at all.

"Well, that's good," I told Berthe, having heard most of her answer. Melissa, eyes clouded over with that before-school ennui, spiced with I-just-woke-up-twenty-minutes-ago, stomped into the den, created another café au lait for herself, didn't really acknowledge either of us and stomped out. "But if someone saw something, it would be easier for the police to unravel this whole thing. Did you know Bill Mastrovy?"

"Who?"

"The man who passed away Sunday night."

Berthe's eyes got wider and narrower in succession. "Oh, no," she said. "Never laid eyes on him before. I didn't even know that was his name. Did you know him?"

Me? When did I become a suspect? "I met him once," I said. "The night before it happened."

"Really." Now Berthe was clearly going to go home and tell her friends she'd stayed at the home of a murderess. This interview wasn't going exactly as I had hoped.

"I mean, I didn't really know him."

Paul was dragging—and I *mean* "dragging"—Maxie down through the ceiling. She was dressed in a bathrobe large enough to conceal the laptop (plus a baby elephant if that became necessary) and also to communicate that she had been "sleeping" (or something like that) and didn't appreciate being forcibly awakened.

"I'm coming!" she shouted. "What's the hurry?"

"You have to tell Alison what we found," Paul told her. "Now?"

"I hope not," Berthe said. "I wouldn't want you to lose a friend like that."

What? A friend? Oh, yeah. "No," I told her. "I'd only talked to him that one time."

Berthe nodded slowly, a small move probably meant just for herself. "Well, I didn't see anything. I really didn't see much even after it happened. I didn't want to look once I heard what was there."

"Yes, *now*," Paul told Maxie. "Get out the laptop."

"It's too big," she protested. "The lady will see it. I need a tablet or something smaller." She'd barely had her precious notebook computer back for a month and she was already lobbying for something more up-to-date.

"Maxie," Paul said.

"Yeah, yeah."

"Um . . . how did you find out?" I asked Berthe. "Who told you what had happened in the hallway?"

Maxie positioned herself behind Berthe so she could uncover the laptop without the guest seeing it. It wasn't exactly a necessity with the Senior Plus guests; it was more of a courtesy so they wouldn't constantly be distracted by floating objects. She opened the computer and pressed a couple of keys.

"It was Maureen," Berthe said. "She said a man had been stabbed and I shouldn't look."

Maureen? "But she was all the way at the back of the room," I said. "You were in the front."

"I walked around when the lights came up," Berthe said. "I sort of wanted to see, but then I got a little nervous and decided I shouldn't get a look. So I went to Maureen and asked her."

"Look here," Maxie said, indicating the computer screen, which was close enough to Berthe's head that I could pretend to be looking at her. "We figured out what kind of knife it was."

"It's not a kitchen knife," Paul said. "This knife is something less precise. Its blade is very sharp but fixed and probably had a three- to five-inch blade."

"So Maureen knew what had happened?" I asked Berthe.

"Yes. She didn't seem especially upset about it, but she's short, so she said she had just barely seen him."

"It's a box cutter, not a knife," Maxie said. "Paul's telling you all the details you don't need, but the point is that it's a box cutter."

"It's not a box cutter," Paul shook his head. "It's a utility knife, but an outdoor one, not the kind of disposable or movable blade commonly called a box cutter."

"Where in town would someone buy that?" Paul asked.

"There's a place," Maxie told him. Maxie spends a decent amount of time on the main drag in Harbor Haven and knows all the stores. "It's called Cut It Out. Specializes in all kinds of knives, and I bet you they have some box . . . utility blades."

"Well, the waves are waiting and this is my last day here," Berthe told me.

"Yes! Don't let me hold you up. You have a fun day, Berthe."

"Alison, you should go there and talk to the owner today. See if he or she recalls anyone buying a fixed utility knife, just one, in the days just before the murder." Paul seemed positively giddy.

"Can I go back to bed now?" Maxie moaned, and before there could be an answer, she flew up into the ceiling again. I assumed the whole "go back to bed" thing was metaphorical.

"This is getting close," Paul said. "I would guess we'll have an answer within a day." Pleased with himself, he sank through the floor.

Berthe stopped at the glass doors leading to the deck and the beach. "It's a fine morning," she said. "I'm glad we had this time to talk alone." She waved and walked outside.

"Yeah," I said now that no one else could hear. "We should do this more often."

# Twenty-five

"I didn't want to be a bother," Maureen Beckman said.

With the rest of the guests out enjoying their last day at the guesthouse, Maureen had opted to stay indoors, saying the trip had been a little tasking on her knees and she felt that rest was the way to go. It was the perfect time to interrogate sorry, chat with her about the events of Sunday night. She'd had the best vantage point, theoretically, of anyone in the room when Bill Mastrovy had met his end.

I'd had no luck in finding Jeremy. I'd called Ace and found he was not in his office again today. His cell phone went straight to voice mail. For all I knew he'd hopped a plane to Venezuela or he was in the next room. Either was equally possible. So I was talking to Maureen.

We were sitting in the library, where Maureen had taken up residence with her e-reader. I was nosy enough to try to get a look at the title she was reading, but she was cagey. At the angle she was holding the reader, even if the book were

*How To Kill a Guy Using a Utility Knife* I wouldn't have been able to see it.

"A bother?" I asked.

She seemed to be embarrassed, staring at the tennis balls on the feet of her walker (which did no discernible good on the rug in the library). "With my knee I don't get around as well as I want to, and the walker makes noise. I didn't want anyone to be distracted while the movie was on, so I came in through the rear entrance to the room and I sat all the way in the back. I stayed there the whole time. The walker makes noise." She said the word *walker* like it tasted bad.

"You didn't have to worry about that," I said, trying to be the gracious innkeeper as well as the probing private eye. Paul, who was watching from the science fiction section, looked disapprovingly at me. He wanted me to be all business, and the business he wanted me to be all was not entertaining guests in my house. "No one would have been disturbed. You should have sat wherever you wanted."

Maureen sniffed. "I didn't mind. The screen was big enough and I've seen that movie before, anyway. Tell the truth, I didn't see what the big deal was."

"I know what you mean. Now, something like *Lawrence of Arabia . . .*"

"Oh, that would have been awful," Maureen said. "I mean, it's so long, and those seats in the back were uncomfortable."

*Well, if you'd sat up front in the cushy chairs . . .* I decided to regain my focus, especially since Paul was practically throwing his hands up to the heavens and lamenting his awful luck at being stuck with such an inept partner. "But you must have seen some movement from back there," I suggested. "When that poor man was killed." I'd decided I had to keep calling Mastrovy "that poor man." I wasn't sure about his financial status, but showing some semblance of sympathy made me seem like a concerned and empathetic person. Calling him "the stiff in the hallway" would not have elicited as much in terms of response.

"I saw something," she said. She was speaking slowly, staring past my left shoulder. Paul hovered in a little closer to watch her face. "I didn't know what it was at the time, but I did see some flash of light or something in that direction." Then the spell seemed to break and she looked directly into my eyes. "But I told this to the policewoman who was here asking about it. She knows."

"Tell her you're aware Lieutenant McElone knows about it but she didn't share the information with you," Paul said. "Tell her you're concerned because it happened in your house."

So I did. "Well, I can see how that would worry you," Maureen answered. "I'm sure you're expected to supply some security to your guests."

I shot Paul an acid look, which wouldn't have been able to do any damage even if it had contained real acid. "It's more that I'm always trying to provide a relaxing vacation," I said, trying to keep the edge out of my voice. "After all, the man who died was not one of my guests."

"The poor man," Maureen said.

"Yes. The poor man."

This was getting me just a few feet short of nowhere. "What did you see?" I said, trying desperately to move the conversation back to something useful. "You said you saw a flash. What did it look like?"

Maureen looked at me like I'd asked her if she could please jump over the Empire State Building and bring back a cheese danish. "It looked like movement."

"Yes, but what kind of movement? A man? A *woman*?" I might have pushed that last word a bit too hard. "Did you see Mr. Mastrovy come into the hallway?"

She no longer appeared to be interested in the conversation; her mouth sort of puckered and she let out a long breath. "I don't know if it was a man or a woman," she said with an edge. "It happened too fast. And I didn't see the man at all, but I heard him."

"You heard him?"

There was no longer any pretense to Maureen's expression: She clearly thought I was an idiot. "Yes. I heard him walk in from behind me and then there was a thump in the hallway, which is, I guess, when he fell down. He grunted, sort of. The policewoman knows this. And you know what happened after that, I'm sure." Her hands fluttered a bit, the last vestige of ingénue behavior left in her.

It seemed the right time to end the interview. I reached into my tote bag and pulled out my phone, asking if I might take a picture of Maureen (as I had with Berthe previously) to add to my "Guest Hall of Fame," an institution I'd instituted that very morning. Maureen looked less than thrilled but allowed the photograph to be taken. If we found a clearer picture of Claudia, we could compare it with these. But so far Maxie had not had any luck.

Maureen picked up her e-reader with great ceremony and without a word—but with a stern look—got back to her book. I couldn't argue with that.

I gave Paul a head shake that indicated we should leave Maureen to her reading and went back into the movie room, where I inspected Maggie's work. It was impeccable. You'd never have known that a man had bled to death on this floor less than forty-eight hours earlier.

It took Paul about a minute to follow me, which was a little odd. "I wanted to see if Maureen would act differently once you were out of the room," he said. "She just sat there and read."

"So that would be a no, then."

"You still need to talk to Tessa Boynton," Paul reminded me.

"She's out."

"She's in," he said. "I just saw her in the den."

*Fine.* I found Tessa at the coffee urn, yawning. "It's already been a long morning," she said. "Jesse and I were out early shopping. You always leave souvenirs until the last day, don't you?"

"It's been my experience that most people do, yes," I told her. "I'm glad this was still an enjoyable vacation for you."

"Oh yes," she said, not looking up from the creamer she stirred into her cup. "But I'm giving Jesse the old heave-ho once we get home." Then she looked up at me. "The boy has the brain of a fruit bat."

"I'm sorry to hear it," I lied. "I hope this wasn't a result of what happened at the screening Sunday night." I had to create an opening. Paul was watching now but not saying anything just yet.

"What happened Sunday night?" Tessa asked. "You mean the man who got killed? What would that have to do with me and Jesse?"

I shrugged. "Sometimes people make decisions when they're upset about something unrelated." When The Swine had moved out to California, I'd bought a cappuccino machine despite the fact that I was living in a two-bedroom apartment and didn't drink cappuccino. It's sort of the same thing.

"Well, no," Tessa said, smiling at the suggestion. "It wasn't related to that."

"You and Jesse were sitting together that night," I said. It sort of sounded relevant at the time. "All the way at the front, weren't you?"

"Yes. Jesse said he didn't want anyone sitting in front of him to block his view of Demi Moore. Seriously. I'm asking you."

"So you didn't see anything," I said. Paul frowned. He doesn't like it when I give the suspect the chance to get out of a question.

"We saw everything." Tessa sounded surprised.

The hairs on the back of my neck stood up. "You did?"

"Yes! Every pore on that woman's face. We were in the front row and that's a very big TV."

So much for my neck hairs; they sat down and pouted. "You didn't see anything related to the murder?"

"No," Tessa said. "By the time I turned around Jesse was back in his seat."

Wait. Whoa. "Jesse had gotten up?"

Tessa nodded. "Yes. He went and got a bottle of water from the cooler near the back." Then, as if she hadn't just said something significant, she took a sip from her coffee cup and walked out of the den.

I looked at Paul. "Do we add Jesse to the suspect list?" I asked.

"I wasn't aware he was off the suspect list," Paul said. "Just because there's circumstantial evidence that Claudia Rabinowitz has been here, there's no reason to think she killed Mastrovy herself, or that she was involved at all."

"Are we actually progressing?"

"I suppose. This case is going in a number of directions at once. We need to confirm some information with Lieutenant McElone."

I had given up my reluctance to talk to the lieutenant and nodded. "Let's make a list," I said.


"A list?" Lieutenant Anita McElone looked at the piece of paper in my hand. "Am I the supermarket?"

"No, you're a police detective lieutenant and I'm an innkeeper who moonlights as a private investigator," I said. "Your memory is even worse than mine. You should probably make lists to help you remember."

"Put this on your list: I don't have to tell you everything about the Mastrovy murder. I'm not required to tell you anything at all."

It was so nice we were back to a comfortable routine. "I'm aware, Lieutenant. But if you want to know what I've found out, you might want to negotiate a trade."

She sat down behind her desk, having ushered me to the chair I was starting to think of as mine. "You've found something out?"

"I don't know what it means yet, but yes. I have information. So let's share."

I sat there and looked at her. She, in turn, sat there and looked at me.

"You start," she said. "I've played this game before and what you have is never as good as what I have, so you start this time. Then I can decide what I want to tell you."

"That hardly seems fair." More sitting and looking. "Okay. For one thing, green fibers were found under the body."

"Your cleaning lady told me about that. The fibers are being analyzed. I'm guessing if you'd recalled someone wearing a horrifying green sweater you'd have already mentioned it. Give me something *new*." She was enjoying this. That didn't seem right.

"Come on. How about telling me about the angle of the knife wound? How did the killer approach the body?" I tried not to glance at the list but this was a new tactic and I had not practiced. Enough.

McElone's eyebrows arched as she considered. "Okay. That was kind of interesting. The stab wound was from the side and seemed to have been delivered on the run. It was just good luck that it landed so perfectly and killed him so fast. You were in the next room. What does that tell you?"

"Not that much. It lets out a couple of the guests who definitely couldn't have been running, like Maureen Beckman. See? I told you something valuable."

"You're a citizen. I'm a police officer. That's what you're *supposed* to do."

She was good at this.

"Lieutenant," I said. "Here's what I know: Vanessa Mc-Tiernan's death and Bill Mastrovy's murder are clearly connected. From what I hear, Vanessa's music was worth a decent amount of money but there was a dispute as to who owned it. Mastrovy might have been one of the people with a claim. So I'm thinking we need to find out who is now the owner of that music and if there was some obstacle—in the form of say Mastrovy—in the way. I think it's important we find Claudia Rabinowitz." It was a plan.

But apparently McElone did not think it was a great one. This time she did lean back in her chair, but not in a smug way. She closed her eyes wearily. "If I tell you something new, will you go away?" she asked.

I know an opening when I hear one. "Absolutely."

"And there are no ghosts in the vicinity?"

I looked around and saw one ghost in a police uniform from about the 1970s, judging from the sideburns. I knew she didn't mean him. "No," I said.

She didn't open her eyes. "Good. I'm going to say something and then I'll count to six and open my eyes. When I open them, that chair should be empty. Okay?"

I said nothing, not wanting to jeopardize the deal. My list had long since been discarded, since it was clear McElone was going to tell me just what she wanted to and nothing I was asking about specifically.

"I did some digging after I got the report from the Davenport, Iowa, police. It seems Claudia Baxter Rabinowitz took on the name Judith Holbrook and moved to Iowa because she was involved in some tax fraud that involved the construction business where her son works."

That was a lot to take in but the solution seemed simple. "So get Iowa to send her here and question her," I said, knowing McElone would have thought of that already.

"I can't. She died of pneumonia six months ago."

"That isn't possible," I protested. "She was going to meet her daughter Vanessa the day she died. *Four* months ago."

"The Iowa State Police confirmed it. She died in Davenport in March. That's all I know."

"How is that supposed to help?" I protested.

McElone did not open her eyes. "One. Two. Three . . ."

I was out of the chair and gone by "five."

# Twenty-six

"Dead!" Vance McTiernan looked absolutely astonished. "Claud is dead?"

"It's confirmed," I told him. "She's definitely dead. And before you ask, she died of natural causes, for certain."

"I can't believe it." Vance was less substantial than usual, more transparent. I've seen that happen when ghosts are especially taken aback. "I was sure I sensed her presence here in Harbor Haven."

"That eliminates one suspect," Paul said. "Our next step is to find Jeremy. I need Maxie." He looked up at the ceiling; it's possible he was doing some Ghosternet Local type of thing to summon her, but he didn't seem to get any results.

"I'm getting ready to have Josh's friends over for dinner," I told Paul.

When my phone rang earlier and the Caller ID showed Josh's name, I wasn't expecting him to say that he'd essentially

invited A.J. and Liz to my house for dinner that night. And
yet, that's what I heard.

"I figured it would be a good way for them to see you
and you to see them without all the hoopla of the other
evening," he said when I expressed (perhaps inadvertently)
some trepidation about the timing. "I want them to see that
someone doesn't get killed in your house *every* night." It
was hard to argue with that.

"We can only hope," I said. It was fair—I *had* said I'd
invite his friends to dinner, and after Sunday night's disaster,
he wanted to clear the air as soon as possible. I asked Mom
and Liss if they would cook so Liz wouldn't judge me for
feeding my daughter takeout, but rather for forcing her to
cook my dinner.

Now, Paul sort of stared at me. I'm not sure he understood
that I was serious, but when Maxie dropped down through
the ceiling with Everett in tow, he spoke to her and not to
me. "Alison is preparing a dinner party when there's a case
to solve," he said. He shook his head incredulously and
seemed to be appealing to Maxie's (!) common sense.

"Uh-huh," was the answer he got. He looked toward the
ceiling but sank down into the floor and vanished.

Maxie followed me into the den, where I started to clear
one of the side tables, the one on wheels. "Hey. Doesn't
dinner get taken care of in the kitchen?" she demanded.

"Maxie," Everett said. "There clearly is a plan of action.
Let the Ghost Lady work it out at her own pace." There are
days I want to thank the heavens for Everett, but since he's
dead, that seems somehow cruel. It's hard to explain.

"Have either of you guys seen a dog around the property?" I asked. "I've been sneezing my brains out for days
and I thought I heard some howling at night."

Maxie, for all her posturing and attitude, is a remarkably
poor liar. She looked at Everett, and even as he said, "I have

not seen a dog here," which I'm sure was true, I could tell Maxie was trying to come up with an answer that I wanted to hear.

So I watched her as I rolled the newly cleared side table to the center of the den and opened the leaves on each side to make a dining table that we'd use tonight. I was pretty sure there was a tablecloth in the sideboard. I probably hadn't used it since I'd moved in two years ago, but this was an occasion, right?

"Um . . . I don't know anything about that," Maxie said. Her facial expression, on the other hand, was screaming, "I know all about that!"

"Okay, Malone, you're busted. What do you know?"

"I just told you I don't know anything. Is there going to be an afternoon show today? Everett wants to try out a new bit where he does a military fitness workout in midair." This appeared to be news to Everett, who regarded Maxie with a quizzical look.

"And how are the guests going to see that?" I asked her.

"We haven't worked out all the details yet."

"The dog, Maxie. Is there a lost dog somewhere outside? If there is, we should see if it has tags and call the owner, or get it to a vet to check out before we call a shelter. So stop stammering about how you don't know anything and tell me what you know."

"Honest, I don't know of any lost dog," Maxie said.

I stopped. What was she really saying? "Maxie . . ."

"Be back for the show. Come on, Everett!" She started to drag him out through the wall and toward the shed in the back, but Paul rose back out of the basement, apparently remembering what he'd needed from her before my cavalier attitude had so offended his sense of purpose.

"Maxie!" he said, stopping her escape attempt. "Have you got a possible location for Jeremy Bensinger yet?"

"Jeez!" She looked disgusted. "Do I have to do *everything* around here?"

"We did ask you to find him," Paul reminded her. I wanted to get to the bottom of the dog situation, whatever it was.

"He hasn't left the country," she said without referring to the laptop, which I don't think she had with her. "He hasn't boarded an airplane for anywhere. If you're sure he's not staying in his apartment, I'd look for a friend or a girl-friend or something, but you haven't given me a name to research. Okay, so bye! Come *on*, Everett! I'm not waiting for you!" And she tugged on his arm again.

Everett, who has a sense of humor that he doesn't let show often enough, let it look like she was pulling him against his will and said, "Yes, ma'am," as he went. But he was smiling. Either it's true about opposites attracting or they're not as opposite as they seem. I didn't have time to think about that.

So there was something going on with a dog near my house. I'd be going to pick up Melissa in an hour. That would be the time to grill—*discuss it with*—her. But it wouldn't be easy; my daughter is a tough nut to crack.

Because I am destined never to spend more than three con-secutive seconds alone, Vance McTiernan wailed again. "She's dead!" We'd forgotten that he was the grieving party here.

"You knew her for one night forty years ago," I told him. "You can't be this upset."

He regarded me with something he wanted to feel like contempt but was playing more like mild irritation. "Have you no pity?"

"I'm not heartless, but I think this is about something else, Vance."

"Alison," Paul attempted. "Please. Jeremy."

Vance wasn't listening to him, either. He decided to change topics. "You know, love, what you said about me to that lady policeman really cut to the quick."

The tablecloth had, as might be expected, folds and wrinkles in it from the previous presidential administration, which annoyed me despite its predictability. I like using an iron as much as I like hearing from my ex-husband, invariably explaining why the child support check will be just a little late again.

"It's always about you, isn't it, Vance?" I shot back. "You know, when you first showed up and told me your sad tale I thought you really were torn up about your daughter's death and wanted only justice for her. I believed the songs you wrote—or claim you wrote—and the shows you put on. But everything you do is about making sure everybody knows what a great guy Vance McTiernan is, and that sort of cuts the nobility out of it." I flared the tablecloth out over the table, thinking that maybe I could just put enough heavy things on it to flatten it out. But that didn't seem terribly plausible once I got a good look. Where had I put the iron?

"You believe that?" I wasn't looking at Vance but he sounded legitimately hurt. "You really think I didn't care about Nessa?"

I exhaled. "I honestly don't know, Vance. I just know my life was a lot less complicated when you were just a voice on an old piece of vinyl. I—"

"No need, love," Vance cut me off. "If that's what you think of me, I'll sod off." And before I could blink, he was no longer in the room.

"I'll sod off"? What had that meant? Was he going off to lick his wounds or was he leaving and never coming back?

For reasons I couldn't quite explain, it mattered to me. Even now, with all he'd put me through and all the lies, I didn't want to end things with Vance McTiernan on bad terms. The lyrics to "On My Own," an early Jingles song, kept playing over in my head all of a sudden:

*Don't leave me*
*On my own*
*Even now*
*Not alone*

Okay, so it was an early effort, but if you've heard the original recording, you know how affecting the plaintive singing became in Vance's capable throat. I called to him, not loudly, a couple of times, but there was no response.

Suddenly, finding the right dishes for tonight didn't seem all that urgent.

None of the guests required anything and it seemed that I'd be left to ponder my possible (okay, probable) rudeness toward Vance and its repercussions for a while, but Paul followed as I was heading up the stairs to get another allergy pill from my bathroom medicine cabinet. I stopped on the stairs and looked at him.

"What do you know about a dog?" I asked him.

"What dog?" he asked back. "Is this related to the Mastrovy murder or Vanessa's overdose?"

"Neither. It's related to my sneezing and watery eyes."

"I don't know anything about a dog," Paul said. "Nor should you be concentrating on that right now. We have too many suspects and not enough facts. The only person left whom we can locate is Sammi Fine, and I don't think we've explored her motives enough yet. Do you have time to see her again before your *dinner party*?"

"You're going to get mad at me for having company for dinner? What have you been up to, Sherlock? Have you figured out the green fibers?"

Paul looked away. "I don't have a strong theory yet."

"Let me know when you do," I said, and went upstairs for some Allegra.

But Paul, cognizant that he shouldn't follow me, was still waiting when I came back down just a minute later. "Alison," he said. "Please."

I probably rolled my eyes like Melissa. "Okay," I told Paul. "But if I talk to Sammi again, will you leave me alone for this dinner?"

He actually crossed his heart with his finger. "You'll never even know I'm here," he said.

Sammi Fine agreed to meet me at a Starbucks around the corner from her office. I got a bottle of water and Sammi found a double chocolate chip muffin to go with an iced latte.

"I don't know any more than I told you already," she said, just picking at the muffin. Her mood was more somber than emotional now; she'd had a couple of days to absorb Bill's death. "I spoke to the cops. They asked me all the questions. What's left?"

I dove in. I had just enough time to get back and pick up Liss after a short interview, so directness was key. "Where were you on Sunday night?" I asked.

She didn't react; she'd been asked by McElone before. "I was home, watching *Game of Thrones*," she said. "Want to know who got knifed on that show? That I can tell you. And no, nobody was with me. If I was a smart killer, I'd have worked out an alibi."

Maybe I could play one suspect against another. You can sometimes get people to say things they shouldn't if you're not asking about them. "What do you know about Vanessa's brother, Jeremy?" I asked.

"He used to come around to rehearsals and some gigs," Sammi said. "Thought Vanessa was Joan Jett or something. Told me her staring off into space was her 'communicating with her muse.' Seriously. I mean, she had an okay voice but he thought he was going to make millions off of her."

"*He* was going to make millions?" Jeremy's line had been all about how Vanessa was a star-in-waiting and how cruel it was that it had been robbed from her. "How did he factor in her career?"

"He was, like, her manager or something," Sammi told me. She picked a chocolate chip out of the muffin and ate it somewhat daintily. "He shopped her record around and got Vinyl Records interested enough to sign her, but Vanessa was going to turn it down, Bill said."

*Turn it down?* First I was hearing about that. "Why?"

"She used to say fame and success had broken her family and she thought it destroyed her father." Sammi took a sip of her latte, which she seemed to think was too sweet. "Said she made the music for herself and her friends. She wanted to distribute it for nothing. But Jeremy and Bill were trying to talk her out of that."

"Jeremy and Bill? Together?"

"You didn't know this? Yeah. Jeremy produced the record, put his heart into it when all Vanessa was doing was singing. She wrote a couple of the tracks, but mostly it was Bill. Then Jeremy said *he'd* written four songs that Bill knew were his and they started to fight about it. Until then, they'd been thick as thieves, those two."

"How about after Vanessa died?" I asked.

"I don't know. Jeremy stopped coming to the gigs and Bill and I were a thing—or at least I thought we were. Now I don't know anything. Can you ever know anything?"

"Actually, I'm starting to think I can." I thanked Sammi for her time and left. I had a daughter to retrieve and a report to make to Paul.

When I picked Melissa up from school, I was feeling less allergic, but I knew that effect would last roughly until I got home. I didn't tell Melissa about the progress in the case because I had a question for her.

"Have you seen a dog around?"

"Why, have you?" she responded. It was a cagey answer. Melissa loves dogs and I suspected that if I admitted that I hadn't actually seen a dog, she'd fall back on flat-out denial.

"No, but I've certainly inhaled some of one," I told her as we drove through what we unironically referred to as Harbor Haven's "downtown," the two-block strip of little shops and

Phyllis's *Chronicle* office. "If you know about a dog living near our house, you need to tell me about it. Right now."

"A dog living near our house?" she repeated.

"Don't divert," I warned. "I'm asking you directly. And you know we don't lie to each other." We've been very careful about that all her life. I'm proud to say I haven't lied to my daughter for quite a while, possibly since the Santa Claus debacle of five years earlier.

"There's no dog I know about living on our land," she said. There was no waver in her voice.

Wow. That took the wind out of my suspicious sails because I trusted her. "Any other ideas why I'm sneezing and itching like this?" I'd like to make it clear that I wasn't actually asking my daughter but stating the problem out loud, rhetorically.

"Maybe somebody's wearing that perfume Grandma used to use," Melissa suggested. She's heard the family lore and I supposed it *was* possible that one of the guests was wearing White Shoulders . . .

There wasn't much to say after that. So I told her about my various adventures. She asked me if I trusted Sammi and I said I didn't know. Because I didn't know. But she had seemed convincing.

The immediate order of business upon arriving home was the afternoon spook show, at which I would undoubtedly have to explain to a disappointed group of guests why I had failed them yet again and was therefore unable to produce Vance for a song or two at their last official gathering. It had not been my best week as an innkeeper or an investigator.

Liss went up to her room to drop off her backpack and prepare for the "flying girl" sequence and I went into the kitchen to prep it for the cooking she and Mom would be doing for tonight's dinner. With Josh's friends coming, there was no way I'd trust my own "skills" as a chef with the evening's meal.

And so I was the first one to find the small kitchen knife on the counter. The one that didn't belong in my block with the other knives I didn't use. The one with a fixed blade that was sharp on one side.

The one that looked like the utility knife that had killed Bill Mastrovy.

Was someone making a threat?

I took in a strong breath and called for Vance. But he didn't come.

So I called Paul, and he did.

# Twenty-seven

**"How did you marinate this chicken?"** Liz Seger asked.

I had, personally, *not* marinated the chicken, so I turned toward Melissa, sitting very straight in her dining room chair (which was really a den chair, since this was the first time we'd used the space as a real dining room) and said, "What did you use?"

"Well, I can't tell everything because Grandma says it's a secret family recipe," Liss said as Liz's eyes widened a bit. "But it had to marinate for at least an hour in salad dressing, lemon juice and two other ingredients, and I covered the bowl with plastic wrap to hold all the flavor in."

Liz's jaw dropped. "You cooked this?" she said to Melissa. "Really?"

Usually when an adult condescends to my daughter, I either turn my rapier wit on her (it's usually a woman, and I'm sorry about that but it's true) or better yet, let Melissa do so herself. But this was a special circumstance: I'd vowed against all odds to do nothing tonight but be especially nice to Liz.

I suppose I should back up: After I found the knife on the kitchen counter, Paul appeared in a nanosecond of my shouting his name, perhaps thinking someone had already used it on me. We'd discussed the object, which I had been cool-headed enough not to touch, and he said the best thing to do was to call McElone immediately. I saw the logic in that, hit speed dial (that's right; I have the local police lieutenant on speed dial) and told the lieutenant about my discovery.

She thought the culprit was indeed sending a message, and although she felt it would be fruitless, sent a uniformed officer to very carefully pick up the knife (which she told me not to touch despite my informing her of my cool-headedness at not doing so) and bring it back for official examination.

Other than that, McElone added, "The only thing to do is continue on as if nothing had happened. Maybe that's how we can smoke this person out."

Lovely. A killer was loose in my house and the cops wanted to put me, my daughter and my guests at risk in order to "smoke this person out." There was a flaw in the logic, and I was beginning to think it was me.

Paul agreed with the lieutenant—he's always taking her side—and asked what I'd had planned for the rest of the day. I told him the afternoon spook show and then dinner with Josh, A.J. and Liz. Mom had offered to take Melissa home with her after preparing the meal, leaving me with my boyfriend and his friends, but anyone who wants to get to know me had better get to know my daughter, so I declined her offer.

Once Mom heard about the knife (from Paul), she insisted on leaving my father behind at the house "in case there's trouble." So although the other three adults at the table didn't know it, the dining room was getting pretty crowded, since Paul, Maxie and Dad were all present. I'd given Paul a pass on his promise to stay away during the dinner because, you know, killer loose in the house and all that. Paul looked interested, Dad looked concerned and Maxie was moving things around behind A.J. and Liz just to annoy me and amuse Melissa.

"Yes," Melissa told Liz. "I've been learning cooking from my grandmother for a while now." She gave me a funny look, which translated into *why aren't you using your rapier wit on her?* Or something to that effect.

"From your grandmother?" Liz said, pushing the point. "Not your mom?"

Josh put down his water glass and motioned toward his plate. "It's really delicious, Melissa. Thank you for cooking tonight." Definite boyfriend points there.

Tessa Boynton walked into the den, saw us around the table and put her hand to her mouth. "Oh, I'm sorry!" she said quietly, as if she'd just made a loud noise in a library.

I stood up. "No reason to be, Tessa," I said. "What can I do for you?"

"Oh, nothing!" Tessa seemed horrified. "I'm fine, really. I'll just leave you to your dinner." And she turned and left before I could protest.

I looked at Josh. "Should I go after her?"

"You probably should," Liz volunteered. "She's your guest, and you're in the customer service business." Liz ran a successful consulting firm, so I took her at her word.

"You're right, thank you," I answered. "That's just what I should do." I walked into the hallway, saw no sign of Tessa and walked back into the den to resume my seat. "Well, that was easy. Thank you, Liz."

"You're going to let her tell you how to run your place?" Maxie seemed appalled when I would have expected her to be amused. Practiced, I ignored her.

I thought Melissa was going to feel my forehead for signs of fever. Even Josh's eyes had lit up with curiosity. Dad, in the corner over the fireplace, paid no attention to the commotion and looked up the chimney, head through the brick, no doubt checking to see if I needed to fire up a creosote log before the season began in earnest.

"Not at all," Liz said. She had probably never heard of sarcasm, but to be fair, I wasn't showing any intentionally. "We businesswomen have to help each other out when we can."

Jesse opened the glass doors from outside, letting in a cool breeze. Everyone looked up (except those who were floating overhead and had to look down). "Anybody seen Tessa?" he asked. "I think she's hiding from me."

"If she has a brain," Maxie offered.

"I haven't seen her," I said lightly, resisting the urge to give Maxie a stern look. I do that so often the urge barely even makes itself noticed anymore. "Have you looked on the beach?" I asked, despite it being clearly where he'd just come from.

"I'll have to go back and check," Jesse said. "Hey, is that chicken?"

We admitted it was, and while he didn't actually ask for any food ("I had a salad for dinner and I'm stuffed"), he did look longingly at the table until Melissa offered him a biscuit. He took it like a grateful puppy and headed back from whence he'd come.

"Maybe having the dinner in this room wasn't the best idea," I said to no one in particular.

"I was going to say something, but I figured I'd be polite." Liz.

A.J. bailed me out this time. "I think it's a lovely room," he said. "Would someone pass the green beans, please?"

Josh did so, but not before Berthe Englund walked in from the library side. "I should just open up an ice-cream stand in here," I muttered, then stood up. "Hi, Berthe! What can I do for you?"

She reacted much like Tessa had, seemingly stunned to encounter people eating in here and somehow embarrassed, as if she'd intruded on us doing something private. "I'm so sorry," she said. "Didn't know you were eating."

"It's absolutely fine," I said, walking toward her before she could turn tail and run. Liz could *not* have another chance to tell me how a good businesswoman operates. "Please. I'm at your service. What do you need?"

"You're sure it's not an intrusion?" She looked mortified.

"Of course not. Would you care to sit down?" I gestured toward the table, only then realizing the only available seat was my own.

"On what?" Maxie asked, laughing.

Paul, I'd noticed, was watching each guest who walked in, getting close to their faces and examining them intently. He doesn't really think he can determine who is guilty of a crime this way, but he does seem to get some information about each individual character. I'm not sure if it involves close observation or some odd intuition.

"No, I'm fine," Berthe said. "I was wondering if we might—that is, some of the people staying here—mostly Tessa and me—we'd like to put on a movie in the room, you know. Is that okay?"

"As long as it isn't *Lawrence of Arabia*," Maxie offered. She was in an especially wise guy mood tonight, which only made me more irritated. I had guests besides my guests, I was trying to make a good impression and there was a decent chance there was a murderer in the house. Listening to Maxie be "hilarious" was the step too far, but I couldn't say anything for fear of looking rude to the invisible person. Ghost etiquette is very tricky.

"I'm planning a game night for later, but of course you can," I told Berthe. "Do you need help setting it up?"

"No, thank you," she answered. "It's pretty simple. We've already done it, to tell you the truth. Just thought it would be a good idea to say something to you before you heard noise coming from in there."

"Feel free. Enjoy the movie," I said. "What are you watching?"

"*Die Hard*," Berthe said, heading toward the movie room. "The first one."

Well, at least nobody seemed especially upset about spending time back there when a man had been knifed to death the last time we tried to show a movie.

Once Berthe was gone, I resumed my seat, although dinner was almost over by now. Melissa had not mentioned a dessert, which was just as well. Liz struck me as one of those women who hears the word *chocolate* and goes into a diatribe about how unhealthy anything that tastes good must be.

Still, it was my mission to convince her that I was the greatest thing since sliced kale, so it was back to work. "So tell me about consulting," I said. "It sounds fascinating."

"I've already told you twice," Liz answered.

"She steps in when a business is faltering and sees to it that the bottom line improves," A.J. jumped in. He turned to Liss. "It's really a pretty simple process."

"Fascinating," I repeated.

"Hardly *simple*," Liz muttered.

Melissa, who had likely decided I'd gone mad, asked, "May I go watch the movie after we clean up?"

"You can go ahead now," I told her. "You cooked. We'll clean up."

Faster than one of John McClane's speeding bullets, she was up and gone. I stood to start clearing the table, undoubtedly missing the incredulous look Liz was giving me.

"*Die Hard*?" she said.

I picked up my own plate, plus Melissa's and Liz's,

deciding I'd get the other two on the second trip, but Josh was up and at it before I could say anything.

"Yeah," I told Liz. "It's an action movie with Bruce Willis."

"I know what it *is*," she answered. "Are you sure it's appropriate for an eleven-year-old?"

I wanted to point out that the real question was whether the movie was appropriate for a nine-year-old, since that was the age Melissa had been when she first saw it, but then I remembered my mission tonight was to be nice to Liz. This presented, unsurprisingly, a conundrum.

"I know it gets a little raw," I said, "but Liss is really very mature for her age, and I'm sure she can handle it." Based on the six other times she'd seen it and had not been outwardly affected other than to ask why Professor Snape was pretending to be German.

Josh and I cleared the plates while A.J., over my protests, picked up the glasses and some silverware to bring into the kitchen. Liz, I noticed, was not moving from her seat.

"I just don't know that I'd let my daughter see a movie like that at this age," Liz huffed, despite not having any children at all. I wondered if this would be an issue if Melissa had been my *son*, but that just led to me wondering why I'd name a boy Melissa.

My goodwill tour was about at its breaking point when Maureen Beckman ambled slowly into the den, eyes on her feet and the fuzzy green tennis balls on the legs of her walker. She did not seem as shocked as the other guests had been at the spectacle of people eating dinner in what had once clearly been a dining room. She just moved through as well as her arthritic hip would allow. "I'm heading to the beach for the last night," she said. "This is the most direct route."

"Of course," I told her. "You feel free to come through whenever you like."

Maureen stopped and stared at me. "I do," she said simply.

Josh took the plates out of my hands and he and A.J. headed into the kitchen. If there was a guest in the room, he knew I needed to be available.

"It's just so bloody and violent," Liz said. She had tenacity, if you consider that a plus.

"What is bloody and violent?" Maureen said, her tone sharp.

"My friend is saying she thinks the movie they're watching inside might be a little rough for Melissa," I explained. "And she's probably right." I actually reached over and squeezed Liz's shoulder.

Josh, behind Liz's shoulder, mouthed, "Who are you?"

"I'm concerned about Melissa," Liz told her, intimating that perhaps I, Melissa's mother, was not.

"That's what makes us love you so," I said. Okay, there was probably an edge of irony in my voice by this point, but then . . .

It was the fuzzy green tennis balls on Maureen's walker that did it. Not really, but sort of. Because I finally realized they reminded me of the green fibers found under Bill Mastrovy's body, and then I remembered where I'd seen that color green before.

On the carpet pads protecting the floor of Jeremy Bensinger's car.

I stood straight up like Roy Scheider does in *Jaws* when he sees the shark at close range for the first time. I avoided telling anyone we needed a bigger boat, but looked up at Maxie and Paul and hissed, "*Get Vance.*" They gave each other a confused look, then Maxie headed out toward the movie room. Maybe she knew something I didn't about Vance's whereabouts.

Paul swooped down, questions in his eyes. "What happened, Alison?" he asked.

"Vance who?" Liz asked.

Maureen shook her head. "Vance McTiernan. He plays guitar here." Then she walked to the beach doors and left.

"Who's Vance McTiernan?" Liz asked, cementing my opinion of her.

Paul's eyes were intent on me. "You know something," he said. "Tell me."

"It was Jeremy Bensinger," I said. "He killed Bill. I'm guessing about Vanessa, but he definitely killed Bill."

From behind me I heard the very voice I'd been hoping not to hear. "I don't know what you're talking about," Jeremy said. "I didn't kill anyone."

"Oh god," Liz said. "They're all talking about killing again."

"Him?" Paul asked. "How do you know?"

"It was the carpet in your car, Jeremy," I said, really answering Paul's question. "You got out of your car after you followed Bill here and when you killed him, and some of the fibers from that carpet landed beneath him."

Jeremy, dressed for the office and not the beach, had no weapon that I could see. I don't know why, but somehow that didn't make me feel better. "Why would I kill Bill?" he asked, ignoring my remarks. "He was a friend." He started to walk toward me.

"I'm going to find a cell phone and text the lieutenant," Dad said. He was out the door before I could fish mine out of my pocket. My father is a problem solver.

"Because once he heard from me that Vanessa was murdered, he put two and two together and figured it was you who did it. And because he wanted his due on the songs he wrote for Vanessa's album but you didn't want to share, did you?" I was prodding Jeremy to keep his focus on the conversation and not the objects moving around the room. Vance and Maxie appeared from the ceiling. Maxie, sizing up the situation, headed for the fireplace to get a poker. Vance just looked shocked.

"Why should I?" Jeremy demanded, getting just to the table where Liz was staring at him as if he were a madman, which might have been the first time Liz was right that evening. "I was entitled! I worked on every one of those songs, and now they were going to pay off! And he was going to ruin it. I didn't want to kill him but he was going to go to the police and lie to them about what happened with Vanessa."

I was instinctively circling back away from Jeremy and toward Josh, who is always a source of security. "Lie? You're saying you didn't kill your sister? If you didn't kill Vanessa, who did?" I asked. Not only did I want Jeremy to keep talking, I also wanted to know the answer.

"Vanessa was an accident," he said defensively. "I didn't know there was soy in her food."

I shook my head as Maxie circled around him, but Jeremy, even without seeing the poker flying (Maxie had secreted it in her jacket) must have felt the threat because he picked up a knife from the table and reached . . . for Liz.

"You didn't know there was soy in soy sauce?" I asked. Maybe I could lunge toward him; Maxie was positioned badly and would have to float around.

Jeremy pulled up on Liz's chin with the flat end of the knife, and Liz, who was trying to protest, stood without speaking, but she did make a gurgling sound. "Vanessa had a million-dollar voice she wanted to give away for *nothing*!" he shouted. He was sweating heavily through his suit jacket. "Her father had screwed up his fame and fortune and she thought that was the way it was had to be."

Vance stopped in space, stunned. "Me?" he said. "It was my fault?"

A.J. pushed in through the kitchen door, smiling, then stopped in shock. "What the hell is going on?"

"It's a situation," I told A.J. "We're going to make sure Liz doesn't get hurt, right, Jeremy?"

But he wasn't necessarily hearing what anyone but he was saying right now. "I had to do what was necessary," he said. "Vanessa would be heard, and heard more because she'd be dead. I held a gun on her while she drank what she had to drink. She kept begging me to call the rescue squad, and I *wanted to* but I *couldn't*!"

Maybe sympathy was the way to get through to him. "I totally get that," I told him. "She was wasting her talent and all you wanted to do was show it off. She was being unreasonable."

"Don't condescend," Jeremy said. He shook his head as he pulled back on the knife and tried to maneuver Liz backward with him. She, characteristically, was being stubborn and resisting. But Jeremy was talking directly to me. "You're going to do exactly as I say or your good buddy here gets her throat cut."

"You're making a huge mistake," I told him. "I don't even like her."

"Excuse me?" Liz croaked.

"Huh?" A.J. chimed in. I couldn't tell what that meant.

"It's true," I told Jeremy. "She's a really annoying know-it-all. She's been getting on my last nerve all night."

Maxie looked down. "I can't guarantee he won't slit her throat if I hit him," she said. "Should I hit him?"

I shook my head again. Maxie looked a little disappointed.

"Here's how it's gonna work," Jeremy said. "You're not going to do anything. I'm going to take your friend here and drive away in your car because I actually had to walk here from the beach. Couldn't let anyone hear me drive up, could I? Then the two of us are going to drive away. If I'm confident no cops are following us, I might let her go in a couple of days. That's how it'll work."

"No!" Liz protested. "I don't want to go!"

There was only one card left to play. "You can't have my car," I said.

"What?" Liz stared at me, eyes wide.

Jeremy also stopped and looked, but his eyes were clear and focused. "I'm taking your car."

"You don't care what he does with *me* but he can't have your *car*?" Liz shouted.

I stole a glance at Josh, who was suppressing a grin. He knew what I was doing.

"I can't let you," I told Jeremy, buying time. "I need that car."

"You have insurance," he suggested. "Mine's too far away." He was going to reason with me now.

"The thing's too old. They won't give me what it's worth and I won't be able to replace it."

"Ex*cuse* me?" Liz said. "I'm the one being kidnapped here!"

Jeremy looked at Liz. "I'm starting to see your point about her," he told me.

A.J. frowned. "Hey." He took a step forward, but Jeremy held up the knife and A.J., chastised, held his ground.

From the corner of my eye came movement, but I forced myself not to look so Jeremy wouldn't know what was coming. Maxie with a shovel? Dad with a cop? The lady with the wagon looking for Lester? I had no idea.

And that's why it was such a surprise when Vance, launching himself like a projectile at Jeremy, hit him low, below the waist and just about at the knee. He dropped the knife and let go of Liz while letting out an "oof" noise that sounded exactly like the ones in old cartoons; it was perfect.

He struggled, but Vance was unrelenting; he was a machine, automatic and unforgiving, almost suffocating Jeremy with his being, holding him down. He finally passed out, presumably from lack of oxygen.

"You killed my little girl," Vance said deeply. "You're lucky I didn't kill you."

I had no time for his triumph. "Get something to tie his hands," I said to Paul. He started to take the tiebacks off the drapes near him to the right. A.J. watched them fly by and mouthed some words but no sound came out of his mouth.

Liz, having fallen to the floor, slowly propped herself up on one elbow. "What the hell was that?" she demanded.

"I told you, it's a haunted house," I said. "What did you expect?"

Paul started in on tying Jeremy's hands as Josh moved to my side and A.J. walked—a little casually, I thought—to Liz. He knelt down and asked if she was all right.

"Of *course* I'm not all right!" she wailed. "That nut was holding a *knife* to my throat and Alison told him to go ahead and kill me!"

"I didn't go quite that far," I muttered. Josh put his arm around me and made a noise that was trying not to be a laugh.

Suddenly the room was a beehive: Dad emerged from the front room, saying he'd found Berthe's cell in the movie room and had texted McElone, who would no doubt be calling me any second.

Morrie floated in from the beach side, hands on hips. "Where the hell'd you go, mate?" he admonished Vance. "I thought we was getting somewhere."

Melissa showed up in the doorway and assessed the scene: Paul finishing up tying Jeremy's hands, Morrie floating over a smiling Vance, Josh holding me close and A.J. helping Liz off the floor with one hand.

"And I thought Bruce Willis was busy," she said.

# Twenty-eight

When Lieutenant Anita McElone comes to my house these days, it is with less anxiety than she used to show, but no more joy. Of course, coming to deal with the aftermath of a murder isn't often call for dancing, but McElone seems to take out her irritation on the house. She acknowledges the ghosts, but isn't happy about it.

"So based on the initial interrogation, what I've got is that your Mr. Bensinger forced soy sauce down his sister's throat because she was going to pass on a big money contract," she said to me while the group of us—me, Dad, Paul, Morrie, Vance, Maxie, Josh and Melissa (since A.J. and Liz had left after McElone okayed it)—sat in the movie room, having once again cut short a screening for the guests, who appeared somewhat discouragingly to be getting used to it.

"Not exactly," I said. "From what he was saying before you got here, he held a gun on her and made her drink it. Which is somehow even colder."

McElone nodded at that. "Then he followed Bill Mastrovy from his apartment to here and knifed him because Mastrovy, once he knew Jeremy had killed his sister, was going to turn him in. But he didn't want the cops involved, so he was coming here to tell you. Is that it?"

"That's what I gather," I answered. "Jeremy thought if he could hold out long enough to get the record money he could fly to some cushy country without an extradition treaty and lie on a beach. On a first album. That's some serious crazy."

"Did he confess when you arrested him?" Josh asked the lieutenant. McElone shook her head. "He says you all are lying. But I paid a second call this evening to Sammi Fine and she confirms that Bill and Jeremy saw each other the day you went to the club to see Once Again. They argued about the record again and Bill was foolish enough to suggest he knew Jeremy had killed Vanessa McTiernan."

"Bill said he was in the apartment the day it happened," I remembered.

"I'm guessing he wasn't there at the actual time of the murder," McElone said. "He might've tried to stop it, and there was no sign of a struggle in the apartment. But I'm thinking he may have found her and been the one who made the anonymous 911 call."

"Poor Nessa," Vance said, his face pained now. "All she wanted to do was get her music out and let her loved ones hear it."

"Unbelievable." I shook my head. "I'm having a hard time getting my head around it."

"Unfortunately, it's not that crazy a story this time," McElone said. "At least your ghosties didn't have a hand in it."

There was considerable avoidance of eye contact in the room despite the fact that the people in question couldn't be seen by the lieutenant anyway.

"I guess not," I told her. "Of course, it was Vance who first told me about Vanessa and started this all rolling."

McElone's eyes went dull, like she'd heard something she'd like to un-hear. "Right," she said. Then she said her good nights and headed for the door. "Oh, there was one thing." She turned back and looked at me.

"What's that?"

"The record company is going to pass on the album," she said. "They decided a debut album with no chance of a follow-up was a bad business risk. Sammi said she'll see to it that the songs get distributed for free the way Vanessa wanted.

"You see what happens when someone tries to claim they wrote something all by themselves?" Morrie shouted at Vance.

"Are you starting that again, you old swine?"

There was a good deal of shouting as they left at a very high speed.

Melissa, reminded there was school the next day, very reluctantly headed upstairs. Josh stood, telling me what I already knew—that he had to open his store early the next morning. But he kissed me nicely and then we headed for the front door.

"A.J.'s breaking up with Liz," he said casually when we got there.

"What? I did all that pretending to like her and giving a murderer the wrong impression for nothing?" I pulled him close. "You owe me."

He was about to lean down and start paying off when I heard the sound of the dog howling again. I turned my head.

"What?" Josh asked. He looked concerned and assessed my face.

"Didn't you hear that?"

"Hear what?"

And then it made sense.

Phyllis had called to do the usual follow-up once she'd heard ("on my police scanner, for goodness sake, Alison") about the arrest at my house. I'd told her what I knew (minus Vance because that would make it too complicated), she'd admonished me a few times for not calling her immediately and we'd left it at that.

Jeannie had called to say she'd told Tony about the coming baby and he'd reacted exactly as I'd said he would. He was now calling his family and friends to celebrate. Why she'd ever doubted he would was beyond her comprehension. She never once asked about the murder investigation. Jeannie is among the best in the world at not dealing with things that she'd prefer weren't there.

The next morning I rolled out the coffee and tea urns on my new cart, which I'd lugged home and assembled last night because I knew I wouldn't be able to sleep. It was especially early (see previous comment re: no sleep), and instead of waiting for Melissa to appear downstairs, I went up to her bedroom in the attic to wake her.

I'd taken an allergy pill but was already tearing up by the time I hit the second step. I'd expected it, but that didn't make the feeling any easier to handle.

I found my daughter hanging halfway off her bed, faced away from the stairs I was climbing, as if she were looking for a stray shoe she'd shoved too hard under the bed. I climbed up to floor level and closed the staircase.

"Okay," I said. "You're busted. Where's the dog?"

"Dog?" The voice came from under the bed, where I also heard a little scratching of clawed feet. "What dog?"

I sneezed. "*That* dog," I said.

Melissa sat up, resigned to her fate. "Oh. *That* dog."

From under the bed, a small dog, no bigger than the average beagle but clearly something in the golden retriever family, squirmed out and jumped up next to Liss. He (and it was clearly a he) snuggled up against her and tried to lick her face, but his tongue went through her cheek.

He was a ghost.

"Who's your friend?" I asked my daughter. Then I sneezed again.

"I'm calling him Bonkers," she said. "Can I keep him?"

"Bonkers?" My throat was scratchy and itchy at the same time. It's not good.

"I don't know. That's the fifth name I've given him. I couldn't think of anything else. Can I keep him?"

The dog ran through Melissa and off the bed. He hovered there for a second, confused, but then lowered to the floor, where he ran in a circle and then lay down. He seemed to have more connection to the material world than most of the human ghosts I'd met.

"I don't know," I rasped. "Can you hear my voice?"

"I'll keep him up here, Mom, I promise. And he can't shed, or, you know, need to go out or anything. Please?"

I decided to go in another direction. "Where'd you find him?"

"He showed up on the beach on Friday all by himself and he looked scared," she said. "Maxie thought we should bring him up here and make him feel secure, so she picked him up and brought him in."

I had figured Maxie was involved. "And you hid him from me because you figured I'd say you couldn't keep him," I said.

She scrunched up her nose. "Um . . . yeah."

"Come on," I said. "I think my head will be clearer outside."

"Can Bonkers come?"

"That's the idea," I said. She coaxed the dog out with a tennis ball in the air, which he had not yet figured he could float up and get. We started down to the main floor.

None of the guests—who would be leaving via a noon van—were up yet. Paul was in the front room when Melissa, Bonkers (oy) and I walked out toward the front door. It was impossible for Melissa to leash the dog, but of course there was no danger of him getting hit by a car and besides, he did not seem to want to leave my daughter's side. They had bonded in only a few days. This was going to be tough.

Paul looked guilty. "You've found out about Toby," he said.

"His name's Bonkers now," Melissa informed him.

"Oh."

"Yes, I did," I told Paul, "and I'm not thrilled that this was kept a secret from me."

"I tried to argue against it, but Maxie was . . . persuasive." Paul looked away. Maxie can indeed be persuasive, or intimidating, depending on one's point of view.

Before we got outside, Vance and Morrie appeared in the hallway, floating in from the direction of the movie room. And immediately informed us they were leaving.

"We're getting the band together and taking it on the road," Morrie said.

I looked at Vance, who surprisingly had become the more reliable source of information. "We have a gig with some of the Grateful Dead in San Francisco in March," he said.

"March? So you're leaving now?"

"It's a long walk. Look, love, I wanted to thank you for all you did and for putting up with us all this time. It wasn't always exactly like we wanted it to be but in the end we did what we could for Nessa, yeah?"

That reminded me. "Hang on," I said. I walked to what my mother calls the telephone table despite it having no such instrument on top of it. But it does have a drawer, and I opened it and pulled out a CD in a jewel case. I held it out to Vance.

"What's that?" he asked, taking it. I hadn't marked the disc at all.

"It's music by Vanessa McTiernan," I said. "Find a player somewhere along the way. I think you'll like it."

Vance looked like I'd handed him the key to the meaning of life. "Really," he said quietly.

"Really."

He looked at me carefully. "You've heard it?"

I nodded. "I burned another copy for myself."

"Is she good?"

"She's very good."

Vance punched Morrie on the arm. "Come on, you old tonk," he said. "We've gotta find ourselves a CD player." They flew out through the front door and were gone without a look back.

I sneezed again and Bonkers barked. Melissa looked like he'd pulled a gun on me. "Bonkers," she said.

"It's not his fault," I said through congestion. "Let's go outside."

The front porch was better. It was chilly that morning, a preview of coming attractions for the season. I didn't have to rake leaves yet, but that wasn't too far in the future. Then would come the winter and that's the slow season for us Shore businesses.

Bonkers ran out on the lawn when Melissa walked down there. He'd have loved to chase a ball, I'd bet, but we had left it upstairs. I really wanted to tell my daughter I couldn't possibly keep a ghost dog in the house—really a ghost puppy, judging by his size—due to my sinuses. But she looked so happy, and that's always a problem when denying her something. I walked down the steps toward where the dog was circling my daughter.

And that's when I saw the ghost woman with the wagon, standing on the edge of my sidewalk.

"You found Lester!" she said.

It took me a moment. "The dog? Lester is a golden retriever?"

"Sure. Light hair, short, generous mouth, right?" The woman floated a few feet closer and watched the dog with Melissa, who was confused and looking like something bad was going to happen.

Lester ran over and let the woman pet him but then he went back and sat by Melissa.

"I think we have to give Lester back to his friend," I said to Liss. "She's been looking all over for him." Then I turned toward the woman. "Haven't you, Claudia?"

"Claudia!" Paul said.

"Claudia?" Melissa asked.

Claudia Rabinowitz looked at me and smiled. "How did you know?"

"Vance McTiernan was here and he said he sensed you nearby. Then it was obvious that Vanessa visited with you just before she died but nobody else saw you. You were already dead. Vanessa used to stare into space and talk to herself, or so people thought. Could she see ghosts?"

Claudia nodded. "Some. Not all. I'm not even sure she knew for a fact what she was seeing. But she saw me, and I could talk to her. It was a real blessing; we worked out our differences. If I'd stayed just a few hours longer, I might have been able to . . ."

"You couldn't have known," I said. But now there was the business at hand. "Now, about Lester."

Liss looked like she might cry. Still, she nodded. But I noticed Lester/Bonkers wasn't sticking to his previous mistress and appeared to favor my daughter. "I'm sorry," Liss told the ghost. "I didn't know he was yours."

Claudia held up her hand. "No. You keep him."

Well, there went my easy way out. "Huh?" I'm nothing if not eloquent.

"I just found him on the road in Kansas. Been looking to leave him with a good home, where people would love him. Looks like we found it. Besides, a girl should have a dog." She actually turned and started up the street without even consulting us.

I had visions of allergist visits in my future.

"Maybe I can find Vance!" I shouted after her. "He'd love to see you—Paul, can you—"

"Please don't," Claudia called back. "We were never any good together."

"Will you be back?" I said as she shuffled off again. She answered, but was too far away for me to hear her.

Melissa, her face a mixture of relief and confusion, turned toward me. "Can we keep him?" she asked.

I looked at Paul and noticed Maxie, stretching her arms and yawning, floating out of the house. She noticed the dog playing in the yard, saw me and stopped in her tracks. "Uh-oh," she said. She turned back toward the house.

"Don't move," I told her. "I don't like being lied to and kept in the dark."

Maxie hung her head and sing-songed like a fourth-grader, "Sorry."

"Mom?" Melissa was pushing the point.

Lester ran up to me, sat at my feet and looked up into my face. Clearly, he was a born salesman.

So that is how we adopted a ghost dog.

That's my story. And I'm sticking to it.